CRUEL
HEART
BROKEN

Suddenly I remember that night on the beach,
when Charlie swam out to the pier and I thought
he'd drowned. And everything that followed.
And I can see now. That's all it takes.

One mistake.

One moment where you make
the wrong decision.

And lives are lost,
or wrecked for ever.

USBORNE

Emma Haughton

CRUEL
HEART
BROKEN

For Hetty

First published in the UK in 2016 by Usborne Publishing Ltd., Usborne House, 83-85 Saffron Hill, London EC1N 8RT, England. www.usborne.com

Copyright © Emma Haughton 2016

A CIP catalogue record for this book is available from the British Library.

JFMA JJASOND/16 ISBN 9781474906494 03945/1 Printed in the UK.

Prologue

These are the things you should know:

My name is Laurie Riley, though close friends call me Lee. I'm fifteen years old; sixteen in August, three months from now.

I live in Hove, the posh end of Brighton. I attend Hangleton High, and am about to take ten GCSEs. I'm hoping to do well – *need to do well* – because I'm going to be a doctor.

I know this with a certainty that comes from desperation; it's the only thing keeping me going. All I have left to hang on to.

My chance to make amends.

My family? Nothing out of the ordinary. Two parents, still together after twenty years. Mum a GP; Dad retired from the police force, now retraining in IT.

A sister, Katy – also in my year at school though she's eleven months older. And my brother, Walt. He's seven, and exactly what you'd expect in a little brother: annoying, endearing, forever asking questions.

I had two best friends, and now only one. Her name is Maya Patel.

These are the facts of my life. Tack on the things people think they know about me. That I'm a good girl. The good sister. The quiet, easy-going one. Katy is all edges and sarcasm and slammed doors, and I'm sweetness and light and lots and lots of homework.

This tells you nothing, of course. Perhaps all you really need to know is that eight months ago, my life changed for ever. Ice grew in my heart. Poison seeped into my blood. Nothing will ever be the same again.

I am a murderer.

It is a secret. My secret.

Never to be told.

PART ONE: NOW

Chapter 1

Really though, this isn't my story at all. This story begins now, in the middle of our GCSEs, and it belongs to Charlie Forrest.

What can I tell you about Charlie? I'll start with his hair, because it's the first thing people notice. It's deep-brown and grows in crazy tight curls, standing up from his head like an electric shock. Along with his olive skin, he says it's the only thing he ever got from his dad.

Back when we were small, when the three of us – Charlie, Maya and me – all sat at the same table in the infant class, his hair fell in long corkscrews down his back. Most of his life Charlie wore it like that, tying it up for PE.

But now it's gone. Charlie cut it off.

Turned up at school one day with it clipped back to a buzz.

I don't know why. It was around the time I became a murderer, and we pretty much stopped speaking to each other. About the time he got serious with my sister.

And my cruel heart broke.

* * *

You'd think, wouldn't you, that a heart could only break once? If only that were true. Whenever I see Charlie mine cracks and splinters all over again. Like now, getting home from my history exam to find him sitting at our kitchen table, shoulders slumped, staring at the floor.

A trap. An ambush, snaring me as always.

"Hey, Lee." He turns his head in my direction, but we've perfected the art of never quite looking at each other straight on. Blood pounds in my temples. My heart collapses into a dark star, devoid of warmth or light. Instantly that hot feeling behind my eyes, the one I get if ever I'm close to him.

"Hi." I keep my tone bright and even as I dump my rucksack on the table; heavy with books, it thunks hard against the wood.

What's he doing, I wonder, sitting alone in here? Shouldn't he be upstairs with Katy?

When the pair of them aren't over at Charlie's, they hide up in my sister's bedroom. Most times I don't even know he's in the house unless we bump into each other on the landing. Once I emerged from the bathroom and found him right in front of me, hand reaching for the doorknob. Only a few centimetres between us.

A knife in my guts. A lurch of something so pure, so piercing, I thought I might pass out.

"How did the exam…?" Charlie stops as Katy walks in, carrying the medical kit Mum keeps in the utility room. My sister scowls when she sees me, putting the box on the table and removing one of the little medicated wipes in a foil packet.

Why does she need that? It's only as Charlie turns to face her that I notice; I've been so busy not looking at him that I missed it before. A gash across the side of his temple. About three centimetres long, oozing blood.

"Shit," I gasp, despite myself. "What happened?"

Katy carries on pretending I'm not there, but Charlie manages a weak smile. Our eyes meet for a fraction of a second, before skittering away.

"It's nothing." He tips his head back as my sister gently swabs the wound. A faint sharp smell of antiseptic fills the room.

I watch, frowning. It looks a whole lot more than nothing. The surrounding flesh swollen, the colour already deepening to purple.

Not a knife then. Something blunt bruised as well as split the skin. I glance at Katy.

Does she know what happened?

But my sister's still blanking me. We may be pretty close in age, but that's it. We're worlds apart, Katy all blonde highlights and cheerleader looks. Me mousy and geeky. Utterly forgettable.

Mum claims we were close, back when we were tiny, too early for me to remember. But any affection we might once have had for each other has well and truly evaporated. I wish I knew why. I've tried talking to Katy a few times over the years, but all I get is a shrug. An eye roll.

A look that says I'm a lost cause.

"Where's Mum?" I ask. "Shouldn't she check that over?"

My sister ignores me. Charlie glances over, then lets his eyes slide away again, like I make them hurt.

"Katy?" I persist.

"I've rung her," my sister says with a sigh. "She's just finishing up at the surgery."

As if on cue, Mum walks in, her thick brown hair pulled back into a clip, her face set in that tired, harassed expression it always has after seeing patients. She raises a hand in greeting as she pulls off her jacket. I catch her glancing at the half-finished bottle of red wine on the countertop, before turning her gaze to Charlie.

He's mustering another smile, but I can tell the effort hurts his head. Has Katy offered him any painkillers?

"Okay, let's take a look." Mum drags out a chair and sits in front of him, observing the wound for a few moments before lifting her fingers to examine it more closely, careful not to touch the broken skin.

"How exactly did this happen?"

Charlie shrugs. "I got into a fight."

"Who with?"

"One of the kids from Patcham Comp."

Mum purses her lips, but doesn't pursue it.

"I was just cleaning it up." Katy holds up the wipe, now smeared with streaks of red. I try not to think what it reminds me of as Mum takes it from her and dabs away more blood.

"This is going to need stitches," she says finally.

Charlie grimaces. "Really?"

"'Fraid so."

"Can't you do them?" he asks.

Mum sighs, considering. "I could, Charlie, but you should go to A&E. They can give you an X-ray, make certain there's nothing more serious."

My sister's eyes widen. Her face takes on a dramatic expression.

"I'm sure he's all right, Katy," Mum reassures her, with a quick glance at me. "But you can't be too careful with head trauma. Best to get it checked out."

She glances at her watch. "Do you want me to take you in?" she asks Charlie. "Or will you call your mum?"

He blows out air between his lips, clearly not keen on either option. Not that he dislikes Mum or anything. Probably can't handle a three-hour wait in the local hospital.

"Honestly, I'm fine," he says. "I'd rather just go home—"

"Charlie, you need to get that looked at. Seriously." Mum's voice has that my-word-is-final tone.

He sighs. Gives in. "Okay. I'll ring her." He gets up and walks out to the garden, even though the low cloud that's hung around all day has turned into a light summer drizzle. Not wanting to make the call in front of us, I guess.

"How did it really happen?" Mum asks Katy the moment he's gone.

My sister pulls her I-dunno face, shrugging up her nose and turning down the corners of her mouth. "A fight, he said."

Mum gives Katy a meaningful look. "It doesn't seem the kind of injury you'd get in a fist fight, to be honest. Not unless somebody used a weapon."

"Well, maybe they did." Katy doesn't so much as blink, but there's something shifty in her manner. The way she presses her lips together, as if sealing in the truth.

Then again, you can never tell with my sister. She goes through life acting like the most ordinary things are secret. Who her friends are. Where she's going. What time she plans to come home.

I've no clue why she does it. Maya says it's because Katy's such a drama queen, that she wants people to think she's more interesting than she actually is. More likely she does it just to be difficult.

The impossible sister.

Mum rubs her forehead in frustration, then gets up and pours herself a glass of wine. She seems exhausted. Clearly an afternoon of heart-sink patients. Possibly a practice meeting; it's Mum's job to work out the budgets.

I glance at the first-aid stuff spread across the table. Look at Katy, but she just sits there, raking her fingers through her long fair hair and gazing absently at her phone.

I see Mum's frown of annoyance, but she doesn't object. Letting Katy get away with it – again – lacking the energy for another confrontation.

"I'll clear up, shall I?" I say pointedly to Katy.

She lifts her head and smiles. "If you like."

I bite back the urge to argue. I can't face it, especially in front of Charlie – or Mum, who shoots me a grateful smile as I stuff everything into the medical box and return it to the utility room.

When I get back, Charlie's come indoors, rain glistening on his hair. "She'll be over in ten minutes," he says, looking worse somehow. More shell-shocked. His eyes meet mine and, just for a second, they linger.

Too much.

I pick up my bag and retreat upstairs. I can't handle this now, and no way do I want to bump into his mother again.

Besides, this has nothing to do with me.

What I feel doesn't matter any more.

Chapter 2

Next day, the skies are clear and blue. It's quiet in the common room at lunchtime, most people outside enjoying the sudden eruption of sunshine. Over in the corner I spot Tom Rochester, headphones in his ears, listening to something on his phone, tapping his foot while keeping an eye on the entrance. Watching out for his dad, no doubt. Must be tough having a parent as a teacher. Feeling you can never get away.

He glances up, gives me a wave. We're not friends exactly. Tom keeps himself to himself, but sometimes he hangs out with our crowd and we chat a bit. I like him; his dry, humorous take on the world. His passion for cheesy eighties music. The way his cheeks dimple when he laughs. He looks a lot like his dad, though his brown hair is straighter, his face more serious somehow.

I smile, then drag my focus back to my textbook. I'm supposed to be swatting up for my maths exam next week, but I can't concentrate. My mind wanders off again, so I pick up my pen and make a list of words, all beginning with E.

Erase

Expunge

Eradicate

Extract

Exterminate

Extinguish

Eliminate

Execute

Maya appears out of nowhere, grinning. I do a double take. She's gelled her hair into spikes, slicking down the sides for extra effect.

"What do you think?" She turns her head so I can see the back. "Erin Massey did it in the loos for me. You like it?"

"Very punk," I say, "but your mum is going to freak."

"That's what I'm hoping."

That makes me laugh. Maya had her long black hair cut into a short bob a few weeks back, prompting her traditional Indian mother to dissolve into tears and ground her for a fortnight.

"It suits you," I add, truthfully. It sets off Maya's heart-shaped face, and makes her brown eyes look even bigger.

Pleased, she glances over my shoulder. Her smile fades into a frown. "What are you doing?"

I shut my notebook quickly. "Synonyms," I say, but I don't mention what for.

She narrows her eyes, her dark brows nearly meeting

above her nose, but she doesn't comment. "You coming to biology?" she asks instead.

I check the time. Somehow I've wasted a whole hour doing nothing but dwell on what can never be undone. I gather up my things and follow Maya to C block. As usual we're early, but that's fine by me. Even without Maya's obsession with punctuality, I always try to be first into class. That way I can choose somewhere at the back, as far away from everyone else as possible.

As far away from Charlie as possible. He always sits at the front, stretching his long legs out before him. Charlie likes to speak up in class. To get involved. Be seen. Be heard.

Katy, thankfully, is in a lower set, so at least I won't have to watch her sitting beside him, their knees touching. The little glances they give each other. The smiles. I have enough of that in French. And English.

Kids file in, get out textbooks. Maya studies the chapter on genetic variation, making notes in preparation for the exam in a couple of weeks. But I've gone over it a million times already, anxious to do well, to have a fighting chance of getting into medical school.

I lean my head against the window, watching a hockey game over on the far pitch, but really I'm just waiting for Charlie to arrive. Despite myself, despite everything, I'm always waiting for Charlie to arrive. I try and focus on other things, go over my work, distract myself with something outside, but part of my mind is biding time till he walks into the room.

I always know when he's there, even if I'm not looking. My skin prickles. A tension in my stomach, something small but seismic, a blip on my internal Richter scale.

Aftershocks.

Today, however, there's no sign of him. Nor Mr Rochester. I glance up at the clock. The lesson should have started ten minutes ago. What's going on?

Around me, the rest of the class is getting restless. Johnny Hopkins is playing a game on his iPad. Most of the other girls are fiddling with their phones, defying the rule against using them in lessons. Two desks away, Harry Lawes and Sam Church are arguing about football and whether the Seagulls – Brighton's home team – will make it into the next division.

Who cares? I think, closing my eyes. Hardly a matter of life and…

My heart shrinks, and I feel myself sinking.

"Hey." Maya nudges my elbow. "You okay?"

I look at her. She's frowning at me again. I know she wants to ask what's wrong. I also know she's given up hope of a straight answer. I wonder if I should tell her about Charlie getting into that fight. Having to go to hospital.

I decide against it – Maya has no time for Charlie since he went off with my sister. Has dropped her attempts to repair the friendship between the three of us.

"Where's Mr Rochester?" she whispers, leaning in so no one else can hear.

I shrug. "No idea."

"Do you think we should get someone?" She chews her lip, clearly deciding whether to do it. That's what I love about Maya. She's so…responsible. Always ready to do the right thing. Which is exactly why I can never tell her the truth. I couldn't bear the look on my best friend's face.

The horror.

The disgust.

At that moment Mr Nevis walks in. One of the part-time science teachers.

"Settle down." He seats himself at the desk and glares at Johnny till he puts away his tablet. "Sorry about the delay, everyone. I'm afraid Mr Rochester can't take the lesson today, but I've been told that you're working on chromosomes."

His hand dives into his briefcase and pulls out a textbook. "Please go through Section Three. There's some revision questions at the end of the chapter." With that he extracts a bunch of exercise books from his bag and gets on with his marking.

Maya leans over. "Odd," she whispers. "I mean, Mr Rochester was in first thing this morning. I saw him before registration."

"Who knows?" I shrug again. "Maybe he's gone off sick. Or there's a family emergency."

I'm more worried about Charlie. I haven't caught sight of him in school today. Is he all right? Did the blow to his head turn out to be something more serious? Concussion? A bleed in the brain?

I run through the possibilities. But Mum didn't seem that concerned, did she? Just a routine examination, she said.

All the same I feel a cold blast of foreboding. Perhaps Charlie really is ill. The ice in my heart shifts and cracks. Bits break off into slivers, lethally sharp. For a second I'm tempted to get up and leave, to go off to look for him, pretending I'm sick or something to Mr Nevis.

But Maya would be suspicious. She'd know immediately something was up, and I can't face another interrogation. I've spent months fobbing her off about Charlie, evading all her questions, especially when he and Katy got together. Maya couldn't get her head around that any more than I could.

I had no answers to give her. Just plenty of questions of my own.

So I endure the lesson. Reread the stuff on cell division and mitosis, though I practically know it off by heart. Somehow I make it all the way through to double maths – still no sign of Charlie – until it's time to go home.

Usually I walk back with Maya, who lives just a few streets away. Today I make an excuse about having to stay behind, then wait for her to head off.

Now what? I ask myself as she disappears through the school gates. What I really want to do is get a bus straight over to Alice Street, to Charlie's flat. Make sure he's okay.

But I can't.

Not any more.

So I opt for the only other thing I can think of – wait around for Katy. But as the crush of kids thins to a trickle, I realize I must have missed her.

Nothing for it but to head home, praying she'll be there, and that somehow I can persuade her to tell me what's going on.

Chapter 3

There's no one home.

I cry for a while, relieved not to have to hide the noise. Then wash my face and sit in my room and do a practice question for English, throwing in some of the things I've read up on Dickens and his life. Stuff no examiner would expect me to know.

Overkill.

Half an hour later I hear the front door open and close. Voices. Katy and Charlie. I stand by my door, opening it a fraction to catch what they're saying.

...your mum said you have...

...I don't want to, Katy. I told you that...

They move deeper into the house, into the kitchen. I can't hear the rest.

At least Charlie is all right, I tell myself. He wouldn't be up and walking around if it was serious.

I sit back at my desk. Finish the question on *Great Expectations*. The same strategy I've been using since last autumn: work as a distraction. Study as an antidote. A painkiller.

Pretty much all I've got left.

The sound of the front door again. Mum's voice calling hello, then Walt protesting about something. Not getting a new game for his PlayStation, probably – that's usually what my brother has on his mind.

No sign of Dad. Still at college maybe? Or up on the allotment. He spends more and more time there these days, when he's not studying for his course. His therapy, Mum says. More effective than antidepressants.

"Laurie?" she calls again. "You up there?"

I take a deep breath and head downstairs. Everyone's sitting in the kitchen, Charlie and Katy too. Mum glances at me. "Aren't you going to change before we go?"

I blink, then remember. It's curry night – Riley family tradition. Every Friday evening, we eat at the Indian restaurant in Kemptown, the one Mum swears does the best dansak in the whole of Brighton.

I swallow. "I think I might give it a miss."

Mum fixes me with one of her looks. The kind I imagine she gives patients pretending to have a sore throat, reluctant to admit why they've really made an appointment. "You okay?"

"I'm just tired," I say. "Too much revising."

Her gaze lingers. I can see the worry on her face. Watch her trying to push it down, knowing, like Maya, that she won't get any more out of me.

She fails. Puts a hand to my face. "Lee, you sure that's all it is? You're awfully pale. I wish you'd talk to me."

I force myself to look brighter. Pray she hasn't noticed the telltale redness around my eyes.

"I just need a bit more sleep, Mum. I'll be better once the exams are over," I add, for good measure.

She gazes back at me. "All the more reason to come on out. You obviously need to take a break."

I hesitate.

"C'mon, Laurie…" Walt pleads, tugging my hand and making his big brown eyes all soulful and yearning.

He knows I can never resist. "Fine," I say, smiling. "I'll go change."

"Yay!" Walt cheers, ridiculously pleased. "And Charlie's coming too."

He is? I frown in surprise. Curry night is family night – strictly Rileys.

Charlie flashes me an apologetic look; clearly this isn't his idea.

"His mum's out," Katy says, her expression challenging, daring me to object. "Mum doesn't want him at home alone, on account of his head."

I glance back at Charlie, at the dressing covering the left side of his forehead and think of that fight. What was it about? Charlie's always been a bit reckless, always enjoyed winding people up, but it's never got to this before.

Though he's changed so much this last year, it sometimes feels like I never knew him at all.

"Can't be too careful," says Mum, gauging my reaction. Making me wonder again just how much she's worked out.

"Great." I try to sound enthusiastic, but underneath my heart is sinking. That's all I need. An evening stuck with Charlie and Katy, trying to act like I don't care.

And like I never did.

Chapter 4

I sit as far away from Katy and Charlie as possible, at the opposite end of the table, next to Dad and Walt. Even so, it's obvious from their body language that something's not right.

Charlie's face is edgy and strained. He keeps checking his phone, while Katy sits there, withdrawn and quiet, studying the patterned floor tiles and the lurid maroon-and-gold wallpaper as if she's never been here before.

What's going on? Have they had an argument?

Mum chats cheerfully to Walt and the waiter. If she's noticed something's up with Charlie and my sister, she's clearly pretending otherwise. After all, I've given her plenty of practice with that.

In the end it's Katy who cracks. Right after we've placed our orders and been served our drinks.

"Terrible," she says, when Mum asks her how school went today. "Mr Rochester's been suspended." Charlie groans in protest and Katy spins back to him. "It's all going to come out anyway."

"What do you mean?" Mum gazes at the pair of them.

Charlie clears his throat. "Um…" He falls silent again.

"*Tell her*," urges my sister.

He blinks a couple of times. "It was him…Mr Rochester who…you know…"

Mum looks puzzled. Clearly she doesn't know.

"He's the one who hit Charlie," Katy blurts, like a dam burst. Unable to hold this in any longer. "Yesterday. Mr Rochester assaulted him."

Mum's head jerks back in surprise. "Paul Rochester hit you? That nice biology teacher?" Her expression a cross between horrified and disbelieving.

I don't blame her. I'm half-winded myself.

I glance at Dad, who's frowning, his gaze locked on Charlie. "You mean, he was the one who did *that*?" Dad nods at the gauze covering Charlie's head wound.

"And he broke his tooth," Katy adds, ignoring Charlie's pissed-off expression. I'm guessing he asked her not to mention it.

A teacher hit Charlie? And broke his tooth?

It seems too astonishing to be true. And especially Mr Rochester, who must be the school's most popular member of staff. All scruffy hair and a ready smile, easy-going and easy to like. Young-looking, despite his age. Half the girls in our year have a crush on him, even though he's a teacher and Tom's dad. Half the girls in the whole school probably.

"What happened?" I gasp, unable to keep my mouth shut any longer. I stare directly at Charlie, no longer caring what my expression might be giving away.

His face clouds. His eyes flick in my direction, just long enough not to appear rude. "We got into an argument," he mumbles, as if it's too painful to articulate the words properly.

"What about?" Dad asks, still frowning. Clearly he's finding this as difficult to get his head around as the rest of us.

My mind is reeling. I can't imagine what Charlie could have said or done to make Mr Rochester hit him.

"His work," Katy butts in, indignant on his behalf. "Mr Rochester accused Charlie of deliberately flunking some stupid revision test, then when Charlie answered back, he laid into him."

Mum looks more astounded. "Is this true?" She turns to Charlie.

He shifts in his seat, then nods. "Not the test bit. I didn't flunk that on purpose."

I believe him. All his life Charlie's wanted to fly planes, even back when we were little. He used to make me and Maya be his co-pilots as he zoomed around the playground, pretending we were airborne.

You need decent grades to get into aviation.

But I still can't imagine Mr Rochester hitting him. I mean, I remember Tom saying once that his dad was strict at home, always on his back over schoolwork, but he never once mentioned him being violent.

"This isn't some kind of joke, is it?" I look from Katy to Charlie, ignoring my sister's furious expression. "Cos if it is, it's not very funny."

"Of course it isn't," Katy erupts. "Trust you to—"

"Where?" Dad cuts in with a tone he must have perfected in the police. Forceful, like you'd use to interview suspects. "Where did all this happen?"

"In the science lab." Charlie sounds sheepish, like he wished everyone would just drop the subject. "After school."

"Yesterday afternoon? Before you came round to us?"

Charlie nods again.

Our meals arrive, but no one except Walt touches their food. We're all too stunned by Katy's revelation.

"Which tooth?" Dad asks Charlie once the waiters have disappeared.

Charlie doesn't respond. He's examining the thick white linen tablecloth, clearly wishing my sister had never brought any of this up.

But that's Katy for you. A law unto herself.

"Show them." She nudges him. There's something defiant in her gaze, like Katy knows Charlie will object.

His face twitches. I get a sense that he's having some sort of battle with himself, but he pulls up his lip to reveal a large chip in one of his top teeth, halfway back. Premolar, I think.

Shit. It looks as if it's been snapped in half.

Nasty.

"Have you had a dentist look at that?" Mum asks.

"Not yet. Nicole's going to make me an appointment."

Ever since I've known Charlie, he's called his mum Nicole.

Once or twice I've asked him why, but just got a shrug in response, as if the answer was obvious. Or impossible to explain.

It still puzzles me though – like they're more friends than mother and son.

Mum gazes down at her chicken dansak. Then up again at Charlie. "I'm surprised there's not more bruising. Around your mouth, I mean."

A pause before Charlie answers. "I was about to say something and he caught me with his elbow." He clears his throat. "It was a weak tooth," he adds. "It had a big filling."

"So it was an accident?" Dad's expression gives nothing away. You could see why he made a good detective. Though he left two years ago, I often wonder if he misses his job more than he lets on.

"No..." Charlie hesitates. "No, not an accident exactly."

"So who have you told?" Dad persists, not about to let the matter drop.

Charlie swallows. He looks really uncomfortable. Like he'd rather be anywhere but here.

"Nicole informed the school this morning," Katy cuts in quickly. "They suspended Mr Rochester and sent him home."

God, poor Tom, I think, hoping none of this comes out. Whatever his father has done, he doesn't deserve this. The gossip. The shame. People whispering behind his back.

"Nicole's taking me to report it to the police tomorrow," Charlie says, his voice quiet. "I have to make a statement."

"He doesn't want to," Katy pitches in. "He just wants to drop it. I've told him his mum is right. You can't let something like this go."

Mum raises her eyes to Charlie, who's looking increasingly unhappy. But then, I suppose he would. It must have been pretty traumatic, getting into a situation like that. Having to deal with the fallout.

"He's been suspended," he says. "It's enough."

"I don't think so." Mum loads rice and curry on her fork. "That was a nasty cut. And your tooth…"

I see Charlie's tongue go automatically to the broken molar. Testing it, the way you do when something feels new and unfamiliar.

Lucky it won't show, I think, remembering how he hated wearing braces for those first two years of secondary school. It'd be a shame to spoil that hard-earned smile.

I start to eat, but at the same time stealing glances at Charlie. He's changed even more in the last few months, his features leaner now, less boyish. He's let his hair grow out too, long enough to twist into tiny curls. My fingers itch with the memory, the feel of it beneath their tips.

Then Katy looks across and catches me watching. Gives me a cool hard stare, loaded with meaning.

My heart falters. Is it possible she knows what happened between Charlie and me? Apart from Tom, I haven't told anyone. And Charlie swore he'd keep it secret.

Promised on his life.

Surely he wouldn't go back on that?

Chapter 5

Monday morning, and I'm looking out for Tom as we file into the sports hall. Wondering if he's come in today. Wondering what kind of weekend he had, with his father being suspended.

Wondering too why the head has called a whole school assembly. Monday is usually Years Seven to Nine – the rest of us and the Sixth Form get our assemblies on Tuesdays and Fridays. So there's a buzz in the air when we're told to go straight to the sports hall after tutor group, the only place big enough for everyone.

Even so, there aren't enough chairs to go round, so latecomers and the younger kids have to squat on the floor. Me and Maya get there just in time to bag a couple of seats right at the back; we wait, apprehensive, as one by one, the teachers file in and sit down facing us. The air of excitement and expectation builds as all the pupils clock their sombre expressions. People giving each other what's-going-on looks and leaning over to whisper.

Something is definitely up.

I search the faces around me; can't see any sign of Tom.

But outside, beyond the glass double doors that lead into the hall, I glimpse Mrs Railton, the head, talking to a man and woman in dark uniforms.

Police officers.

Shit. What is this all about?

I look around for Charlie. Spot him sitting next to my sister, over by the folded trampolines. He's staring straight ahead, still wearing that dressing on his forehead, the white of the gauze stark against his olive skin.

Another five minutes drag by. Everyone is getting restless and fidgety, the noise level rising as kids strike up conversations with their neighbours. Several of the teachers glance at their watches, peering out through the double doors.

Finally Mrs Railton walks in, her expression solemn and serious, and takes her position in front of the other staff. She stands perfectly still, waiting for the chatter and coughing to die away. It doesn't take long. Everyone is eager to know what she has to say.

"I'm sorry to keep you all wondering what this is about…" Her voice trails off and she lifts her gaze to the skylights in the ceiling, one hand clutching a piece of paper – even from here, I can see it trembling.

Jesus. I've never seen Mrs Railton lose her cool. Never. Whatever this is about, it must be bad.

She clears her throat and starts again. "I've gathered you all in here today because I'm afraid I have some tragic news to relate, following an incident that occurred this weekend."

Several of the teachers look down – clearly they know what's coming. Probably had a meeting in the staffroom first thing. With a frisson of shock I see that Miss Castell is crying, her shoulders shaking as she gives in to silent sobs. Mr Portesham reaches across and offers her a tissue.

"You all knew Mr Rochester, from the science department, who worked at this school for the past seven years." Mrs Railton pauses again. Visibly swallows to regain control. "I'm very sorry to have to tell you that, regrettably, he passed away yesterday."

A collective gasp of dismay echoes around the hall.

Mrs Railton clears her throat again. "Since I've just been reliably informed that there is no question as to the cause of death, and it's likely to be reported in the local newspapers, I thought it best to inform you that Mr Rochester, tragically, took his own life."

No gasp this time. Just the sound of a thousand kids holding their breath in stunned silence.

"Clearly this will be a very difficult period for Mr Rochester's family," Mrs Railton continues, her other hand clutching her stomach as if it aches with the news she's telling us, "and I would ask that you all refrain from speculation about the—"

The sudden loud smack of a chair as it hits the floor.

I'm already looking at Charlie, so I see all of it. The expression on his face as Mrs Railton announces the teacher's suicide. His features so shocked, so appalled that one thing is clear.

Charlie never, ever saw this coming.

I'm watching as he leaps to his feet, the chair pitching backwards from the momentum, my gaze following in his wake as he runs towards the exit, the tide of bodies shrinking back to let him through.

Seconds later, Katy hurries after him. In the rush of murmurs and disbelief that erupts, as everyone tries to process what just happened, it takes every ounce of willpower I have left not to follow them both.

PART TWO: THEN

Chapter 6

Charlie, Maya and me. Always the three of us, right from that first week at primary school.

Those days are a jumble now in my head, a blur, more of a feeling than a memory. But I remember how we gravitated towards each other, like elements in a kind of human chemical reaction.

Charlie, loud and boisterous and always laughing. Unpredictable too; sometimes thoughtful and considerate, other times careless, almost oblivious to his effect on people.

Maya, sharp and funny, even at five, with a wicked smile and a crooked way of looking at the world.

And me. Quiet and serious, in awe of the pair of them. Their energy and noise. The confident way they declared whatever was on their minds. What they wanted or needed. What they liked or didn't. Whereas I always worried what the other person thought. Whether I'd given the right answer, the one they wanted to hear.

The three peas, Dad called us, back in those early days when it was his turn to pick us up from school. Not that we were alike, even to look at. Maya, small and delicate, with her dark straight hair and huge almond eyes. Charlie, her polar opposite, tall for his age and hair as wild and curly as hers was sleek. Me, somehow lost between the two of them, pale-skinned, my hair mousy, neither straight nor curly.

I was amazed they wanted to be friends with me. To include me in their little gang. But there I was, always sandwiched between them, like peas in those fat swollen pods Dad grew on his allotment.

I remember Maya and Charlie going up there once, when we were eight or so. It must have been summer, because the peas were ready to be picked.

"Have some," Dad offered, so I plucked three pods from the tangle of wiry stems, passing two to Maya and Charlie. Showed them how to split the skin to reveal the perfect little spheres inside, nestled tight together.

Charlie seemed amazed, his eyes wide with surprise. I realized then he'd probably only ever seen peas frozen in a bag, or hot on his plate.

I pulled one out and put it in my mouth, smiling at the fresh juicy taste. Charlie and Maya did the same, though I could tell by the furrow that appeared on Maya's forehead that she wasn't keen. Charlie, however, grinned and scoffed the lot.

"Like sweets," he said. "Little green sweets."

So we were the three peas to Dad, but I thought of us more as a triangle. An equilateral triangle, three points, each an equal distance apart, each linked to one another.

It's the most stable shape, our teacher explained in junior class. The strongest in nature.

And so it was for years. At primary school we always sat together, though at first the teacher tried to put me with Katy, assuming I'd be happier with my sister. Katy, however, was having none of it. Insisted on sitting at a different table, having her own friends.

So I got to be with Maya and Charlie, and even when we moved up to Hangleton High, we stuck together, though it was harder with desks that only came in twos.

We solved it by alternating. Sometimes Maya and Charlie paired up, with me in front or behind. Or I was with Charlie, and Maya had to sit next to someone else. Other times, me and Maya sat side by side, leaving Charlie out in the cold.

After school it was easier, and we moved like a shoal, spending most of our evenings and weekends together.

When we were small, we'd beg an adult – usually Maya's mum – to drive us to the summer paddling pool on the seafront. We'd spend hours sitting in the water, kicking our legs and competing to make the biggest splash, squealing when we got our faces wet.

We loved it in all weathers; would happily have gone there in the rain if we could have persuaded anyone to go with us.

Eventually, though, we grew out of paddling pools, graduating to the park on The Level, where we watched the older kids swoop and spin on their skateboards. Sometimes we nagged Maya's older brother, Raz, to take us to the pier. Half the time he'd bump into someone he knew, leaving us free to wander on our own, wasting our pocket money in the arcade or on the stalls in the funfair at the end of the pier.

When it was cold or wet, we'd just hang out at one of our houses. I preferred Charlie's flat in Alice Road. It was only a short hop from the seafront, and I loved how it was all on one level, no effort needed to get from room to room.

Charlie liked Maya's place best, because her mum would bake cookies or brownies. But more often than not we ended up at mine, huddled in the summer house at the bottom of our garden where no one could overlook or hear us. Avoiding Katy, though she ignored us anyway, flat refusing if we ever asked her to join in. As if there were years between us rather than months.

And of course there was the beach. Looking back, it feels like we spent half our lives on that sloping shingle, staring at the waves as we talked, or seeing who could throw stones furthest into the water. Charlie usually won, though I was better at skimming when the sea was flat and calm. And Maya had the best aim. She could hit anything you pointed out to her – a can, another rock, a piece of seaweed. The moment the stone left her hand, you knew it would land on its target, every single time.

We three. Always.

"So if you had to marry one of us, which one would it be?" Maya asked once, when we were twelve or thirteen. The question made me uncomfortable. I wasn't sure I wanted to know the answer. It might not be one I liked.

"Can't I marry both of you?" Charlie's grin showed all his teeth.

Maya shook her head, her own eyes crinkling into a smile. She enjoyed teasing people, finding their edges. "Two wives is illegal."

"Not everywhere," Charlie retorted. "It's allowed in some countries."

"But we live here," I said, before realizing I was encouraging them both.

Charlie picked up another stone and lobbed it into the sea. It made a loud "plup" sound as it hit the water. He looked at Maya, then he turned to me, his gaze serious.

Did I see something back then? There, in his eyes. Was he trying to tell me something?

"I'd let you decide." Charlie lay on the shingle, squinting up into the sky. "You could both flip a coin, see who wins. Or you could make bids, like on eBay. Or maybe you could fight over me, you know, like a jousting contest. Or I could set you both a challenge—"

"Oh, shut up," Maya laughed, thumping his shoulder. "Who says either of us would want you anyway?"

I liked the way Charlie dealt with Maya's question, preserving the triangle.

Equilateral. Every side the same. Everything equal.

Most of our lives it had held fast. Eternal, I thought. Indestructible, I assumed.

But one night, that's all it took.

One single night, and it was broken for ever.

Chapter 7

It happened last year, a fortnight into the summer holidays, a week or so after my fifteenth birthday. A bunch of us went off to celebrate Ria turning fifteen too; our first proper night out alone. Old enough now to leave our parents at home. Old enough to pretend we could be trusted.

"Ring me if you need a lift home or anything." Dad offered his cheek for a kiss as I was leaving, then took a step back and eyed me appraisingly. "You look nice."

I was only wearing jeans, Vans and a floaty top I got online, though I'd put on a bit of the make-up my sister left in the bathroom. Nothing much, just a swipe of mascara and lipgloss; I didn't go the whole Katy. But even I could see the difference it made: my eyes appeared larger, my face brighter.

"Thanks," I said, pleased Dad had noticed. Pleased too that he'd seemed happier this last week or two. For the first time since he'd been pensioned off from the police a year before, his low mood appeared to have lifted. He'd even cracked a few jokes this morning, at breakfast.

That had been the worst thing about those long months

of Dad's depression – the sense that he'd left us somehow. That part of him had gone missing, the fun, happy, cheery part that liked to fool around and draw silly doodles on the kitchen whiteboard. The part that always planned a special treat on anyone's birthday, or pulled daft faces just to make you laugh.

I'd thought perhaps that side of Dad had vanished for good. Thankfully it seemed I was wrong, and I set off for Maya's with a lift in my heart. I felt buoyant. Elated even. Not just about Dad, but everything – the glorious days of summer stretching ahead, my first night out with friends, still something new and exciting, filling me with a sense of freedom and possibility.

Only one blot on the horizon, already fading: that stupid argument with Katy after breakfast. "Little Miss Bloody Perfect" she'd mouthed as I unloaded the washing machine, seeing Dad was busy with Walt and Mum was late for work. Normally I ignore my sister's jibes, but today I gave her the finger. Told her to do it herself, then left her to it.

Charlie would be proud, I knew. Stick up for yourself, he always said, whenever I complained about Katy. Live dangerously. Tell her to shove it.

He was right, I decided. Time to ditch the good girl image and enjoy myself more.

After all, what did I have to lose?

*   *   *

"Wow!" Maya said when she opened the door. "Get you!"

I laughed. "You don't look so bad yourself." It was true. Maya looked amazing in her tight black jeans and ballet shoes, and a punky grey T-shirt with *Death or Glory* printed on the front.

I waited on the step as she called goodbye to her parents. Her mum said something from the kitchen, but it was in Hindi so I hadn't a clue what it meant.

"Whatever," Maya replied in English. "Bye, Mum!" She closed the door behind her and we headed towards town.

"What did she say?" I asked, once we were clear of the house.

"Oh, the usual. No alcohol. No bad language. No 'consorting' with boys, that sort of thing."

I laughed, and watched as Maya pulled out a make-up bag. Resting it on a nearby garden wall, she took out a mirror and some black eyeliner and drew a couple of dramatic swoops around her eyes, applying another layer of mascara to heighten the effect.

"Couldn't do it at home." Maya gave an apologetic shrug. "Didn't want to set Mum off again."

She added a light brown gloss to her lips, quickly messed up her hair with a tube of gel, then checked out her reflection.

"Gorgeous," I said.

"It'll do," she sighed, linking an arm through mine.

It took us twenty minutes to get to the pizza place in the Lanes, the one that does three courses for fifteen pounds. Charlie was waiting outside.

He gave me a quick up-and-down look. "Not bad," he said, smirking in that way that always ended with me punching his arm. "You look...great. Both of you," he added, grinning at Maya.

"Thanks." I stared back at him. Truth was, he looked pretty good himself. I hadn't seen Charlie since we'd broken up from school. He'd got a job doing the deckchairs on the seafront, setting them up in the morning, then taking them down again once the crowds had gone. Collecting all the money in the meantime, pacing the length of the beach.

The work obviously suited him. Charlie appeared fitter, leaner. The constant sunshine in the last few weeks had tanned his face to a warm glow.

More than that, he seemed older somehow; more mature than his fifteen years.

"C'mon." Charlie nodded towards the doors. "Ria and Soph are upstairs already. Let's get a seat together before the others turn up."

Ria waved when she saw us, getting up to kiss us on both cheeks, the way our parents did to their friends. Her eyes looked a bit glazed, I noticed, and she was grinning hard, like we'd turned up at the tail end of a private joke.

We grabbed the spaces next to Sophie, Charlie sitting between me and Maya. Tom Rochester and others from Ria and Soph's crowd arrived, joining us at the end of the table.

"Looking good, Laurie," Tom said, as he sat down by me.

"Thanks." I gave him a smile as the waitress handed out the oversized menus. Out of the corner of my eye, I glimpsed Sophie slipping Ria a silver hip flask. Ria took a surreptitious sip, grimacing slightly. Whatever was in there, I was guessing it was strong.

As the meal progressed, the pair of them got more brazen, taking swigs between bites of their pizzas, giggling and glancing around in an obvious way. Once or twice they offered the flask round the rest of the table. Me and Maya shook our heads, but Tom and Charlie both took a large mouthful before giving it back to Ria.

Just before our desserts arrived, Sophie and Tom sneaked off towards the kitchen. A few minutes later, a waiter advanced towards our table, carrying a plate of tiramisu stuck with several candles, and a fizzing, spitting sparkler. Most of the restaurant broke into a chorus of "Happy Birthday", while Ria grinned and pretended to be mortified.

"Like she isn't enjoying every moment," Maya whispered to me.

By the time we reached the pier all the neon lights were on, a dazzle of different colours. "C'mon," yelled Ria, heading for the dodgems at the end. The three of us looked at each other when we got there. It was only two to a car.

"You go with Charlie," I told Maya, climbing into the neighbouring car with Tom.

"Want to drive?" he asked.

I shook my head. "I'm fine."

It was true. I felt another rush of happiness as we sat

there, waiting for the dodgems to start. The air was still warm with the day's sun and I was enjoying myself. Properly enjoying myself, wanting to savour the moment.

"Hold on," said Tom, as the ride jolted into life. I squealed as we tore round the rink, chasing after Charlie, who was weaving in and out of the slower cars, trying to shake us off. Maya hanging on to the side panel to keep her balance.

The blare of music overhead. I felt dizzy, laughing as we swung past Ria and Sophie. Then suddenly Charlie yanked hard on the steering wheel, spinning round so we smashed into them head-on. I just had time to brace myself for the impact, but Maya, who'd been waving at Ria, was thrown violently forward.

"Ouch!" I heard her yell, putting her hand up to her neck and glaring at Charlie. "That bloody hurt."

In that instant all the other cars came to a halt. The end of the session. Charlie raised his hands in a gesture of surrender. "Sorry. It was an accident."

Tom eyed him without speaking, but Maya glared at Charlie. "You shouldn't have been driving so fast," she complained, massaging her neck.

Charlie shrugged. "Sorry," he said again, clearly subdued. "You okay?" he asked, watching as Tom offered me a hand to climb out the car.

I nodded, turning to Ria as she bounced towards us. "Hey, guys. You coming on the rollercoaster?" She looked even more buzzed than earlier. Had she and Sophie somehow refilled that flask? What was in it anyway?

We followed her to the entrance. "After you," Charlie said gallantly to Maya as we approached, trying to get back in her good books. But she just shook her head. "You two go. My neck hurts."

Charlie looked a little annoyed, but he didn't say anything. Maya could be like that sometimes, spiky and quick-tempered. We'd both learned it was best not to argue. Let it blow over.

"You up for it?" He turned to me. I glanced back at Maya, but she was already walking off in the other direction, chatting to Tom. I should go after her, I thought, check she's okay, but Charlie was gazing at me, waiting for my answer.

Truth was, I wasn't good with heights, and though the coaster was quite small, it was still a long drop to the sea below. And it was set close to the edge of the pier, like you might fly off at a corner and fall into the water.

Live dangerously, the voice in my head reminded me. Go with the flow.

So I sat with Charlie at the back. "Hope they've got the track fixed this time," he said as we began to climb towards the first drop.

"What do you mean?" I swung round to look at him. He was grinning from ear to ear. Beneath us the pier was receding. I could see miles into the distance, all the way to Shoreham.

"Nicole told me about it. It was years ago now. They

removed some track for routine maintenance, but forgot to inform the blokes operating the ride. They sent eight people off on it."

I swallow, my skin prickling. "You mean they died?"

"Duh," said Charlie, the track flattening out as we curved round on ourselves. Underneath, seeming far below us now, the dark mass of the sea.

"Better hold on tight," he whispered as we tipped over the brink and plummeted downwards. I squeezed my eyes shut, biting back the urge to whimper. Up in front, I could hear Ria and Sophie screaming and laughing, somehow both at once.

Oh, god. My hands began to sweat as I clutched the guard rail. *Please let this end.*

All I could think of was those poor people, plunging to their deaths in that missing section of track. The split second when they realized they were in free fall.

"Lee?" Charlie's voice in my ear, half lost in the rush of noise around me. "You okay?"

I opened my eyes briefly, just in time to see us hurtling towards the loop-the-loop. I shut them again quickly, tightening my grip on the bar to counteract the sensation of collapsing in on myself.

Please let this stop. *Please.*

Aeons later I felt the car slow as it slid back into the station. I opened my eyes. Charlie was peering at me, laughing. "You should see yourself, Lee. Like you've seen a ghost."

I glanced at my hands, my knuckles white where I'd clung on so hard. When I got to my feet, my legs felt shaky and weak.

Charlie offered me his hand and helped me off. "I was only kidding, you know."

"About what?" I stammered.

"The accident. They didn't die, those passengers. Someone saw what had happened and stopped the ride. It was a pretty close call though."

I frowned, uncertain. Was he trying to make me feel better?

"Really," Charlie said. "Google it if you don't believe me. They were all fine."

I snatched my hand away and glared at him, but that only made him laugh even more.

Chapter 8

After Ria had spent half her birthday money in the amusement arcade, we walked along the seafront to the opposite pier – or rather what remained of it. That ruined hulk looming out of the water, black and skeletal.

It always made me sad to look at it. Abandoned decades ago, left to collapse and fall. Most of it gone now, home only to the hordes of starlings that roosted there in winter.

We picked our way towards the water's edge, spreading jackets over the stones to make sitting more comfortable. On the horizon, the sun was beginning to set, the sky turning orange.

"You okay?" I asked Maya, who'd been quiet ever since our collision on the dodgems.

"Sure," she said, nodding, but Charlie curled his lip.

"Girl stuff?"

Maya frowned. "What do you mean?"

He shrugged. "You know…*girl stuff.* Nicole is always in a right mood beforehand."

"Hey!" Maya eyeballed him. "Sexist much?"

"I'm not being sexist. Just saying how it is." He turned to me for backup, but found me staring at him.

"You mean, *Nicole tells you*?" I couldn't imagine even Mum, who was a GP and used to discussing all sorts of stuff with patients, ever mentioning her period.

"What's the big deal?" Charlie shrugged again, as if that kind of mother–son conversation was the most normal thing in the world.

It was moments like this that made me wonder. No matter how well you thought you knew someone, no matter how much time you spent together, perhaps other people remained strangers, their internal landscape as different to yours as Earth's to the moon. Maya was obviously thinking something similar, because she glanced at me, her eyebrows raised.

The three of us were sitting a little apart from the others. Not deliberately, but somehow we always ended up that way, set back from the crowd. Comfortable together.

That's how it was with Maya, Charlie and me. We'd got so used to each other that it was an effort to hang out with anyone else; when we did I was more on my guard, never free of a slight tinge of anxiety. With Maya and Charlie, however, I felt relaxed. I didn't have to overthink everything. Could simply be myself.

Turning towards the sea, I noticed Tom look away quickly, as if caught in the act. He too seemed to be on the edge of things; one of our crowd, sometimes hanging out at school with Sophie and Ria, but always a bit aloof.

I guessed it was down to his dad being a teacher – that would set anyone apart.

Though of course, it could just be the way he was. Quieter, more private. I could relate to that.

I studied the deepening sunset, Ria and Sophie and the others chattering away in the background. The whole sky now alight with red and orange as the sun sank into the sea, the vivid colours in sharp contrast to the wreck of the pier, turning it darker and more foreboding.

A small cheer went up. I turned to see Dan Lawrence making his way towards us, several packs of lager dangling from each hand.

"Sorry I'm late." He bent to kiss Ria on the cheek. "Happy birthday," he declared, raising the cans to indicate they were his present.

Ria giggled as he flopped onto the stones. She'd always fancied Dan, who at fifteen looked more like twenty-five, and never got ID'd in supermarkets.

"Yes, please." She held out her hand as Dan pulled cans free from the plastic mesh, passing them around. Charlie took one for himself, another two for Maya and me.

"Cheers." Charlie ripped the ring pull, then clinked the tip of his can against mine and Maya's before leaning across the pebbles to do the same with everyone else.

"Cheers," we all echoed. I took a sip of my lager, trying not to grimace at the sour taste. I didn't want the others to know I'd never had alcohol before. But I looked up to see Tom smiling at me.

"You'll get used to it," he said, and he was right – after the third mouthful or so it stopped tasting so bad.

I lay back on my elbows, listening to the rhythmic suck and swish of the waves, the sizzling sound as they retreated over the shingle. It was such a beautiful evening. Most of the day trippers had gone, leaving a few locals. A couple walking arm in arm. Several people with dogs. And further along, a hundred metres or so towards Hove, the lights and tents of a group of fishermen.

"Roll on next year," Maya sighed, crossing her long brown legs.

"How do you mean?"

"We can go off somewhere else to do A levels, if we want. And I'll be sixteen, which means my mum will have to get off my back."

"You reckon?" Charlie smirked, and I smiled too. I couldn't imagine Maya's mother ever admitting defeat.

"Seriously, I can't wait," said Maya. "Bring on the rest of my life."

Charlie laughed, though I wasn't sure why this was funny. It seemed kind of sad, in a way. Sure, I was excited about the future, but it wasn't like I wanted to abandon the past. The life I was living right now.

What was wrong with it anyway?

The sunset faded to indigo. Far out in the channel, the lights of a boat slid slowly across the horizon. Dan went off to buy more booze, returning with a litre of vodka and a couple of large bottles of cola.

Part of me felt concerned that things were getting out of hand, but another part was slightly numb and buzzy, like it wasn't worth the worry.

As Maya said, we were growing older.

Almost grown up.

So I didn't object when Dan poured vodka into each of our empty beer cans, topping it up with cola. "What we need is a drinking game," he said, sitting back down. "How about Never Have I Ever?"

"Only if we keep it clean," said Maya, sticking out her tongue at him.

"Okay." Dan looked around and grinned. "Never have I ever…read *Wuthering Heights*."

"But that's one of our texts for English," protested Ria. "Of course we've all read it."

"Not me," Dan laughed, waiting for everyone to take a swig from their can. "No cheating…" He gave me a meaningful look, so I forced myself to try a sip. It wasn't too bad, tasted mainly of cola with a lagery tinge.

"Never have I ever –" Sophie paused to think – "been to Paris."

I had to swallow another mouthful. Mum and Dad took me and Katy to Disneyland before Walt was born. Katy had sulked the whole way there, refusing to sit by me in the back of the car; in the end Mum swapped seats with her just to shut her up.

Maya was next. She seemed confused about the point of the game. "Never have I ever eaten bacon-flavoured crisps," she said eventually, forcing everyone – herself included – to take another drink.

"You're supposed to pick something that lets you off the hook," I hissed under my breath.

Maya shrugged. "Oh well."

"Never have I ever…been to the zoo." Charlie looked around triumphantly, expecting everyone but himself to tip back their cans.

Sophie stared at him, eyebrows raised in surprise. "You're joking, aren't you? Didn't you ever go with your mum?"

"Nope," Charlie said casually, catching my eye. I gazed back at him. Had Nicole not taken him when he was small, even to that little one over in Alfriston? I'd never thought to ask. Assumed it was the kind of thing all parents did.

We each took a swig, then Tom broke the silence before it could get awkward. "Never have I ever…ridden a horse."

Dan, Sophie and Ria gulped more of their drinks and suddenly it was my turn. "Never have I ever…" I tried desperately to think of something, but my mind had gone blank. "Um…lost a game of Scrabble."

God, how lame could I get? Everyone laughed, and downed another mouthful. Dan got up and refilled our cans.

"Never have I ever…" Ria started, then paused when Sophie nudged her and leaned over to whisper into her ear.

"No way," Ria hissed.

Sophie looked at her defiantly. "A dare is a dare."

Ria sighed, then turned to the rest of us, her eyes flashing in the dwindling light. "Never have I ever... done it."

There was a silence. "Done what?" I asked, confused, before catching the expressions of everyone around me.

"Oh, for god's sake, Laurie," Ria sighed again. "Don't make me spell it out."

I felt my cheeks flush. Turned and caught Charlie peering at me through the darkness. His eyes lingered for a moment before sliding away.

A general air of hesitation while we all considered what to do. Drink or not drink? Either way, you were damned.

"This is a stupid game." Charlie downed the rest of his can in one go.

Maya and I exchanged glances. Out of the corner of my eye, I saw Tom watching Charlie, his expression unreadable.

"Time to cool off a bit," Sophie exclaimed. Slipping off her sandals, she edged across the shingle. Stuck a toe into the water.

"Cold!" she squealed, making us all laugh.

But Charlie leaped up. "Last one in gets more booze," he declared, stripping off his T-shirt and shorts, leaving on a pair of black boxers. With a roar he ran down the beach and plunged into the sea.

Tom stared after him, seemingly transfixed. Then got up and ran after him, Dan on his heels. They shrugged off their clothes and charged into the waves, their arms held high, groaning as the water rose up around their waists.

None of us girls moved. Too embarrassed, probably, to strip to our underwear. Certainly I was.

We sat there watching as they waded past the breakers, Charlie and Tom plunging into a crawl, Dan adopting a more uncertain breaststroke.

It took a moment or so to realize where they were heading. Out towards the end of West Pier. Several minutes later we saw Charlie pull himself onto one of the horizontal crossbars that ran between the corroded iron struts.

"They're mad," said Sophie, gazing at them.

"Idiots," agreed Maya.

As Dan and Tom caught up, I watched Charlie, one hand clutching an upright girder, turn and wave at the shore. My chest tightened. The whole structure looked insanely precarious, like it might collapse at any moment.

Still, I raised my arm and waved back. There was a pause, then Charlie let go, diving into the water again.

I waited for him to surface. Counted the seconds till his head appeared above the waves.

One…

Two…

Three…

Four…

Still no sign of him. I peered into the darkness.

Six…

Seven…

Eight...

Nine...

"Shit, where is he?" Maya's voice was urgent as we both scrambled to our feet. "Can you see him?"

I ran down to the shore, heart pounding.

Twelve...

Thirteen...

Fourteen...

Charlie, where the hell are you? I could make out Dan and Tom hanging onto the pier, eyes scanning the water, evidently asking themselves the same thing.

Fifteen...

Sixteen...

"Lee," I heard Maya yell after me. "What on earth are you doing?"

I didn't stop. I waded in, ignoring the shock of freezing water as it swirled around my legs, my waist, my chest, soaking my clothes as I plunged forward. My breath ragged with cold and panic.

Nineteen...

Twenty...

Charlie, was all I could think. *Charlie...*

It was at that moment I knew, as I started to swim towards the pier, legs kicking against the waves. Knew for certain what he meant to me.

Suddenly, out of nowhere, someone grabbed my leg. Charlie surfaced right in front of me, his face contorted into a grin.

"Bit overdressed for skinny-dipping, aren't you, Lee?"

I glared at him for a moment, my feet feeling for the bottom, toes grazing the pebbles beneath.

"You stupid…" I thumped him on the chest, pushing myself away.

Then burst into tears.

Chapter 9

"Won't your mum mind?"

I stood in the doorway while Charlie searched his jacket pockets for his key. I was shaking with cold. My clothes had stopped dripping, but my jeans and top clung to my skin. I was freezing, despite the loan of Charlie's fleece.

"She's not here," he said, finally locating the key and opening the door. "She's gone to Bristol to see a friend."

I felt a shiver of relief. Lately I'd started to feel like an intruder in the flat whenever Nicole was home. As if I were in the way somehow.

"Don't you mind staying here on your own?" I asked.

Charlie shrugged. "Why would I? I'm old enough to take care of myself." He groped in the airing cupboard in the hallway and handed me a towel. "Here." He nodded towards the bathroom. "You go first."

Closing the door behind me, I stripped off and turned on the shower. My legs were weak and tired and I still felt trembly – whether from the shock, the cold or the alcohol, or all three.

I'd planned to go straight home, walking back with

Maya, but Charlie insisted I come to the flat first to get warm and dry. I think he felt bad about the whole diving-in-to-rescue-him thing.

Plus I was worried about the booze, the smell of it on my breath. If I went home now, Mum and Dad were bound to notice. And the fact that I was soaked to the skin might just tip them off that we hadn't exactly been behaving ourselves.

The shower was gloriously warm, but I didn't stay in long. I knew Charlie must be cold too, and desperate to wash off all that seawater. So I didn't bother with soap or anything, just rinsed my skin and hair.

It was only when I got out that I remembered I had nothing to wear. Unless I was going to put my wet clothes back on.

Right at that moment I heard a knock.

"Laurie? You decent?"

"One sec." I grabbed a towel and wrapped it around me, then opened the bathroom door.

"Thought you might need this." Charlie grinned, holding out a white towelling bathrobe. "I'll chuck your stuff in the tumble dryer."

"Thanks." I took the robe and handed over my clothes, but Charlie lingered, his gaze intent.

"Do you like Tom?" he asked suddenly.

I frowned. "What do you mean?"

"Tom Rochester. I just wondered if maybe…you know. You might have a thing for him."

I laughed, taken aback. "Why would you think that?"

Charlie stared at me for several seconds. "No reason," he said, but for a moment he seemed relieved. "He was watching us, that's all. I reckon he has a crush on you."

I pulled a face. Not because I didn't like Tom, or anything; more that the whole conversation was making me uncomfortable.

Why was Charlie even bringing this up?

"Want me to get you Nicole's hairdryer?" He reached out and picked up a lock of my wet hair.

"Please."

While he was gone, I put on the bathrobe and rubbed toothpaste round my gums with my finger. I could still taste the vodka.

How long were my clothes likely to take? I wondered, then asked myself why I even cared. What was the hurry? It was only ten. I told Mum I'd be back around eleven.

Live dangerously, I repeated to myself, but the truth was I felt awkward hanging around in just a bathrobe. It was not having Maya here, I realized. Charlie and I had seen each other half-naked dozens of times over the years – at the swimming pool and down on the beach – but Maya had always been with us. Three's a crowd, after all. It felt less of an issue.

But here, somehow, it *was* an issue. And there was something else. A year or two ago we were barely in our teens. Now, all at once, I felt worlds older, and everything seemed to have shifted. Become more uncertain. More ambiguous.

"Sorted." Charlie reappeared, a towel wrapped round his torso that emphasized how his shoulders had broadened, the muscles on his legs become more pronounced. It made me aware how much he'd changed, losing the slight chubbiness of a few summers ago. Puppy fat, as Mum called it.

Charlie was definitely no longer a pup. He was growing taller and more angular with every passing day.

"Make yourself a hot chocolate or something," he said. "I won't be long."

I stood in the kitchen while he showered. Watched my clothes revolving in the machine. "There's some oven chips in the freezer," Charlie called from behind the bathroom door. "Stick them on, will you? I'm starving."

I rooted through the freezer drawers. Found the bag of chips and tipped the lot onto a baking tray, then shoved them in the oven.

I was hungry too. The pizza we ate seemed more like days than hours ago.

Five minutes later Charlie joined me, dressed in a fresh white T-shirt and a pair of navy cotton tracksuit bottoms. His hair smelled faintly of lemon shampoo, and when he rubbed it with a towel, dozens of little ringlets bounced up all over his scalp.

I resisted the urge to reach out, to press the palm of my hand against them. Feel their springiness.

"Smells good," he said, like I was cooking some kind of gourmet meal.

"What?" I laughed. "Oven chips? Have you got anything to go with them?"

I hadn't seen much in the freezer, beyond a few packets of burgers, some frozen peas and sweetcorn. An ancient tub of caramel ice cream. Nothing that would actually do you any good.

Everything about Charlie's home life seemed like this. Slightly neglected. The way his mum had been happy to leave him alone since he turned twelve, sometimes for several nights in a row. How he often had to fend for himself when it came to food, taking cash from the pot Nicole left in the kitchen.

Charlie never seemed bothered. Never saw it as odd. Appeared to think it was a bonus that Nicole trusted him to look after himself. He didn't seem to mind not having a father around either. "Can't miss someone you don't know," he said the one time I asked.

Though I wasn't sure that was true. It would still leave an absence in your life, wouldn't it? Losing out on what most people took for granted?

"When did you say you'd be back?" Charlie asked, pulling bottles of tomato sauce and mayonnaise from the cupboard.

I glanced at the clock on the wall. Half ten already.

"Soon." I peered into the washer-dryer, but my clothes were still wet, nowhere near ready. Anyway, the chips would take another twenty minutes, I thought, considering whether to ring Dad and warn him I'd be late. He always worried when Katy stayed out longer than agreed – the ex-policeman in him never off duty.

"Hey, relax." Charlie handed me a drink, then flopped on the sofa in the living room. "Why not call and say you're sleeping over at Maya's?"

I frowned. "But I'm not."

"I know that, Lee. But you can stay here instead. Keep me company."

Heat rose to my cheeks. "Why don't I just let my parents know I'm here?"

Charlie didn't answer.

And I read everything into his silence. I couldn't say that to Mum or Dad, cos they'd ask if Maya was with us. Or Nicole.

Why was it weird, that I couldn't tell them I was alone with Charlie? I mean, last year Maya and I had slept over at hers, when her parents were away for the night, and Charlie was too tired to bother. Neither of my parents had objected to that. Why was this so different?

Because it was, said a little voice in my head. It just was.

And Charlie knew it too. I could tell by the way he couldn't quite meet my eyes.

Oh god. Suddenly I wanted to leave, immediately, embarrassment coursing through my veins like the alcohol I'd had earlier. But I couldn't. I needed my clothes.

Maybe I should borrow something of Charlie's? But he was miles taller than me. I'd look absurd, and it would only alert my parents to what we'd been up to. Start them off on a train of questions which would almost certainly lead to the booze.

It was a skill I hadn't yet developed – the art of evasion.

"Reckon those chips must be ready." Charlie went into the kitchen and removed them from the oven, piling them onto one large plate, with a little mound of ketchup and mayonnaise on the side. "Salt and vinegar?"

I nodded. He dowsed them in both, then brought the plate back to the sofa, placing it between us. I tucked my feet under the bathrobe, picked up a chip and nibbled the tip. It was hot and insanely delicious. I grabbed another, and soon Charlie and I were racing, shoving them into our mouths, half choking and laughing.

I tried to snatch the last one but Charlie got there first. He put the empty plate on the floor, then dangled the chip in front of my face.

"Come and get it."

I made a lunge, but Charlie whisked it away, forcing me to lean back to recover my balance.

He grinned. "Not fast enough."

Teasing me. No, *flirting* with me, I realized, self-consciousness rushing back. Somehow, in the space of a few hours, we'd moved from being friends to being…what?

Charlie caught my serious expression and his smile faltered. "What's up?"

"Nothing." I got off the sofa, went to retrieve the plate. But Charlie's hand shot out and circled my wrist.

"Don't go."

I hovered there, resisting his attempt to pull me back down. Still time to turn this into a joke. Pretend nothing was meant by it.

"Lee…"

"What?"

"Come here."

I sat back on the sofa, and as I did, the front of my bathrobe gaped open. I put a hand up to adjust it but Charlie's fingers tightened around my wrist.

"Come here," he said again.

I closed my eyes. Stalling.

"Lee." His voice was quieter, almost breathless. "Look at me."

I forced my eyes open and Charlie held my gaze, daring me to break it. Then lifted his hand and ran a finger down my cheek.

"Lee," he whispered, as he leaned forward and his lips closed on mine.

And I let him.

I let him and it wasn't weird any more. It felt like something that was meant to be. Something that had always been lying in wait. Waiting for us to arrive.

I let him lead the way, and it was like waking to sunshine, everything smooth and golden.

And love settled around me, taking root in my heart like a seed sown in summer, bursting with life and promise.

Chapter 10

Damn.

As I came in through the back door, I found Mum in the kitchen, folding laundry. I'd thought she was at the surgery this morning. Had been hoping to sneak in unnoticed.

"Good time?" she asked, as she tackled a pile of Dad's shirts. Despite not working, he still wore long-sleeved shirts every day – though he no longer bothered with a tie.

"Great." I forced myself to meet Mum's gaze, but could only stand the contact for a second or two. "Ria had a fab time."

"How's Maya?"

I held my breath. Why was she asking? Mum only saw Maya the other day, after all; they'd chatted in the garden about their favourite TV shows.

Had Mum guessed I wasn't at Maya's last night? Could she possibly know?

"She's fine." I kept my voice light and airy, relieved when Mum returned to grappling with the laundry. She was on autopilot, I realized, going through the motions.

You could always tell that with Mum. You could be

having a whole conversation with her, then it would dawn on you that she wasn't really listening to any of it. She was talking off the top of her head, her mind a million miles away, pondering a patient or problem at the practice, or deciding what to cook for supper.

Then Mum straightened up, and from the way her eyes fixed on mine I knew I'd landed back in her thoughts. "You look tired, honey." She paused, the basket of clothes suspended in mid-air. "Up late?"

"A bit." I tried desperately to think of some way to distract her, to change the subject.

I felt Mum could see right inside me. Could tell I hadn't been tucked up in a sleeping bag in Maya's bedroom, chatting and gossiping late into the night. Could tell I'd been with Charlie.

My stomach clenched. What if Mum suspected something? What if she mentioned it to Maya next time she was here? Asked about our supposed sleepover?

I should warn Maya, I decided. Ask her to back me up. But in that instant I knew I wouldn't tell her anything about what happened with Charlie, though I wasn't exactly sure why. It felt…too private, too precious.

Even thinking this way gave me a hot flush of betrayal. As if somehow I was shutting out my friend. Breaking our triangle.

"I need a pee." I skirted round Mum and headed upstairs. Bumped headlong into Katy as she emerged from her room.

"Hey, watch it." She held her hands up like I was some kind of hazard, and I saw the Barbie pink polish drying on her nails. I went to pass her but my sister blocked my path, gazing at me in that inscrutable way she has where you can't tell what she's thinking, but you just know it isn't good.

"Where have you been?" she asked.

I blinked. Since when did Katy care what I did with myself? She always behaved like my life was too boring to contemplate. As if my utter lack of cool might be contagious.

"Maya's," I lied.

She didn't respond to that. Just carried on giving me a hard stare.

"Anyway, what's it to you?" I asked.

She shrugged. "I heard there was a bit of a party last night. Down on the beach."

She had? News travelled fast.

"It wasn't a party – just Ria and some friends. It was her birthday."

Her mouth twitched. She was jealous, I realized. Miffed she hadn't been invited. Even though Katy hung out with a completely different crowd, and wouldn't normally be seen dead with any of my friends.

But that was my sister for you – the slightest sniff of me having anything, and she wanted in on it.

"I need the loo." I pushed past her and locked myself in the bathroom. Taking a deep breath, I stared into the mirror. My reflection gazed back at me, looking much the same as usual. Same brown hair, unplucked eyebrows. Slightly long nose.

Only the shadows beneath my eyes were a little darker, more pronounced. Probably the wear and tear of the vodka and not enough sleep. Or simply the remains of the mascara I'd forgotten to wash off.

I replayed what had happened, going through every moment in my head. Last night had been a first for me in so many ways. Not only the alcohol – I'd never even kissed a boy before, unless you counted those stupid playground games at primary school.

Yet somehow, despite my lack of experience, it had all felt completely natural, one thing flowing on to another. I hadn't even been embarrassed at Charlie seeing me naked.

I peered into the mirror again, unable to believe that something so significant had left no trace. But what was I expecting? Some mysterious inner glow? That I'd look… what…older? More experienced?

My reflection smiled at that.

I glanced at the bath. I fancied running one, deep and hot and full of that lovely honeysuckle bath oil Maya gave me for my birthday. But I could still smell Charlie on me, his scent lingering on my skin. I didn't want to wash away the only reminder that last night was real.

I peed, then shut myself in my room and lay on my bed, examining all the familiar objects. My wardrobe, rescued from one of Mum's de-cluttering campaigns. It was old, with chipped white paint and a door that didn't close properly, but I liked to think of it as vintage.

My desk, loaded with files and textbooks, and pens in the various mugs I'd collected over the years. My bookshelf crammed with my favourite novels. The beanbag Mum and Dad got me for my fourteenth birthday, the seams already splitting from Walt's habit of rolling around in it whenever my back was turned.

All my things. The same as they ever were. Hard to believe the last time I was here – just yesterday afternoon – nothing had happened. I felt like a whole other person now. That the world, somehow, had been remade in my absence.

How could I not have known? Not have sensed what was coming?

Love.

And what love meant.

A shiver as my body flashed back to the sensation of Charlie's skin against mine. My pale white against his warm gold. His muscles taut and hard under his flesh. The feel of his lips, soft but firm. The scent of him, new and yet familiar.

My feelings for Charlie had crept up on me so slowly I hadn't noticed. Like watching the minute hand move on a clock – you couldn't detect the motion, but it was there.

Till one day…one night… It was like I'd always loved him, and always would. And he felt the same. I was certain of it. I remembered his smile as he nuzzled against me afterwards. The way he kissed my ear.

"I love you."

I was sure I'd heard him say that, later, just before we fell asleep. I hadn't imagined it, had I?

But when I woke in the morning, after nine, he was gone. Back to the deckchairs. Back to the day trippers and the tourists, the noise and the sweat and the banter. Like working in a fairground, he said. Or a bar. Acting cheerful. Cheeky.

I sighed and closed my eyes. Saw Charlie's face hovering over mine. His honey smile. Maybe I'll go and see him later, I thought, longing to be near him again, to make sure it was real. That I hadn't just imagined the whole thing.

I picked up my phone. Went to call his number, then remembered he never answered it when he was working. Not wanting to get in trouble with his boss.

My next impulse was to ring Maya. Confess everything. The urge to talk about last night was almost overwhelming.

But then I pictured the hurt in her face...how she'd feel like a gooseberry now, whenever the three of us got together. The odd one out.

Besides, who said Charlie wanted her to know? I felt the ache of loyalty divided, the weight of the dilemma I'd created for myself. Charlie and Maya – my best friends. The two people I cared about most in the world, beyond Mum and Dad, Walt and my grandparents. Perhaps Katy.

Nothing must come between the three of us.

I'll wait, I told myself. I'll wait till I see Charlie and I'll ask him what we'll say.

He'll know how to handle it. Charlie always knows what to do.

Chapter 11

"What's up, love?"

"Mmm…" I lifted my head. Dad was standing by the kitchen table, giving me one of his concerned looks.

"Nothing," I mumbled.

"Laurie's been in a right mood." My brother stopped eating his cereal and glared at me. I smiled back, but he stuck out his tongue. Walt could always read me, with that uncanny radar small kids seem to have for other people's feelings.

"It's only a headache," I told Dad. "I'm fine, really."

Lies. All of it. Three days since that night with Charlie, and already I was getting better at hiding the truth.

"Have you told Mum? She'll give you something." Dad shrugged his coat onto his shoulders. It was a warm day, way too hot for coats, but Dad always wore his up to the allotment. It had deep pockets that held everything he needed: secateurs, bits of string for tying plants, plastic labels and an indelible marker.

"I took some ibuprofen," I said, wishing he'd leave and take his scrutiny with him. But he didn't move, waiting for

Walt to finish his breakfast. When he wasn't at school, my little brother always went with Dad to the allotment. Loved the place almost as much as Dad, who'd given him his own patch of ground by the shed.

Walt had sown it with sweet peas and marigolds, flowers he could pick and give to Mum.

"You do look a bit peaky, Laurie," Dad persisted.

A bit peaky. I wondered if that was something Mum studied at medical school. Off colour. Under the weather. Out of sorts. They probably even had pills for it these days, I thought, before remembering that they did: Dad went on antidepressants when he gave up work.

I'd never really got to the bottom of why he left the police. A couple of difficult cases, Mum had said. Long hours, overwork. But she didn't give any details, and I never felt I could ask Dad. Didn't want to remind him of things he'd probably prefer to forget.

I inhaled, forcing myself to appear brighter. "I'm fine," I repeated. "Really. Stop worrying."

Dad waited for Walt to swallow the last of his cornflakes and stack his bowl in the dishwasher. Katy's, I noticed, was still lingering on the table like an afterthought, so I got up and cleared it myself.

"Have a nice time." I gave Dad a kiss on the cheek, then ruffled Walt's hair for good measure, but he just scowled up at me.

Not fooled for a minute.

*   *   *

Three days, and no word from Charlie. Not even a text.

Day one, I was okay. Still high on the memories of the night before. He's just busy, I told myself. Caught up with work.

With the second day came a niggle of anxiety, the first dent in my happiness. The afterglow of our night together faded as doubt crept in. Had I read it all wrong? Was it a one-off? Did Charlie *really* like me or would he rather just stay friends?

I longed to hear his voice, have him tell me everything was okay between us, but I fought the impulse to ring him. Better it came from him. Willingly.

By the third day I was beginning to crack. Don't call, I told myself, as I went back upstairs and checked my phone for the thousandth time. Distract yourself, Laurie. Wait for him to come to you.

But Maya was visiting family in Peckham, and I hadn't the heart for anyone or anything else. I picked up a book she'd lent me, been raving about for weeks, but couldn't get beyond the first chapter. Words had somehow drained of meaning, just print on the page.

I fired up my laptop and went online, but the urge to root through Charlie's profiles on social media was overwhelming. I hunted for new status updates, clues as to what he was up to, but there was nothing.

His last post had been the day of the party. A selfie of him on the seafront that afternoon, sun still high in the sky, arm around the shoulder of some guy I didn't know – one of the other deckies, I was guessing. Both of them leering at the camera, eyes widened, teeth bared.

It looked nothing like Charlie. If the photo hadn't been on his account, I would barely have recognized him. Maybe Charlie was getting into a new crowd, I thought. Meeting new people, leaving me and Maya behind.

Maybe I didn't matter to him at all.

I made it through to midday before the desire to contact him grew into a compulsion. One I could no longer resist.

I grabbed my mobile and called Charlie's number. It rang for several seconds before cutting into voicemail.

I didn't leave a message. Just sent a text.

"Call me."

He was probably too busy to check his phone, I reassured myself, when I heard nothing back. It was a glorious day. The deckchairs would be doing a brisk trade, and Charlie covered the whole section from the Palace Pier to the volleyball court beneath The Grand hotel. Some days he barely got time to grab a sandwich for lunch.

By mid-afternoon, however, I was trying to convince myself he'd left his phone at home, or the battery had gone flat.

An hour later I caved. Grabbed my bag and headed to the bus stop. It was nearly five by the time I got to the seafront. I walked along the promenade, scouring the beach for Charlie. There were still a lot of people around, so it was hard work, searching for his face amongst so many. I focused on hair, looking for his trademark curls.

I'd almost reached the Palace Pier when I finally spotted him, down on the shingle, gathering up the vacant chairs. I made my way across the pebbles, uncertain whether to call out. He had his back to me, couldn't see me coming.

"Charlie?" I said, when I was a few metres away.

His body stiffened at the sound of my voice. I caught the tension in his face as he turned to me.

"Laurie."

My proper name, I noticed. Not Lee, his and Maya's pet name for me since we did *Cider with Rosie* in English.

Up to this point I'd been planning to play it cool. To pretend I was out for a stroll, just happened to bump into him. But seeing him now I knew that was stupid. It was obvious why I was here. No fooling either of us.

"How are you?" I asked.

"Okay." Charlie's expression was awkward, fidgety, like someone trying to appear relaxed and failing miserably. "You know, busy." He nodded at the empty deckchairs scattered across the beach. People were leaving, prompted by the evening breeze picking up along the coast.

"Sorry." I couldn't think of anything else to say.

"S'okay." His lips twitched, but didn't manage a smile. "It's good to see you."

Is it? I thought, examining his face. It didn't seem like it. Everything about his manner implied a new distance, a gap opening further between us with each passing minute.

Charlie had somehow become a stranger these past three days.

How could this have happened?

What had I done wrong?

"I was wondering," I blurted, trying not to sound desperate. Knowing I shouldn't be pushing like this, but unable to stop myself. "If you wanted to do something tomorrow."

Tuesdays were Charlie's day off.

He looked to the side of me. Scratched his nose. "I can't. I'm sorry. I'm going away."

Shock jolted through me. "Where?"

"Nicole's taking me up to see my grandad in Norfolk."

I frowned. Charlie always said his mum hardly spoke to any of her family. "That's a bit sudden. You never mentioned anything about it before."

"He's not very well," Charlie replied, but there was something shifty in his gaze. "Mum only arranged it yesterday."

Abruptly, he turned away. Started carrying the deckchairs up the beach, two in each hand.

I stood there, feeling lost, almost winded. Why had Charlie's behaviour changed completely? He was so different from the other night, so different from how he'd ever been. His manner verging on cold. As if he couldn't wait for me to leave.

A pain behind my ribs, like a rupture. Tears stung my eyes.

"Charlie," I stammered, going after him.

He stopped and turned. Saw the anguish on my face. He seemed agitated, his features hovering between indecision and…something else. Something worse. He looked wretched. Torn, like he wanted to leave, but couldn't quite bring himself to walk away.

"Lee…I…" He paused. Ran his hand over his face, let it drop back to his side. "I have to go. My mum doesn't want to go to Norfolk on her own, and it's only for a few days. Let's talk when I get back."

I should have been comforted by his words, but his expression spoke volumes. Sorry, it seemed to say. Sorry, Lee, but you know how it is. Fun while it lasted, but now it's over.

I turned away before he could see me crying. Headed back along the seafront, along the promenade, almost at a run.

Charlie didn't come after me.

Chapter 12

"You heard from Charlie?"

Maya shifted her legs to make more room for mine. We were sitting in my window seat, backs propped with cushions, watching Walt and his friend Ollie play on the lawn below. They'd built an assault course out of buckets and brooms and an assortment of empty cardboard boxes, and appeared to be having a game of who could fall over the most as they tried to leap over them.

Walt was winning. Hands down.

"Nope." I kept my gaze fixed on the garden, afraid that if I looked at my best friend she'd read everything in my face. Maya was like that. One of those outgoing, extrovert types who nevertheless has an uncanny knack of seeing right through you.

"He can't still be at his grandfather's. It's been ages." She laughed as Walt plunged headlong into a pile of boxes, scattering them across the grass.

Three weeks and nothing from Charlie. Not a call, not a text. No updates online. I had no idea where he was. Whether he'd come back from Norfolk after one week, or was still away after three.

"Who knows?" I twisted my mouth into a shrug, wishing I could change the subject without making it obvious. It felt impossible to act naturally. Impossible to get back to that old, easy way of thinking or talking about Charlie.

Who knew one night could change so much?

"I've texted him twice and left loads of messages online, but he's ignoring me," Maya grumbled.

"Maybe he's lost his phone? Forgotten to send us his new number?" I knew I was clutching at straws, but it was possible, wasn't it?

Maya pulled a face, dismissing my suggestion. "You don't suppose he's gone and got himself a girlfriend, do you? You know, done something stupid like fall in love?"

My gaze swung to hers. The shock must have been written all over my face.

Oh god, could Maya be right? Could Charlie have met someone else? Just the thought of it made my stomach ache.

"I know we promised and everything, but that doesn't mean he'll actually stick to it," Maya continued. "He's probably met some girl and forgotten all about us. Jeez… boys," she muttered, screwing up her nose in disgust.

The pact went back to the summer we left primary school. Sparked, I guess, by worries about moving up to secondary school, with all the new experiences and pressures it would bring.

Maya was the one who came up with it, when we were hanging out at The Level. She made us join hands, and each repeat: "I do solemnly swear not to let anyone or anything come between us. Ever."

"Does that mean we can't get married?" Charlie had asked.

Maya thought for a second. "Not necessarily. But only if the bride or groom agrees we three come first. And then only if the other two like them."

It sounded daft now, of course, but at eleven, it seemed deadly serious. Though we'd kind of joked about it ever since. Sure, as we got older, we could see how silly it was and yet…and yet some part of me had always dreaded this moment. The moment it all got real, and our affections, our attentions, were diverted elsewhere.

"Lee…you okay?" Maya was staring at me. She had that look, the one Mum and Dad kept giving me. The one that said *we know there's something you're not telling us.*

"Sure." I did my best to make it sound convincing.

"You're not holding out on me, are you?" She kicked my foot gently. "No secrets, remember?"

That was the other part of the pact – that we'd tell each other everything. No secrets from each other – and no lies.

I made myself laugh, though inside I was cringing with guilt. "Like what?"

"I dunno. You tell me."

I returned my gaze to Walt, who was trying to pole-vault a tower of buckets using a bamboo cane. I grappled with the urge to confess everything to Maya. I wanted so desperately to let it all tumble out.

That night. What had happened afterwards.

The terrible anguish I felt when Charlie dismissed me that way, down on the seafront. So abrupt, like nothing had happened between us at all. Like we weren't even friends. Like the pact had never existed.

I turned back to Maya, her concerned expression. Opened my mouth, then closed it again. It wouldn't be fair. Telling her might make me feel a little better – temporarily – but it would drive a wedge further between the three of us, and I didn't think I could bear that. I didn't want Maya forced to take sides, or ending up piggy in the middle of whatever was going on between me and Charlie.

So I searched for something close to the truth. Something that would sound halfway convincing. "I guess I'm just dreading school starting next week. You know, it being our GCSE year and stuff."

It was true enough, after all. I *was* dreading it.

Another lurch of anxiety as I pictured myself face-to-face with Charlie in registration. No avoiding each other there, and I wouldn't even have Maya for support – she was in a different tutor group.

At least during the holidays I could pretend it would all be okay. That there was some simple explanation for Charlie's disappearance. Ironically, not seeing him was keeping my hopes alive; at school we'd be thrown together, and I'd have to deal with it all.

Maya tilted her head to one side. "You usually like school. Why the change?"

I inhaled. Let it out slowly. "I don't know. I suppose it all gets serious from now on. GCSEs at the end of this year, and deciding what we're going to do next."

"But you know what you're going to do," Maya grinned. "Be an astronaut."

I let myself smile at this. Maya and Charlie had been teasing me about it for years, ever since I declared in Year Five that I wanted to go into space. Though of course I'd long since given up the idea.

But right then I wished it wasn't so impossible. Right then I'd have loved to be on a spaceship heading out towards the stars. I'd watch the planet recede to a pinprick, all my problems left behind. Surely, up in that vast emptiness, a broken heart would seem like the smallest thing imaginable?

"I guess you're right." Maya lifted her legs and hugged her knees. "I'm not looking forward to going back either. Tons of work, then revision and exams."

Downstairs I heard the back door open, then Katy yelling at Walt. Bored with jumping over random objects, he and Ollie were now bouncing a tennis ball against the kitchen wall.

Clearly it was annoying my sister, who'd taken over the sink with hair products. "Experimenting," she'd said, when I asked what she was doing. Though why she couldn't experiment in the bathroom was anyone's guess.

"Still," Maya sighed. "At least there's something to look forward to."

"What's that?"

"The prom. Sophie told me they're holding it at The Grand hotel next year. Right posh!" She grinned with excitement.

I suppressed a groan. The Year Eleven prom marked the end of school, a final get together before everyone split off for the summer, destined for different colleges or apprenticeships in the autumn. I'd barely given it a thought recently, though god knows the three of us had discussed it often enough. Mainly who'd go with Charlie – me or Maya.

The last time we talked about it – before we broke up for the holidays – we'd decided we should all three go together. It wasn't obligatory to have a partner, after all.

"But who would get the first dance?" Maya had protested.

"We'll toss a coin," Charlie said, but that just set us off arguing about who should be heads, and who tails.

Back then, the prom had seemed an age away, a distant ship on the horizon. Though now, suddenly, it was looming. No longer so far away at all.

Not that it mattered, I thought, my heart sinking even further. Not now. I had a feeling Charlie had changed his mind.

Heads or tails, he wouldn't be going with me.

Chapter 13

First day back and my heart was thumping as I made my way to registration. It wasn't far, the next block from the cloakrooms. A limit to how long you could spin it out.

I'd nearly reached the classroom when I lost my nerve. Turned and retraced my steps, keeping my head down.

"Hey, Laurie, you're going the wrong way." Tom caught me a moment before I bumped into him. He laughed, then saw my face. "You all right?"

"Fine," I said, clearing my throat.

"You look...sort of panicked. You sure you're okay?"

I lifted my mouth into something resembling a smile. "Oh, you know. Post-holiday nerves. Takes a while to get back into it all."

Tom grinned. "Tell me about it. Even Dad was looking grim at breakfast this morning. Said he couldn't believe the summer had gone so fast."

"Yeah. Anyway, I'd better go. I need a pee before tutor." I darted off before Tom could ask me what I'd been up to since Ria's party, or anything awkward like that.

I cut into the girls' toilets by the science labs. Thanks to a long-standing problem with the taps, which regularly leaked over the floor, most people used the loos further up the corridor. So I wasn't prepared to find myself face-to-face with Katy and her best friends, Sammy and Jo.

Jo was styling Katy's hair, twisting it into a loose topknot and pinning it up with a large tortoiseshell clip.

That's all I need, I thought, as my sister eyeballed me. She'd taken to watching me recently, I'd noticed. I'd look up during meals and find her staring at me, as if trying to figure something out.

"Hi," I said, ignoring my less-than-enthusiastic reception as Sammy and Jo glanced in my direction then turned away.

"Hi, Laurie." Katy sighed as she replied, like it had cost her everything to bother.

I flashed her a sarcastic smile, then locked myself in the loo at the end. Lowering the lid, I sat down, resting my head on the side of the stall. Dead silence outside. I imagined my sister and her mates mouthing things to each other. Gesturing.

A few seconds later, the sound of the door shutting behind them.

Get a grip, Laurie, I told myself, closing my eyes and breathing deeply. It'll be okay. If I could just make it through today, tomorrow would be easier.

After a minute or two, I was more ready to face the world, though I still felt almost faint with dread. I heaved my rucksack onto my shoulder, and went to tutor group.

Hesitating for a second outside the classroom door, before forcing myself to walk inside.

And there he was.

Charlie.

Not in his usual place at the front, but sitting near the back, chatting to Adam Mallin. He glanced towards me as I crossed to a vacant desk, gave a quick nod of his head, then turned back to Adam.

That was it.

All there was.

Though what had I expected? That he'd leap up and kiss me? In front of everyone?

I faced the window. I felt dizzy, my heart beating so fast I thought I might pass out. I mean, I knew Charlie was going to be here. Of course I knew that. But the shock of actually seeing him, of being in the same room, sharing the same space, breathing the same air, left me jolted and shaky. I focused on a couple of Year Nines hurrying into school, wishing for the thousandth time Maya was in the same tutor group. At least I'd have someone to distract me.

Then again, if Maya were here, she'd probably have sat with Charlie, insisted on quizzing him about where he'd been the rest of the summer, and that would have been even worse.

"Greetings." Ms Ryan walked into the classroom and installed herself at the front. "How is everyone? Good summer?"

I tuned out the buzz of replies. What do I say to Charlie?

I thought desperately. How should I behave? Should I ignore him? Or be friendly? But at the same time cool and unconcerned, like I wasn't bothered. As if that night four weeks ago meant nothing to me.

God knows, all I'd thought about these past few days was how I would deal with this moment. Picturing every possible scenario, from Charlie blanking me completely, to him bounding straight over, enveloping me in a hug that told me everything was back to the way it was before.

As if that were possible.

Somehow, though, I'd never imagined it would be quite like this. So casual, so…lukewarm. As if nothing had ever happened. And nothing ever would.

I held it together till lunch break, when Maya disappeared to sort out a problem with her timetable. Grabbing some food, I took advantage of the warm September day and sat outside. On the bench near the playing fields, underneath an oak that still showed no hint of autumn in its leaves.

I nibbled the cheese sandwich I'd bought in the canteen. It was okay, but I wasn't hungry. Hadn't been hungry for a few weeks somehow – as if all my appetite had disappeared with Charlie.

"Lee?"

I turned, my stomach contracting. So hard I felt sick.

Charlie.

He was standing right next to me, leaving me no choice but to look at him properly. His face was darker, I noticed, more tanned, his hair bleached at the tips from the summer sun. He looked fit, healthy, and somehow that made me feel worse. Charlie had clearly thrived in my absence, while I seemed to be wilting, off my food and increasingly tired, everything becoming an effort.

"Mind if I sit?" Charlie nodded at the empty place on the bench. His question revealing he was feeling as awkward as me; a few months ago he'd have plonked himself right down.

I shifted up against the armrest to give him plenty of room. All at once the bench felt way too small, his legs too close to mine, his body seeming to take up all the space between us.

"You okay?" Charlie turned towards me, but I kept my eyes fixed on the group of boys playing footie on the far pitch. Trying to ignore the loud thump-thump-thump of my heart.

"Not bad." It came out as a croak. "You?"

"All right," Charlie replied, with a half sigh that suggested he didn't mean it any more than I did.

"So how was Norfolk?" I kept my gaze forwards, watching the goalie dive to save the ball, catching it with the tips of his fingers.

Charlie didn't answer for a minute or two. I risked a glance at him. He had his face turned away, pretending, like me, to be absorbed in the game. But I could tell from the tension in his jaw that he was thinking hard about what to say.

Had he been dreading this as much as me? Been agonizing for days how best to breach the gap between us? I fought down the urge to take his hand, fold it in mine.

"Norfolk was…well…strange," he said eventually. "I haven't seen my grandfather in nearly ten years. He'd changed. There's something wrong with his lungs, apparently, though no one seems to know what."

"How long did you stay?" The words came out too fast, like an accusation. Which it was, in a way. And Charlie saw that too. Charlie knew what I was really asking: *where the hell have you been for the last four weeks?*

"Lee, listen," he replied, sidestepping my question. "I'm sorry I didn't call or anything."

"Okay." Though of course it wasn't.

"It was difficult."

"Difficult how?" I heard the anger creeping into my voice. How could he just ignore me for the best part of a month? Cut me off like that?

"Laurie…I…" Charlie stopped.

"*Why?*" I turned to him, my expression full of challenge. "Why, Charlie? Why sleep with me if this is how…how you're going to be?"

He scanned around us, checking no one was within earshot. Afraid we might be overheard. "I'm sorry—"

"Sorry?" I snorted. "What for? Screwing me? Or dumping me straight afterwards?" Tears pricked my eyes.

I took a deep breath, blinked them away.

"I don't understand," I added, my voice quieter, but just as fierce. "I can't get my head around why you'd do that."

Charlie cleared his throat, his right leg jiggling in that way it did when he was getting agitated. "My mum found out."

"What do you mean?"

"I had to tell her." He looked at the ground. Unable to face me.

"Had to tell her what?"

A pause before he answered. "She was home, when I got back from work that next day. You know, after Ria's party. I was going to come and see you, Lee, wanted to have a shower first, but Nicole sort of…ambushed me."

He stopped. I could see the strain in his face, and despite myself, despite everything, I wanted to reach out and smooth it away.

"What happened?" I asked instead.

"She found the wrappers in my bedroom bin."

I frowned. "What wrappers?"

Charlie's cheeks reddened. "The…er…you know. The condoms we used."

"So she knows?" I stammered, my own cheeks burning now. "About us?"

I could have kicked myself the moment the words left my mouth. *About us*. It made it sound like I thought there *was* an "us".

Instead of simply hoping.

"Did you tell her it was me?" I asked.

Charlie nodded and I felt a surge of frustration. Why hadn't he made something up? But then Charlie was always a terrible liar. Even that time he accidentally broke Mum's favourite vase and hid the pieces, he ended up confessing the minute Mum noticed it was missing.

One look at him and you knew when he was fibbing. His features went all...twitchy. Like when you're posing for a photograph and you forget what to do with your face.

"Oh shit," I groaned, as the implications of Nicole knowing began to sink in. "So this was...what...the evening after?"

"Yeah, she practically interrogated me when I got home. Then went mental." Charlie shifted in his seat, glancing around again. "I didn't mean to let on it was you, Lee. Honestly. I held out...but she sort of guessed."

"Guessed?"

He flushed again, embarrassed. "She always knew I liked you."

My heart leaped with pleasure, until I clocked exactly what he'd said. *Liked* you.

Past tense.

"How do you mean, went a bit mental?" I prompted, trying not to read too much into his choice of words.

"She went on and on about..." Charlie shuffled on the bench again, clearly uncomfortable. "You know, about you being..." He paused, swallowed. "You being underage. She knows you're not sixteen till next summer."

"Yeah, but you're not sixteen either. Not for another two months."

"I know," Charlie sighed. "I told her that. I told her it was none of her business anyway." He chewed the inside of his lip. "She wouldn't listen to me, Lee. She was really… frantic. I can't explain it. She was acting like it was the biggest disaster in the whole world."

God, I thought. She was a fine one to talk. Everyone knew Nicole Forrest got pregnant with Charlie when she was still in her teens. Apart from anything, it was obvious – she looked more like his sister than his mother.

"So she doesn't like me." I shrugged, trying not to mind. After all, it wasn't as if I had much time for Nicole; even when we were small, she seemed strange to me. Distant, somehow. Unpredictable in her moods. "It doesn't mean you have to do what she says, Charlie. You didn't have to just disappear."

I could hear the bitterness in my voice. The weeks of brooding, of wondering what the hell was going on breaking through.

"It's not that easy," Charlie replied.

I felt myself growing angry again. "What do you mean? Why isn't it easy? Since when do you do everything your mother tells you? And for that matter, since when does she give a shit what you get up to? Most of the time Nicole couldn't care less what you do."

Charlie kept his eyes averted, but I could see he was gritting his teeth. "She's not that bad, Laurie. Nicole does things differently, that's all. More hands off. She trusts me to look after myself."

"Except now, apparently."

Charlie inhaled, his jaw tightening. Steeling himself for whatever he was about to say next. "She was concerned, Lee, okay? Said I could get into trouble, with you being underage. I could even get a record, once I turn sixteen. And, you know, your dad being a policeman…"

"Ex-policeman," I said.

Tears welled again. I tried to blink them away, but Charlie noticed. His face softened and he seized my hand. "Lee, listen, I'm sorry I went off like that. It was Nicole's idea we stay up in Norfolk, to give me time to think it through. She basically made me go."

"Made you go?" I snatched my hand back. "*How*, Charlie? How could she possibly make you go?"

He leaned in, lowering his voice, though there was no one within fifty metres of us. "She threatened to tell your parents if I didn't go with her. She said it would look bad for them, especially your mum, with her being…you know…a doctor. Important in the community. Your dad too. I dunno, I just didn't want to get you into any trouble."

I was filled with a rush of hatred towards Nicole, hot and pure. No way did my parents need that. Mum had enough on her plate with her job, and Dad's recovery still felt precarious.

In my head the whole argument between them began to unfold. Nicole threatening Charlie, lecturing him about his future. I could picture it all. I'd seen his mother upset a few times over the years. Once when the three of us were bored one rainy afternoon and sneaked into her bedroom, trying on her clothes, playing with her make-up. Another when Charlie decided to make a chocolate cake, spilling flour on the floor and leaving the kitchen looking like a war zone.

Scary, that was the word. Nicole could be very intimidating, even though she was barely five foot tall and skinny too. But there was a fierceness there, something unguarded in her temper.

I'd also seen how Charlie reacted when she got like that. Careful not to wind her up any further. Smoothing things over till she calmed down.

"Okay…" I started, then faltered. Trying to find the words for what I wanted to ask. "So that's it then? We… what…go back to being friends?"

If that was even possible. Somehow I didn't think so.

Charlie shut his eyes briefly, ran a hand over his face. "No, Lee, that's not it. Not for ever. Just for a little while, till things cool off. Nicole will forget about it soon enough."

"So we can't see each other at all? I mean, we don't have to…you know…" I couldn't bring myself to say it. Not here in school.

"What can I do?" Charlie murmured, seizing my hand again, holding it tight. "What can I do, Lee? Nicole said to stay away from you, and I reckon she means it, about telling your parents. I've never seen her so upset."

"But why?" I asked again, my fingers growing hot in his.

My skin reacting to his touch. "I don't understand. What has she got against me?"

Charlie let go of my hand. Leaned forwards on the bench. "I dunno, Lee. I couldn't really make sense of it. It was like there was something else, something she wasn't telling me. But it was clear she meant it – about staying away from you."

He turned back to face me. "And I did think about it, a lot, while I was in Norfolk. That maybe we shouldn't rush into things. We've got our whole lives, Lee. Plenty of time. Maybe it's not such a bad idea to cool it for a while."

"You didn't even call me," I said, my voice choking. I felt exhausted, suddenly. Like all those weeks of waiting to talk to Charlie had drained the life out of me.

"I'm sorry, Lee. That was shitty of me. I wanted…I dunno…I needed to sort things out in my head a bit, before we talked. And I was paranoid Nicole might check my phone or something. You know what she's like when she gets into one of her moods. It's not worth the risk of winding her up any more."

It was a crap excuse. Even he could see that. I could tell by the way he wouldn't meet my eyes. I studied his face, wondering if he was serious. Or was this simply a clever way to fob me off? To get rid of me without a fuss.

A month ago I would never have doubted him, not for an instant. But everything had changed, and I hardly had a clue who Charlie was any more. Could I still trust this boy I'd known most of my life?

Did he really like me?

Did he feel the same?

"You haven't told anyone else, have you?" I asked. "Besides your mum?"

Charlie shook his head. "Why would I?"

"Just promise me you won't." I wasn't sure I could handle the gossip; or having to explain to Maya why I'd kept this a secret from her. Not until I was certain Charlie meant what he said. That he wasn't just spinning me some kind of line.

"I promise, Lee." He reached over, pulled me into a hug. "On my life, I won't say a word."

He released me, lifting my chin so he could look right into my eyes. "Give it some time, all right? That's all I ask. Just give it time, then you'll see, everything will work out okay."

And to think I actually believed him.

Chapter 14

"So, are you going to tell me what's going on?"

"How do you mean?" I glanced at Maya, but she wasn't looking at me. She'd spotted Ria and Sophie across the road, walking home with two boys from the year below.

Maya nudged me, nodding towards them. "Reckon there's something they're not telling us?"

I laughed, relaxing a bit. Thinking she'd forgotten her previous question. But a moment later she turned and said something that knocked the breath right out of me.

"You and Charlie. What's going on? We've been back two weeks and you've barely spoken to him. And he's avoiding both of us like the plague."

Just the sound of Charlie's name made my stomach flip over. Since our talk by the playing fields, I'd only seen him from a distance: in class, in the lunch queue, walking around school. His absence in my life felt almost physical. A dull ache, a kind of hollowness inside.

Every day I asked myself the same question: *how long would we have to wait?* How long before it all blew over with Nicole?

I was praying it would be weeks rather than months. I missed Charlie more than I could say. I missed the three of us too, the way we were together. Without Charlie, Maya and I seemed to have lost the fun in our friendship, all the joking and fooling around. Everything felt more serious somehow. More strained.

"Lee," Maya prompted. "What's it all about?"

"Um…" I began, but Maya cut me off, unable to contain her frustration. "You know, I invited him round this weekend and he made some crappy excuse about coursework. Like that ever stopped him doing anything before." She didn't bother to hide her hurt and annoyance. Her bewilderment at her failed attempts to reunite the three of us.

"That's probably true," I said, hoping to head her off. "I don't know about you, but I've got loads more work compared with last year."

"More like he just doesn't want to know any more," she complained. "He's deliberately avoiding us."

I sighed. Maya was right. Obviously right. Charlie had been avoiding us. And I'd gone along with it. Given the situation, it was easier that way. Being anywhere near Charlie now made me feel stilted and awkward. All our previous closeness, that easy way I once had in his company, had vanished. If he was in the same room, I couldn't even look in his direction, afraid something in my gaze would give me away.

But of course, what gives you away most is your efforts not to betray yourself.

"Well?" asked Maya, gazing at me.

I looked at her. "Well, what?"

Maya sighed, loudly. "Stop dodging my question, Lee. You know exactly what I mean. It's obvious the pair of you have fallen out or something. So how come you haven't mentioned it?"

I inhaled, feeling relieved. At least Maya hadn't guessed the truth.

"It was nothing really," I improvised. "I just made some silly comment about –" I paused, desperately trying to think of something innocent Charlie and I could have argued over – "about this whole pilot obsession he's got. I said he should widen his horizons; shouldn't focus on one thing."

Maya stopped walking, scrunching up her eyebrows in confusion. "Why on earth would you say that, Lee? You know Charlie's had his heart set on flying, like, for ever."

I pulled a face. "I don't know. I just said it. I didn't mean it like that, but he took it the wrong way."

It was the lamest lie in the whole history of lying. I couldn't believe Maya would take it seriously, and it was making me feel crap. I groped around for some way to change the subject, but she got in first.

"So why not apologize? Say you didn't mean anything by it. You can't just stop speaking to each other, Lee. It's horrible, and he's avoiding me too. Like I've taken sides or something."

I shrugged, hoping Maya would leave it at that. I hated

what this situation was doing to our friendship, the tension it was causing. I hated having to lie and be evasive all the time. I hated how much it must be hurting and perplexing her, and I loved her for hanging on in there, and not just giving up and finding new, less troublesome friends to hang out with.

"Seriously, Lee. I miss him. I miss *us*. Do whatever it takes."

I swallowed, fighting back my distress. I desperately wanted to tell Maya the truth, but having held out so long, it seemed worse to confess everything now. She'd feel doubly betrayed.

We turned into Welland Road, and my stomach somersaulted. There was Charlie, up ahead, walking slowly, talking to a couple of girls. I couldn't make out who they were from here, but one of them had the kind of long glossy hair you see on a shampoo ad.

Something twisted inside. I stopped dead.

Maya gazed at me. "What's up?"

She obviously hadn't seen Charlie, or she'd probably be forcing me to run and catch up. Apologize on the spot for our fake argument.

"I'm sorry." I closed my eyes briefly. "I don't feel well."

It was true. I'd been feeling off-colour all day, with a kind of bone-deep tiredness I'd never experienced before. Drunk with it almost, like it was an effort to keep standing. At the same time I felt sort of buzzy and tearful, as if the slightest thing might set me off.

"You do look kind of terrible," Maya admitted.

"Thanks," I sniffed, sinking onto the low wall outside the Baptist church. I wanted to lie back on the grass bank behind and go straight to sleep.

"You know what I mean, Lee. You're super pale. You're not dieting or anything, are you?"

I shook my head, though in truth my appetite hadn't improved. Things tasted odd somehow. Stronger. Off-putting.

"In that case, why not come round to mine? Mum's making chickpea curry. Your favourite."

My stomach lurched again. Usually I love the food at Maya's house. Her mum's curries are divine, all done from scratch, grinding the spices and everything – much better than the ones we get at the Indian. But right now even the thought of eating made me feel queasy.

"Do you mind if I duck out?" I gave Maya another apologetic shrug. "I don't think I'm up to it."

"You should get your mum to give you a check-up," she said, her eyes full of concern. "Seriously, something's not right with you."

I nodded. "I think I'm coming down with a bug. I just need to go home and lie down."

Maya sat on the wall next to me and gave me a hug. "I'm worried about you, Lee. You don't seem your usual self."

I smiled and rested my head on her shoulder. Only for a minute, but it gave me the strength I needed to get myself home.

*   *   *

No one was around when I got in. Katy had probably gone to Jo or Sammy's, and no doubt Dad had taken Walt to the allotment.

I checked the time. Half four. Mum wouldn't be back till six. I made myself a cup of tea and went upstairs to bed.

I must have fallen asleep almost instantly; when I woke, my tea had gone cold.

I still felt odd. Not refreshed by the nap at all. The metallic taste in my mouth had worsened, and as I hoisted myself into a sitting position I could feel my breasts were sore. Like they were sometimes before a period, tingly and tender.

My heart flip-flopped.

My breath stalled.

My period. When *was* my last period?

Suddenly it seemed a very long time ago. I'd never been that regular, sometimes going up to six weeks in between. But it had been longer than that, hadn't it?

I grabbed the little pocket diary from my rucksack, the one Walt gave me for Christmas but I knew really came from Mum, who was inundated with freebies from the pharmaceutical companies. I flicked back through the pages.

I'd never kept a note of my cycle, like you're supposed to. But I remembered the day I last came on – Maya and I had been to see a film down at the Odeon, and I had to rush into Boots afterwards and buy some tampons.

When was that? Around the time we broke up for the summer. Yes, that Saturday. I found the day in the diary, then counted the weeks to today's date.

My stomach turned cold.

Seven weeks ago. Nearly eight.

Shit.

Don't panic, said a voice in my head. It's probably nothing. You're just late, that's all – and anyway, Charlie used a condom both times, *remember*?

I inhaled. Tried to calm myself down. It was bound to be stress, I reminded myself, recalling Miss Bradbury telling us in PSHE lessons how it could upset your cycle.

"Laurie?" Dad's voice calling upstairs. "You there?"

"Coming," I yelled, hauling myself out of bed. At the top of the stairs I met Katy, on her way up.

She frowned at me. "You okay?" Sounding almost like she cared.

My sister scrutinized me, making no effort to let me pass. "Something's going on with you, isn't it?" Her tone made it more a statement than a question.

I forced myself to return her gaze, staying silent until Katy moved out of my way. I went down, then paused at the bottom of the stairs. Should I go after her? Follow Katy into her room and confess everything. Tell her what I was so afraid of.

Katy would know what to do. My sister might be a total bitch to me most of the time, but surely she'd help me in a crisis? If only to get me off her back.

I hesitated for a few more seconds.

"Laurie?" Dad's face appeared at the end of the hallway. "There you are. I thought you hadn't heard me. You fancy shepherd's pie for supper? I've dug up loads of potatoes."

A blare of music from Katy's room. Something loud and trancy. Sounded like that new band she was into, the one whose name I could never remember.

Leave it, Laurie, I told myself as I followed Dad into the kitchen. Better to deal with this on your own.

Chapter 15

I picked the chemist in the centre of town, the one by the clock tower. It was a bus ride away, but I didn't care. It was large and anonymous – less chance of bumping into anyone I knew.

It took several minutes to find the section with the pregnancy tests. I examined all the packages. Selected the least expensive.

As accurate as a doctor, it said on the box. I tried not to think of Mum. Tried not to think about anything as I checked I had enough money in my purse. Just about, but I'd have to walk home.

I was heading towards the cashier when I saw Tom, right in front of me in the queue. Shit. What were the chances? I looked around, but there was no way to escape without making it obvious I was running away.

"Hi," Tom grinned, pulling off his headphones. I caught a burst of music. "The Cure," he said, turning it off on his mobile. "'A Forest' – one of their best songs."

"Hi." I forced a smile, glancing at the item in his basket. A bottle of expensive-looking aftershave.

"Dad's birthday," he said. "This is his favourite."

"Nice," I said stupidly. I saw his eyes stray to the box in my hand. The box I was desperately trying to obscure with my fingers. His gaze hovered for a second before sliding back to mine.

"I'm guessing that's for a friend." Tom kept his expression deadpan.

"Er…yeah."

We both knew I was lying. My guilt must have been written all over my face.

"Next," called a cashier. Two of the tills were now free. Tom went to one, me to the other. I handed over the money, then shoved the box deep into my bag. I hurried away, but as I reached the door I found Tom there, holding it open.

"Laurie," he said. "Wait up."

I turned to face him. Tom was a head taller than me. He too had changed a lot in the last year and I could see he was going to be good-looking, like his dad. I remembered Charlie's question, that night when we got back to his flat. Asking if I had a thing for Tom. His expression of relief when I laughed it off.

It seemed a lifetime ago.

"Listen." Tom nodded at my bag. "If I can help in any way, Laurie. You know…if you want someone to talk to."

Heat rose to my cheeks. "Thanks," I mumbled. "Just don't say anything to anyone. Please." No point pretending this wasn't about me.

Tom fixed me with his deep brown eyes. "Of course I won't. You don't even need to ask."

"Thank you." I let my gaze drop to the ground. "I appreciate it."

"Good luck." He lifted his hand and squeezed my arm before heading off towards the clock tower.

I stood on the steps, taking a deep breath. Above me, a mob of seagulls cawed and wheeled as they rode the updraughts blowing from the sea.

Time to head home, I told myself. No point putting this off any longer.

Chapter 16

In the end I waited till everyone was asleep, then crept into the bathroom. Turning on the light, I locked the door and opened the box. Removed the little stick from its cellophane packet and read the instructions carefully.

Squatting on the loo, I peed on the stick, then wiped it clean with some tissue. My hand was shaking so much I had to prop it on the shelf above the basin so I could see it properly.

Then I washed my hands and waited.

Nothing was happening. The window in the plastic stick remained blank. I checked the instructions again.

Three minutes it said, so I closed my eyes and counted them off in my head.

Second by slow, painful second. Right up to 180. My heart beating time.

Then I opened my eyes.

PART THREE: NOW

Chapter 17

Mr Rochester's funeral, and it's standing room only. Every seat in the chapel is taken, and people are crowding at the back, three or four bodies deep. Someone has seriously underestimated the turnout – half the school appears to be here, including most of Mr Rochester's tutor group, and many other kids he taught.

Not to mention the teachers and the admin staff. With the school immersed in the summer exams, I guess a Saturday service meant everyone could come.

I give up my seat to an elderly man who looks too frail to stand, and hover at the end of the aisles. I spot Tom sitting in the front row, next to a woman and a girl I assume are his mother and sister; the girl looks younger than Tom, but with similar striking features. I see his mum reach across and take Tom's hand, hanging on tight.

On the other side of her a man that has to be Mr Rochester's brother. Same wavy dark hair, though his features are leaner and more angular. A bit older too. I watch as he puts an arm round Tom's mother. She's staring ahead at the coffin, her chin held determinedly high, but even from here the strain in her face is clear.

I check out the other mourners, wishing Maya had agreed to come. "I'd feel sort of…nosy," she'd said when I asked. "I don't want people to think I'm there just to gawp."

Judging by some of the other people here, I can see her point. I spot Fleur Rickard and half her crowd over in the corner, their faces positively excited, like they're watching something cool on TV. I'm pretty sure Fleur wasn't in any of Mr Rochester's classes, or his tutor group.

Fleur catches me staring, gives me a sarky little wave. I ignore it, dropping my gaze to the Order of Service. It's short and plain. I'm guessing Mr Rochester wasn't religious, though he always bowed his head during prayers in assembly. Then again, all the teachers do, except Mr Humphrey, who stares obstinately into space with an air of distaste.

The piped organ music playing in the background comes to a halt. People stop talking and put on respectful faces, waiting for it all to begin. It's then I spot him, right at the very back, his face pale and nervous.

Charlie.

What the hell is he doing here?

I'm pretty sure the school has kept his accusation quiet, no doubt out of respect for the family. But of course Charlie knows what happened between him and Mr Rochester. What has possibly – probably – led to us all being here today. How could it be a coincidence? Even Charlie must see the connection – his reporting Mr

Rochester for assault, and then the teacher killing himself.

I glance around for Katy, but there's no sign of her. Perhaps she's had the sense to stay away. My eyes slide back to Charlie. I haven't seen him since he rushed out of assembly nearly two weeks ago. He's not been in school, or round to our house.

Why is he here?

It's insane. I mean, I can imagine what a shock his teacher's death has been for Charlie, how he must feel responsible on some level, even though it wasn't really his fault. But surely he knows that coming here today is madness? What if Mr Rochester's family sees him? They must have been told, after all, why he was suspended. Charlie's part in it all.

I'm about to go and drag him away when there's a cough from the front of the chapel. I turn to see Mr Rochester's brother standing by the lectern, preparing to speak.

Too late. I have to stay put as Ian Rochester introduces himself and gives a speech about his brother. How Mr Rochester had wanted to be a teacher since he was thirteen years old, when he discovered the kid living next door to them couldn't read.

"That was the kind of person my brother Paul was," Ian Rochester says, his voice trembling. "Always trying to help people, to make a difference."

At the back of the chapel one of the girls starts to cry, noisily. I shouldn't have come, I think, feeling embarrassed. None of us should.

This is private.

But I liked Mr Rochester. His brother was right. He was nice. A good person – at least I'd always thought so.

My mind flits back eight months, to last October. Those weeks after I became a murderer, when homework was an impossible task, and turning up to school at all felt like a superhuman effort. Mr Rochester had been one of the few teachers who hadn't given me a hard time. Had been kind, where others were curt or insistent.

As I stand here, listening to his brother, I remember that afternoon in particular, when Mr Rochester found me sitting in class, still staring out the window after everyone had left.

Lost in my own world.

And what I'd done.

"Laurie?" I'd looked up to find him standing by my desk.

"I'm sorry," I mumbled, assuming he was chasing my overdue biology assignment. "I'll do it soon."

Mr Rochester gazed down at me. "Do it when you're ready."

I almost started in surprise.

"You look like you've got enough on your plate," he added, with a smile.

I stared back at him in alarm. Had Tom broken his word? Told his dad what he'd seen me buying in the chemist?

"Look, Laurie, I've no idea what's going on," Mr Rochester said, reading my expression. "And I'm assuming it's nothing you want to talk about."

He waited for confirmation. I shook my head, though for a second I was tempted. For a second I felt like letting it all burst out, purely for the relief of being able to tell someone.

Anybody.

"You're a good student, Laurie," he continued. "A very good student. I know when this passes you'll make an effort to catch up."

It was a little thing, and I'm not even going to pretend it made much difference. After he walked away, leaving me there, trying not to cry, I'd still been stuck with my life. Alone with the guilt.

But I remember it. I remember what Mr Rochester did for me, and now I'm sitting here at his funeral, tears running down my cheeks, trying to square it with what he did to Charlie.

That cut on his head. The broken tooth.

How could both be true of the same person? Did Mr Rochester's assault on Charlie cancel out his kindness to me? Or did that still count?

Maybe we're only as good as our own worst actions, I decide, as the organ music starts up again and we file out of the chapel, the service over.

In which case, I realize, there isn't much hope for me.

Chapter 18

Two women stand each side of the chapel doors, collecting donations. For a suicide prevention charity, I notice, as I hand over the five-pound note I keep in my purse for emergencies.

I look around for Charlie. I want to ask what the hell he's playing at – and make sure he leaves before any of Mr Rochester's family notices he's here.

But I can't see him among the cluster of mourners lingering outside the crematorium. I scan all the faces again. Could Charlie have left already? But I came out pretty fast. And there's no sign of him on the long drive leading to the exit.

Maybe he's talking to someone? Or nipped to the loo. I hang around for a minute or two, trying to avoid all the students from school. Some of the girls are crying conspicuously, dabbing their eyes with tissues. The boys just look faintly embarrassed, hands thrust into trouser pockets, gaze fixed on the paving beneath their feet.

"Hi, Laurie."

I turn to see Tom heading towards me. Behind him,

his mother and sister are talking to someone in the foyer.

"Hi." I give him a quick smile. "You okay?"

I could kick myself the moment the words leave my mouth. *Of course he's not bloody okay, Laurie.* Who feels okay at their own father's funeral?

But Tom doesn't appear to notice my blunder. "You know…it's hard. But we're coping." He glances back at his mother and sister, but they're still deep in conversation. One of the well-wishers, a balding man in a black suit, cradles his mother's hand, nodding earnestly.

"I'm so sorry…" I start, then can't think what to say. What use are words? Or sympathy?

"I know." Tom nods. "Thanks."

Then I see him. Coming out of the chapel.

Charlie. Heading straight towards us. Jesus, what on earth…?

Tom catches my expression, turns to follow my gaze.

"*You,*" he says, frowning with astonishment. "What the hell—"

"Wait." Charlie holds up a hand, like Tom might run away. "Please. I just want to say…" His voice sounds slurred. He's swaying slightly, his eyes blurry.

Shit. Is Charlie actually *drunk*?

"Say what?" Tom stands his ground. "Say what, Forrest, you lying scumbag?"

Charlie looks stunned. Takes a step backwards as Tom strides towards him. All around us, people fall silent. Everyone's gaze swivels in our direction.

"Tom, who—" His mother's voice.

"It's *him*, Mum," Tom tells her. "The bastard who said all that crap about Dad."

Mrs Rochester's head whips round to Charlie, who gazes back with a pleading expression. "Listen, please…I didn't mean—"

"*Leave now!*" she hisses, furious. "How dare you, after everything you've done. How *dare* you show up at my husband's funeral."

"Charlie." I walk up and grab his arm. "Charlie, come with me."

I try to pull him away but he won't budge. This close, I can smell the alcohol on his breath. In his sweat. How much has Charlie had to drink?

I fight down a rising sense of panic. Charlie feels like a stranger, suddenly, as if he's veered right out of my orbit. A rogue asteroid, heading for some kind of collision.

"Come on," I repeat, tugging his arm. But he won't budge. As if he's rooted to the spot.

What on earth is the matter with him?

I mean, who knows what part Charlie's accusation played in our teacher's death? But you don't have to be a genius to work out that it can't have helped.

So why is Charlie hell-bent on rubbing their noses in it?

"You bastard!" Tom yells suddenly. "Don't you think you've done enough damage?" He launches himself at Charlie and seizes him by the hair, dragging him towards the exit. Charlie tries to grab his arms, to pull away, but though he's taller, he's no match for Tom's fury.

Halfway down the drive, Tom lets go. A second later, he takes a swing at Charlie, his right fist catching him on the jaw.

Charlie staggers backwards, hand raised to his mouth, eyes wide with surprise. Then he leaps forward and throws a punch at Tom. But the alcohol has made him slow, and Tom ducks out of the way and charges into Charlie's stomach, sending them both to the ground.

Just as Charlie reacts, headbutting Tom on the nose, Ian Rochester intervenes. He yanks Charlie away, pinning his arms behind his back so he can't move.

Not that Charlie is resisting. All the fight seems to have gone out of him. He's staggering, whether from the booze or the blow Tom landed on his cheek, already turning an angry shade of red.

"He's a liar…" Tom's voice chokes. He's clutching his nose and I see it's bleeding. "That stuff he accused Dad of…it's all fucking lies."

Ian Rochester releases Charlie, turns to face the pair of them. For a moment they lock eyes and I wonder if it's all going to kick off again. But Charlie steps back, raising his hands in a gesture of surrender.

"Charlie, *go*," I plead. "Just leave."

He glances at me, but doesn't move. It's like he's in shock.

"NOW!" Ian Rochester yells, and with that Charlie

takes off, trying to run down the drive but managing no more than a drunken stumble.

I watch him go, wondering whether I should catch him up. Behind me, I hear Tom give a yelp of distress, and turn to see him bolting round the side of the crematorium.

Oh shit. Could this get any worse?

Tom's mother and uncle stare after him, uncertain what to do. "I'll go," I say, and before thinking twice, I head off after him.

I find Tom round the back of the building, crouched on the grass behind the wall, face in his hands. He's crying. I stand there, trying to decide what to do. Should I even be here? It's not like we're that close.

"You know, don't you?" Tom lifts his head to look at me. "About what he said...I mean, about my dad."

I nod. No point pretending otherwise.

"Why?" Tom asks. "Why, Laurie? You know him, you and Charlie have been friends for ever. So you tell me, why did he do it?"

I stare back at him, confused. Does Tom mean coming here today? Or is he talking about the assault – Charlie's accusations?

Tom fumbles in his pocket for a tissue, using it to wipe the blood from his nose. "You think he did it, don't you?" He peers up at me again. "You think my dad did that to Charlie."

I gaze down at him, helpless. "Tom, I…"

I saw the cut on Charlie's head, the broken tooth.

Facts.

But if you hadn't seen them for yourself, I guess that would make the whole thing harder to believe.

"Dad never laid a hand on me, Laurie, like ever. Even when I was really winding him up. Even the time I lost the watch Grandad left him. Sure, he got angry sometimes, he'd raise his voice, send me to my room maybe, but nothing more than that. There's no way on earth he would have hit some kid at school."

I can see the conviction in Tom's face. I sit on the grass beside him. It's springy and green, like everything around us, the trees and bushes, all bursting with life and the promise of summer.

Funerals should only be held in winter, I think. When the world is less bright, less vibrant.

"This must be really hard," I say. "Charlie should never have come here today." Though I'm assuming he was trying, in his own stupid way, to make amends. To make up for his own part in all this.

Tom snorts. "You're not kidding." He stares off into the middle distance. Out the corner of my eye I see Ian Rochester appear round the side of the building. Clocking us both, he gives me a discreet nod then leaves.

Letting us have some space.

"The irony is I always liked Charlie." Tom wipes his nose again. "I just can't get my head around why he would do this. Why he'd turn up here after everything."

"I don't know," I say truthfully. "I hardly speak to him any more."

Tom sniffs. His nose seems to have stopped bleeding, so he stuffs the tissue back into his pocket. "I failed him," he says suddenly.

"Who? Your dad?"

"Yeah."

"Tom, why would you even think that?"

He looks at me. "Wouldn't you, Laurie? Wouldn't you think that if your dad killed himself? Wouldn't you feel you were somehow to blame?"

I swallow. I guess he's right. I probably would. I'd probably torture myself, wondering if there was anything I could have said or done that might have made a difference. Feeling guilty over any argument, any cross word.

No, I *definitely* would.

"At the very least, I didn't see what was going on with him," Tom continues, "the pain he must have been in, especially after the school suspended him. I mean, I know things got him down, but I had no idea—"

His voice chokes off again. He shakes his head slightly, as if trying to force something out of his mind.

"The paramedic who came...you know, when it happened...she said middle-aged men were the most common group for suicide. And Mum told me, afterwards, that Dad had been depressed for a while."

Tears loom in his eyes again. I glance away, giving Tom

a chance to recover. And think of my own father. His struggles after leaving his job. The way he'd mooched around the house for months, looking like the world had ended. He'd been so much better this year, enjoying his IT course, looking forward to a new career.

Could it all be a front? Putting on a brave face?

I should talk to him, I decide, with a flush of worry. Make sure he's okay and not just covering things up.

"Mum asked him for a divorce," Tom says, out of the blue. "A week before he died."

My eyes widen in shock. "How do you know?"

"She told me." Tom snatches at a blade of grass, twisting it round his finger. "Mum was the one who found him... you know."

I did know. Mr Rochester had hung himself in the garage, a gruesome detail that had somehow made its way round the school since that assembly.

"After the police and the ambulance had gone, she drank half the bottle of gin that had been in the cupboard for ever – and Mum hates alcohol. That's when it all came out, when she started telling me this stuff."

Despite my anger with him, I feel a rush of relief for Charlie. Perhaps Mr Rochester's death had nothing to do with him. Perhaps it was something that had been building for a while.

That would explain, too, the question that had bugged me these last two weeks: why *had* Mr Rochester hit Charlie? Surely it couldn't just have been about his schoolwork?

I mean, I know Charlie can be annoying. Cheeky, a bit cocky. But teachers are used to that, aren't they? He could hardly be the first kid to get on Mr Rochester's nerves.

Then again depression can make you short-tempered – I've seen that. I remember how irritable Dad was, his mood filling the house like a dark cloud. Even Walt felt it, staying out of his way in case he got snapped at for making a mess or too much noise.

It stopped, thankfully. When Dad's mood lifted, he was back to his old self: patient, funny and kind.

"Why did your mum want a divorce?" I ask, pulling my thoughts back to Tom.

He takes a deep breath. "Dad had been having an affair. Mum told me she'd found out and threatened to leave him, but he'd promised to end it. This thing with the other woman."

I shift my weight, feeling uncomfortable all of a sudden. I shouldn't have asked. Shouldn't be hearing all this… private stuff.

Then remind myself that Tom knows some pretty private stuff about me, after all. That in many ways, this boy sitting beside me, devastated, knows me better than anyone.

He knows what I did.

A swoop inside as I recall Tom's face in the chemist shop. His expression when he spotted the pregnancy test. The conversation we had about it ten days later.

I inhale. Push it away. "What a mess," I say, meaning both of us. Both of our lives.

"You can say that again," Tom mutters. "I guess we'll never know exactly why Dad killed himself. I suppose it was…everything."

"Did he leave a note?"

Tom nods. "It was very short. Just sorry – and I love you all." Tears run down his cheeks again, and this time he does nothing about them. I want to reach out, put my hand on his shoulder, but it feels too…awkward.

"Not that it excuses what that bastard did." Tom turns to me, his eyes fervent. "Charlie lied, Laurie. What he said about Dad wasn't true."

But it was, I want to say. I saw it, with my own eyes. The gash on Charlie's head. His tooth.

That wasn't something you could make up.

Not to mention Charlie's a hopeless liar. No way he could have pulled off something like that, even if he wanted to – and I couldn't think of any reason on earth why Charlie would want to falsely accuse Mr Rochester.

I look at Tom, wondering what to say. Decide to stay silent. How would it help if I convinced him Charlie's injuries were real? That his father had obviously been unstable. That Charlie had no way of knowing what it would lead to when he reported Mr Rochester for what he did.

"You didn't tell him, did you, about the baby?" Tom says suddenly. "Charlie, I mean. You let him off the hook."

I don't answer.

"He doesn't deserve it." Anger rising in his voice again. "Charlie doesn't care who he hurts, does he? Going off with your sister like that. Never stopping to consider the damage he does to other people's lives."

I gaze back at him, searching for some response. But what could I possibly say? Because even now – after everything – I still find it hard to believe the worst about Charlie. As if I'm tied to the memory of all those years together, all those shared experiences.

How do you let something like that go? How do you switch it off?

Tom susses me in an instant, and lets out a bitter kind of laugh. "I don't believe it. You still actually care about him, don't you?"

My face goes hot. Is it that obvious?

"Shit, Laurie. I honestly don't know who I feel more sorry for – you or me."

He scrambles to his feet, brushes a few blades of grass from his smart black trousers. They look new. Probably bought for today, I realize, and the thought makes me feel worse. Buying clothes should be a pleasure, shouldn't it? Dressing up something you associate with celebration – not the very worst day of your life.

"Anyway, I have to go." Tom watches as I get up too. "Everyone will be waiting for me. We've got this…whatever you call it back at the house…wake?" He sniffs, tipping his face up to the sun. "Bloody stupid name for it, isn't it? A wake. For someone who will never wake up again."

"I'm sorry," I say, unable to think of anything better. "I'm so sorry."

Tom raises his hand, starts to walk away, then turns around. His expression weary and resigned. "I know you like him, Laurie. I know how you feel about Charlie, but I'm warning you – he's bad news. And not just for going off with Katy, though god knows, that's crappy enough…"

He pauses. Opens his mouth then shuts it again, censoring something he'd been about to say. "Stay away from him is my advice. He doesn't deserve you. He never did."

Tom holds my gaze, his expression softening, as if he really does feel sorrier for me than himself. "For what it's worth, Laurie, I think you made the right decision. I know it can't have been easy, what you had to do, but it was absolutely the right thing."

With that he walks off, leaving me standing there.

Feeling useless. Foolish.

Alone.

Chapter 19

"You heard the rumours?" Maya leans in, whispering, as we wait for the replacement teacher to arrive. Today – Monday – is our last biology revision class.

"What rumours?"

"There was a fight between Charlie and Tom at Mr Rochester's funeral on Saturday. You went, didn't you? Did you see it?"

I nod. Pointless to pretend otherwise, given loads of people witnessed the whole thing. It would only be a matter of hours before everyone in the school knew about it.

Not surprisingly, neither Tom nor Charlie have turned up today.

"Ashley Jenkins told me Tom accused Charlie of somehow being involved." Maya frowns. "You know anything about that?"

"Involved in what?" I ask, praying she doesn't mean what I think she means.

"In Mr Rochester's death. I heard something about Charlie accusing him of assault. Telling the school and the police." Maya studies my face, clearly suspecting I know more than I'm letting on.

People had put two and two together, it seemed. Realized Charlie was behind Mr Rochester's suspension.

Whose side will they take? I wonder: Tom's or Charlie's?

I think back to the funeral. Tom's distress. His fury at Charlie. His denial that his father could have done what he did. I didn't blame Tom. After all, who wants to believe their dad would assault a pupil?

But I'd hoped for Charlie's sake none of it would come out – judging by the state of him on Saturday, he was already struggling to deal with it all.

"Hasn't Katy said anything?" Maya asks, not ready to let this drop.

"Not to me," I reply, but even this is enough of a lie to make my stomach curl. Why haven't I told her? I ask myself. Since when did I stop confiding in my only friend?

You know when, comes the answer. Since you stopped talking to everyone. Keep one secret, and inevitably you start keeping others. The lies pile up like toxic waste, polluting all your relationships.

Maya gazes at me intently. "Do you reckon it's true? Have you spoken to Charlie at all?"

Once upon a time that question would have been ridiculous. Once upon a time – even a year ago – we had no secrets; the three of us told each other everything. Once upon a time, none of us had anything to hide.

But how can I tell Maya about finding Charlie in our kitchen? About his bleeding head, that broken tooth?

I can't help feeling I'd be betraying some kind of confidence. Not that I don't trust her – far from it, I'd trust Maya with my life – but what if it got back to Tom somehow, that I'd added to all the gossip about his dad? How would that make him feel?

Besides, I can't talk about Charlie to anyone. Can't take the risk that if I start, everything that happened last year will come tumbling out.

"Hello, class." Mr Pritchard arrives, saving me from Maya's scrutiny. He hovers at the front of the room, looking uncertain; I don't think biology is his usual subject. Clearly the school hasn't had a chance to replace Mr Rochester yet.

"Right." He clears his throat. "I believe you were…er… revising…" His cheeks flush as he tries to avoid mentioning Mr Rochester by name. "Okay, yes, the unit on human reproduction."

Normally this would raise a titter from some of the boys. Josh Penfell and Toby Riggs at least.

Today it's met with dead silence. Mr Rochester's suicide has cast a shadow over the whole school, and the mood still hasn't lifted.

But life has to carry on. We've filed in and out of exams and revision classes, but it's felt like going through the motions. Several times, in the middle of answering a question, I've found myself staring across the exam hall, wondering what I'm even doing there.

"Right." Mr Pritchard clears his throat again. "I've dug up a short video."

He presses a button on his laptop and waits for it to load onto the whiteboard. He clicks the start arrow, and the class settles back with a sigh.

It's an educational cartoon about human fertilization, skipping all the embarrassing sex stuff. On the screen, a cartoon egg drops down the Fallopian tube, and a cartoon sperm swims up to meet it, burrowing inside.

"After fertilization the single cell splits into two, then the two cells double to four, four to eight, eight to sixteen and..." drones the voiceover and I start to tune out. Nothing I don't know already. "The journey along the Fallopian tube continues slowly for about four days."

Suddenly, unexpectedly, the video switches to an actual film. A woman having an ultrasound scan, showing a real baby in a real womb. It's a bit blurry, but the voiceover explains what we're looking at, as arrows point out its features.

"By twenty-one to twenty-five days the baby's heart is beating. Other internal organs are present in simple form and functioning as they grow. Early facial features appear..."

Inside me, something stirs. A swell of nausea.

"By week eight, the fetus has individual fingerprints; no two sets are ever the same." The picture switches to a diagram showing a cross-section of a pregnant mother, the tiny baby nestling in her womb.

Oh god...

"At ten weeks, the fetus begins to move...it is possible to hear its rapid heartbeat using..."

Ten weeks.

Something detonates in my head.

My chest tightens. I try to inhale but my lungs seem to have frozen.

Maya glances at me, frowning. "Lee? You okay?"

I can't even turn to look at her. Can't tear my eyes from the scene on the whiteboard.

"At this stage the fetus is totally reliant on its mother for…"

The video begins to swim and blur. In my head another film, the one I made myself watch afterwards. How it was done. In all the bare, brutal detail.

Penance.

Punishment.

Those images I can never erase from my mind. Those words I read, on that "right to life" website I stumbled across.

I close my eyes. Hear myself utter an audible groan as her face flashes up again, that woman outside the clinic, brandishing her pro-life banner.

"Murderer!" she screamed, her features distorted by fury and hatred. *"How could you kill your own child?"*

Mr Pritchard is beside me now, his voice full of alarm. "Are you okay?"

I force my eyes open. Behind him, the rest of the class is staring at me, their expressions shocked and concerned.

I don't answer.

Just pull myself to my feet. Then run out of the classroom as fast as I can.

Chapter 20

It's only when I'm halfway down Church Street that I remember I've left my bag at school. In the classroom, with all my textbooks and revision notes for the biology exam on Friday.

But I'm past caring. About studying, about exams, about anything. So I carry on running, down to the Old Steine and past the Royal Pavilion, heading towards the seafront. As fast as I can manage without getting out of breath.

Keep moving, I tell myself. As if I can outrun the pictures in my head. Those terrible, terrible images.

Oh god…I am a murderer. *A murderer.*

Nothing can undo that.

Ever.

I run past the Palace Pier and the Brighton wheel, right along the seafront towards the Marina. Even when I get there, I keep going, following the undercliff path that leads to Black Rock and beyond.

Only when I've left behind all sign of the city do I slow to a fast walk. It's a rainy, blustery day, and there's hardly anyone around on this section of the coast. Some dog walkers, the odd jogger, all giving me strange looks as I hurry past in my wet uniform. Rain is soaking through my trousers and blazer, penetrating to my skin, but I don't care.

Nothing matters but to keep moving.

Suddenly the sun emerges from behind a low bank of cloud, lighting up the white cliffs to the left of me, the lumps of chalk on the beach on my right.

I let myself stop, sinking onto the wall facing the water. My lungs are burning, and I can hardly breathe, but the pictures in my head have receded, finally.

For now.

Slowly my breathing returns to normal, my pulse rate falling to a steadier beat. I focus on my surroundings, the little beach below me, the rock pools, the tideline marked in green seaweed. Beyond, the English Channel, the waves crested in white.

I watch for a minute or two, then close my eyes, letting the sun warm my face. Letting it bleach my mind blank.

For a while I escape all thought. I'm just here, absorbing the warmth on my skin, the smell of salt and seaweed, the sound of the sea slapping against the shingle, the occasional *caw-caw* of the gulls.

If only I could freeze this instant, I think. Stop time's relentless forward motion and stay in this moment for ever.

Almost in response, I feel a buzz in my blazer pocket.

My phone. I thought I'd left it in my bag, the ringtone set to silent.

I pull it out and check my messages. Shit. Seven in the

last hour. I guess I didn't notice the vibrations when I was running.

There's one from the school admin office. Two from Mum. Three from Maya… And one from Charlie.

I open this last one, knowing what the others will say: *Where are you? Are you okay? Please get in touch immediately.*

Charlie, on the other hand, has written just three words: *Can we talk?*

My finger hovers over the delete button, then I relent. *I'm not at school,* I punch in.

A minute later, my phone buzzes again. *Where are you? Undercliff Walk*, I write. *Near Rottingdean.*

Charlie will know exactly where that is. The three of us often used to cycle along here, to get away from the traffic on Brighton seafront. We'd buy an ice cream or some crisps in the village in Rottingdean, then eat them on the beach before riding home again.

I'll meet you by the basketball court, Charlie replies. *Half an hour.*

I sit there, marvelling at his assumption that I'll be there. Even after all this time, even after everything that's happened between us, he thinks that's all it takes.

One call, and I'll follow, wherever he wants to go.

Chapter 21

It takes me another fifteen minutes to walk to Rottingdean, where I skirt round the seafront to the games court on the site of the old open-air pool. We never got to use the pool, sadly – it closed before we were born – but Dad has pictures of him and Mum swimming there, back when they first moved to Brighton.

There's no sign of Charlie, so I sit on a bench and wait, thankful the sun has stayed out, taking the chill off my damp clothes. Ten minutes later I spot someone heading towards me. I don't recognize him for a moment. Charlie's cut his hair again, back to an ultra-short buzz. His skin is puffy and pale, and he looks thinner, almost gaunt. Like he's lost more weight, even in the two days since the funeral.

"Sorry I'm late." He sits down next to me. "I had to wait for Nicole to give me a lift." He's wearing a *Breaking Bad* T-shirt and faded jeans. Next to him I feel awkward, babyish in my school uniform.

"Does she know you're meeting me?" I ask. Does Katy for that matter? I wonder again if he's broken his promise, told my sister about our night together.

Charlie's gaze flits away from mine. "No. I thought we could do with a chance to talk alone." He squints back at me. "You're wet."

"Got caught in the rain."

I wait for him to ask why I'm not in school, but he leans forward, elbows resting on his legs, staring out at the water. Above the salty seaside smell I catch a faint odour of something…something sweet and fragrant.

Beer, I realize. Charlie has been drinking again – though thankfully he seems sober enough right now.

That said, it's only lunchtime. Plenty of day left yet.

"How have your exams been going?" I ask, after a full minute of silence. Annoyed that Charlie wanted to meet, then leaves me to do the talking. "You know." He shrugs. "Not great. Maths last week was a bitch."

"Yeah." It was a tricky paper, and I'm guessing revision hasn't exactly been top of Charlie's agenda.

"Nicole told me not to stress about it. I can always retake."

"Right." I can't think of any response to that.

"She reckons I should take it easy…you know…till things have settled down. Not sweat the exam stuff too much."

Till things have settled down.

I guess Charlie means what happened at Mr Rochester's funeral. I wonder whether to tackle him over that fight with Tom, or why he showed up there at all. But I can't be bothered.

I feel drained of energy, of emotion now. Like I've hit empty.

"Actually Nicole doesn't want me going back to school at all. She thinks I should sit the rest of my exams somewhere else."

"Cos of the rumours?" I'm guessing Katy has told him what people have been saying.

Charlie nods. "She doesn't like all the gossip."

"There wouldn't have been any, would there?" I say, exasperated. "If you hadn't gone to the funeral and got yourself into a fight with Tom. No one need ever have known what happened with Mr Rochester."

He doesn't reply. Just stares out to sea, his expression morose.

"So why haven't you done your exams somewhere else?"

Charlie shrugs. "I dunno. I guess it felt like a cop-out."

"Cop-out?"

"Taking the easy route."

"From what?" I ask, but Charlie doesn't answer. Just kicks at a pebble, sending it skittering across the concrete.

From dealing with the fallout from Mr Rochester's death, I suppose. Was this Charlie's way of punishing himself for what happened? For reporting the whole incident?

I chew that over, thinking of my own situation. Was that what I did last year? Took the easy route? Did I do what I did simply because I hadn't the guts to deal with it all? The consequences? The fallout?

This time the silence runs longer. Deeper. Charlie and I together, by ourselves, for the first time in how long?

Nine months, I realize. *Nine months.* My chest tightens, and I push the thought away.

"Lee," Charlie's voice cuts in. "I just wanted to say I'm sorry."

Another pang in my heart, even sharper, breaking through all the emptiness. What exactly is Charlie apologizing for?

For fighting with Tom at his father's funeral?

Or for what happened between us?

For Katy?

I inhale, pushing down the questions that have tormented me all these months. Why, Charlie? Why my sister? Was it just that she's prettier? Did you always fancy her? Is she simply…a better fit?

"I'm sorry," he says again. Waiting for me to ask why.

I give in. "What for?"

"The other day, for starters. The funeral."

I sigh, facing him. "Why did you go, Charlie? What was that all about?"

"Lee…" He stops. I sense there's something he wants to tell me, but something is holding him back. I know the feeling.

"You're close to him, aren't you?" Charlie gazes at me. "Tom, I mean."

I narrow my eyes. Surely Charlie isn't jealous again? But why would he be? It's not like he cares.

"Not really," I say. "We just talk sometimes." I flashback to Tom, after the funeral. His anger. His anguish at having to deal with Charlie on top of everything else.

"Yeah, I heard you stayed with him…after I left."

He did? I guess another kid told Katy.

"Tom needed someone to talk to…after your fight. He was really upset."

Charlie's mouth twitches. His eyes avoid mine.

"You shouldn't have come, Charlie. To the funeral. It was awful, the last thing Tom and his family needed."

"Yeah, I know." He reddens. Swallows. "What can I say? It was stupid, though it made sense at the time and I didn't think—"

"You never do," I cut in, before I can stop myself.

Charlie blinks. "I had to go, Lee. You know why…what happened." He mumbles the words. Ashamed, I sense. Feeling guilty that reporting his teacher might have led to his death.

I say nothing and we just sit there, in a silence seething with all the things left unsaid.

"Lee?"

I look over at Charlie.

"Would you pass on a message? Please tell Tom I'm sorry."

Suddenly I've had enough. I don't want to be more involved in this than I am already – I've plenty of my own crap to deal with. "Why don't you tell him yourself?" I snap, unable to keep the bitterness from my voice.

Somehow what happened at the funeral and his pathetic attempt to excuse himself just crystallized my worst feelings about Charlie.

His selfishness. His cowardice. His insensitivity.

Not only towards Tom. Never, at any point in the last year, has Charlie ever thought to say sorry to me. To apologize about Katy. Explain any of it. "But the funeral's not the only reason I wanted to speak to you," he continues, his voice softer, almost appeasing. "I…we haven't talked properly. Not since…" Charlie can't bring himself to say it. Not since he walked away from me. No, *ran away*.

Wait, he'd said. Just wait till things blow over.

He didn't even manage a month.

Suddenly I can't hold it in any longer. I'm angry. Really angry. For how he behaved, how he treated me. The mess he left me with.

I get to my feet and head back towards the Undercliff. Charlie leaps up and runs after me.

"Lee." He grabs my arm. I snatch it away. A couple walking a dog along the seafront stop and stare, clearly wondering whether to intervene.

"Listen to me, Lee, *please*. There's things you don't know—"

"I don't *want* to know, okay?" I yell, moving away before those people get involved. "Leave me alone." Emotion rising up in me, refusing to stay suppressed. All the stuff I'd tried to bury, just to survive.

"Please, Lee, let me explain." He makes another grab for

my arm and tries to pull me into him.

"*Too late!*" I scream in his face, wrenching myself away again. "Grow up, Charlie. Tell Tom whatever you need to say yourself. Sort your own fucking life out, and stay out of mine."

His face pales, and right at that moment the sun disappears behind a cloud and we're cast into shadow.

His arms drop, hang by his side. Charlie looks broken. Devastated. And I realize something else as I turn and walk away.

I don't care.

I don't give a shit how he feels any more.

Chapter 22

"A party?" I stare at my sister, incredulous. A week after Mr Rochester's funeral and she's having a *party*?

"Well, I thought everyone could do with cheering up, and it's to celebrate the end of the exams. Besides, it's not a party, it's a *bar-be-cue*." Katy splits the word into syllables for extra effect.

"There's a difference?" I ask, tempted to add that not all of us have finished our exams – I still have physics on Monday. But then I don't suppose I'm invited anyway.

I eye the bottles of beer and cider littering the kitchen table. I can't see much in the way of food. Only a packet of spicy potato wedges by the sink, some paper plates in a carrier bag.

"The food's in the fridge," says Katy, reading my mind. Or perhaps just following my gaze. "And people are bringing their own stuff. Saves having to worry about who's vegetarian."

She gives me a hard look. Daring me to ask.

I oblige. "Have you told Mum and Dad?"

My sister rolls her eyes, like I'm completely predictable. Which I guess I am.

At least in this instance.

"I'll text them," she says casually.

So, no, in other words. Mum and Dad have taken Walt off for the weekend to visit Nana and Grandad in Hampshire. Leaving me and Katy alone.

Should I ring them? Tell them she's planning some kind of party? Or *bar-be-cue*?

But I know my sister will go ballistic if I rat on her and I can't face the inevitable argument. Stay out of it, Laurie, I tell myself; it's Katy's job to let them know.

Nothing to do with me.

I meet Maya at the Rotunda Cafe in the corner of Preston Park. She's brought Dougal, her black Highland terrier, who keeps tugging on the lead, making begging eyes for her to carry on throwing his ball.

We get a couple of cans of lemonade and sit in the rose garden, where a riot of pink, red and yellow blooms give off so much scent it's like hanging around the perfume counter in Boots. Dougal lies next to us on the grass, resting his head between his paws, eyes swivelling as he watches people go by.

"Didn't she even invite you?" Maya asks, when I tell her about Katy's impromptu get together.

I shake my head. "You know Katy."

Maya's expression betrays her long-standing dislike of my sister. Even before Katy hooked up with Charlie, Maya had little time for her and her snarky remarks. Afterwards, Maya could hardly stand to be in the same room as her, on some level clearly holding her responsible for wrecking our trio.

"So you're not going to tell your parents then?" Maya raises her eyebrows.

"Grass up my sister?" I peel the wrapper off the muffin I bought. Take a bite and let the chocolatey sweetness spread across my tongue. "She'd never speak to me again."

"She hardly speaks to you anyway."

I sigh. Can't argue with that. I take another large bite of muffin, the first thing I've eaten all day.

"Careful." Maya laughs. "Don't want you getting sick again."

I smile, but I know what she's referring to. After bolting out of that biology revision class, I told her I'd thrown up in the girls' loos. Claimed I'd made a mess of my uniform and had to go home.

Maya didn't comment when I spun her the story. Didn't ask why I hadn't returned her messages till later that evening. She's learned it's pointless asking me too many questions.

"So I guess Charlie's going?" She takes a sip of her lemonade, watching me. I try and read her expression in return, but there's nothing there; if Maya has her suspicions about us, she's never let on.

"I guess."

I haven't seen Charlie since our encounter in Rottingdean

five days ago, except a glimpse in the biology exam yesterday. I guess Nicole got permission for him to revise at home; it's hardly as if the school would object given what's been going on.

Charlie hasn't been round to our house either, though Katy disappears after supper every evening, presumably to meet up with him.

Which makes life a lot easier for me. And that bit emptier. Some stupid part of me still misses him, even after everything; like the after-image that hovers in your vision when you stare too long at a bright light.

"Don't you think he's changed?" Maya asks suddenly.

I gaze at her. "Who? Charlie?"

"Who else?"

I shrug, but I get what she means. He looked even worse in the exam yesterday. Deep, dark circles had appeared around his eyes, like he'd barely slept. His easy smile seemed to have vanished.

Charlie looked haunted. Hunted, even.

What happened with Mr Rochester is obviously hitting him hard – I almost feel bad for blowing up at him in Rottingdean.

Almost.

"So, you looking forward to the prom next week?" Maya asks, clearly tired of trying to get me to talk about Charlie.

I grimace. To tell the truth, I've hardly given the prom a thought. And I still haven't found a dress. I'll go tomorrow, I think, when the shops are quieter.

Maya, of course, got hers weeks ago, ordering it from a specialist shop online. Katy too – I've glimpsed her dress hanging up in her room, along with the shoes and diamanté clutch bag she bought to go with it.

"You're not going to pull out, are you?" Maya frowns, picking up on my lack of enthusiasm. "Please, Lee. I couldn't bear it if you didn't go."

"I'll be there," I promise, though in truth I can't think of anything I want to do less. All I want is for this year to be over. To put it all behind me. It doesn't feel like there's much to celebrate.

But I know Maya is counting on me – now Charlie is well and truly out of the picture.

"I'd better get back." I finish the last of my lemonade.

"What are you?" Maya frowns again. "Some kind of unofficial chaperone? Why not come to mine tonight, leave them to it? Mum would love to see you. I'll get her to make spinach samosas. And chapattis."

I consider it, seriously tempted. God knows I don't fancy an evening stuck with Charlie and my sister. But if I'm not going to tell Mum and Dad about the party, the least I can do is keep an eye on things.

"I'd love to, but I can't. What if they burn the house down or something?"

Maya sighs. "Always the good sister." She picks up Dougal's lead and he leaps to his feet, panting with anticipation.

I blink. Tears looming out of nowhere.

The good sister.

If Maya only knew…

My friend hesitates, puzzled by my reaction. I wait for the inevitable questions, but they don't come. "You don't have to do this, you know, Lee," she says instead, looking resigned. "Keep it all locked up inside. You could try letting some of us in. You never know, you might even find it helps."

Walking home, I think of going round to see Tom, who I know lives a few streets away from the park. Not to deliver Charlie's apology – I'm pretty sure it would only infuriate Tom more – but to see how he is.

Too soon, I decide. Just a week on from the funeral, the family must still be reeling, trying to come to terms with everything that's happened. They don't need me hanging around. Feeling awkward, making everyone uncomfortable.

So I head back, and hear the music before I even reach the house. Something loud, bassy, reverberating through the late afternoon.

Shit. I didn't think they'd be starting this early.

I let myself in the front door, and the blare of music gets instantly louder. Walking into the kitchen, I see Katy has opened the double doors that lead onto the patio and garden beyond. A dozen people are already milling around on the lawn.

Oh god. The neighbours are going to go mental. At this

rate I won't have to ring Mum and Dad – someone else will.

"Hi, Laurie." Jessie Milton squeezes past me, heading for the downstairs loo. Katy is lifting a tray of foil-covered garlic bread out of the oven, dressed in a sleeveless T-shirt and tiny shorts, silver flip-flops on her feet.

She doesn't notice me, just carries the bread outside and puts it on the garden table. The waft of grilling meat drifts into the house; at the end of the patio I spot Charlie, holding metal tongs, flipping burgers on Dad's portable barbecue. In his other hand is a bottle of lager and I watch as he drains most of it in one go.

I glance at the clock – ten past four. If he carries on like that, he'll be completely wasted by the evening.

Katy catches sight of me as she comes back with the empty tray. Turns away without so much as a murmur of greeting.

Okay…I guess I'll take that as a hint. I go up to my room, dig out my physics folder and try to focus on revising for my last exam. Manage an hour or so before the thump of music, interspersed with bursts of laughter, becomes too distracting.

I give up. Go back down to the kitchen, make myself a cup of tea and a cheese and tomato sandwich, nicking a burger bun from the pack on the worktop. Eat it upstairs, looking out from my window seat.

Charlie is sprawled on one of the garden benches, necking another bottle of beer. Katy is sitting on the grass with Jo, Stacy Bridger and a few of her other friends, pretending to enjoy herself. But between all the shrieking and the laughter, I see her shooting Charlie worried glances, which he studiously ignores.

I turn away, fighting the urge to leave the house again, take up Maya's offer to hang out with her for the evening. But what if something went wrong here? Mum and Dad would be so upset.

So I lie on my bed and close my eyes.

I wake to a knock at my door. Sit up quickly, glancing at the clock. Gone ten. God, I've been out cold.

"Come in," I murmur, knowing it will be Katy. Unable to find something in the kitchen. Or wanting to borrow money for more beer.

But it's Charlie who pokes his head round the door. He looks terrible. Bleary-eyed, his skin sallow and sweaty. And swaying slightly. Drunk. Just as predicted.

Whatever battles he's fighting inside himself, they're obviously escalating. That's how Charlie operates, I think, as he hovers in my doorway – the good and the bad in him always in conflict. The kind, generous Charlie waging war with the reckless, selfish side of him.

But everything that's happened in the last few weeks has clearly upset the equilibrium. Charlie seems to be losing his grip on himself.

"Do you want something to eat?" he slurs.

I shake my head.

"Sure? I saved you a burger."

"I'm fine, thanks. Really."

Charlie hesitates, his hand lingering on the doorknob. I can see the outline of the tendons in his wrist, the muscles standing out on his arm. How much weight has he lost? I wonder. Maybe he's actually ill?

But he doesn't seem ill. Just...defeated somehow. It radiates off him like bad energy. Like alcohol fumes.

"What is it?" I ask finally, when he doesn't speak. "What do you want?"

He gazes at me, hanging on to the doorknob as if for support. His lips move slightly as he searches for his next words.

"It's not what you think, Lee, what happened last year. It wasn't that I didn't care – far from it…" He pauses. Seems to be groping for a way to continue.

"Charlie?"

Katy's voice, calling from downstairs. Charlie actually flinches, shaking his head as if waking up. He blinks at me a couple of times.

I come to my senses. "You'd better go." My tone cold as I turn away. Whatever he wants to say, it's too little, too late. I no longer want to hear it. I can't handle any of it any more.

A click of the door as Charlie gives up and closes it behind him.

Chapter 23

I must fall asleep again, because when I wake the music has stopped. The house is completely silent. All I can hear is birdsong outside my window.

I look down. I'm still lying on top of my duvet, fully dressed.

Nine in the morning, according to my clock. I've been asleep for ever. My mouth is parched and I feel hungover somehow, though I had nothing to drink last night. Nor much to eat, I think, remembering Charlie's offer of food.

Sitting up, I find my slippers and venture downstairs. I'm relieved to see that no one has trashed the living room. Not that Katy's friends would do something like that, but throw a party and word can get around; next thing you've got a house full of people you've never seen before, and anything can happen.

The kitchen, on the other hand, is littered with food packaging and empty beer bottles. There's melted cheese all over the oven, and the sink is crammed with dirty plates and dishes.

I look down. There's something spilled across the

floor tiles. A dark blackish crimson. Red wine – probably nicked from Dad's stash in the garage.

Oh for god's sake. Couldn't Katy have cleaned up a bit before she went to bed?

If she went to bed, I remind myself. I wouldn't be surprised if Katy went over to Charlie's, leaving me to tackle the mess before Mum and Dad get home.

I feel a wave of anger. No way is my sister dumping all this on me. And Mum said they'd set off after breakfast; they'll be back by lunchtime.

"Katy?" I stand at the bottom of the stairs and shout up.

No answer. No sound of anyone stirring.

"Katy?" I yell again, then go up to her room. Open the door to an empty bed.

Hell. She really has gone back with Charlie. At that moment I hate the pair of them. Selfish and careless – neither of them concerned about the chaos they create for other people.

It's then I spot the mobile on my sister's desk. Fluorescent blue case with a big orange smiley sticker on the front. Charlie's. He must have forgotten to take it with him.

I stare down at it, fighting the temptation.

Lose.

Grabbing it, I press the button to wake the phone. It's not protected with a pin code or anything; Charlie's never bothered with stuff like that.

I glance at the message icon. My finger hovers, then withdraws.

No, I'm not even going to go there.

Instead I bring up the photo gallery. I don't know why. I have enough pictures of Charlie, but none taken recently. Most of mine are from back when it was just the three of us – me and Charlie and Maya.

Before we all grew up. And grew apart.

I work my way through. Loads of selfies, many with my sister, who seems to have insinuated herself into nearly all of them. One of Charlie in his rugby kit, covered in mud. Another with Jo and Sammy crowding in alongside him and Katy, taken at school. A rare shot of Charlie with Nicole, sitting together on the sofa in their flat, Nicole with her arm around his shoulder and a forced kind of smile.

I keep scrolling, back and back until suddenly my own face stares up at me. I'm looking right into the camera. The sea in the background.

My heart contracts. It was taken last summer, down on the beach. Before Charlie dived into the water and I thought he'd drowned.

Before...*it* happened.

Without thinking I delete it. I don't even know why Charlie kept it.

I flick forward again, studying the change in him over the last year. Charlie's once carefree expression morphs into something more serious, and as the pictures slide by, he looks older – but not in a good way. More like someone whose world has tilted on its axis, throwing them off balance.

I carry on, past all the photos of that school visit to Fishbourne in April: various selfies with friends taken in different poses, some on the coach, some outside the Roman palace.

I remember that trip vividly. Maya hadn't been able to come, stuck at home with a stomach bug. Which left me pretty much alone, trying to avoid Charlie and my sister and her gang.

A whole day thrown together. Every minute of it agony.

More shots of Charlie and Katy, heads touching, my sister obviously holding the camera, her smile practised. I flick through them, wondering why I'm torturing myself like this. Rubbing salt into my wounds.

I'm about to get a grip, shut down the phone, when something catches my eye.

I pause, my finger hovering over the touchscreen.

What the hell?

I scroll back to the previous shot. One with Charlie and Katy, faces tipped skywards. The entrance to the Roman palace in the background.

My heart stops.

I enlarge the picture, zooming in on Charlie.

My breath flatlines. My heartbeat starts to thud in my ears.

It can't be.

It just can't.

The picture wobbles as my hand begins to shake. I sink onto Katy's bed, cradling the phone to keep it still.

In the photo, clearly visible by the angle Charlie is holding his head.

That tooth.

Broken.

A full month before he blamed it on Mr Rochester.

PART FOUR: THEN

Chapter 24

Ten minutes. That's how long I stood outside the pregnancy advice centre, trying to pluck up the courage to go inside. Not that there was anything particularly intimidating about the place: an ordinary red brick building set back from the main road, surrounded by large trees, leaves turning autumn-brown.

But somehow I couldn't bring myself to walk through the front door. As if taking those last few steps would make all of this real.

Fate intervened. Two women emerged; one of them, seeing me standing there, held the door open, assuming I was on my way in. I forced myself to step forward.

Finally, I was inside. An ordinary waiting room, chairs arranged round a low coffee table covered in magazines. A large pot plant in the corner. Posters covering most of the walls.

"How can we help?" asked the woman at the reception desk. About Mum's age, her smile warm and welcoming. I glanced at the people seated in the waiting area – a woman in her twenties, flicking through a magazine. Another, older, reading a leaflet. Her eyes drifted up to mine, and I looked away.

"Um…" I tried to formulate what I needed to say. But all the words in my head had disappeared. I stared at her blankly, fighting the urge to bolt back out the door.

"Here." The receptionist handed me a laminated card. On it were various symbols and options. One for help with contraception, another for tests for STIs. I pointed to the one showing pregnancy advice, relieved I didn't have to say it out loud.

The smiley woman typed something into her computer, then gave me a form and a pen, indicating a chair near her desk.

I sat down and filled in my name and date of birth. For a second or two I thought about lying, making up a different surname or pretending I was older. But what would be the point? I'd read all the stuff online. I knew they were obliged to keep everything I told them confidential – even from my parents.

"I'll get someone to have a chat with you," the receptionist said as I handed back the form. She nodded towards the waiting area. "Won't be long."

As I sat down, the woman reading the magazine looked up and gave me a once-over, her face deadpan. I squirmed in my seat, feeling exposed. Could she tell how old I was? I felt stupid. Foolish. Like everyone was thinking I was another teen statistic, another silly girl who hadn't been careful.

I was also scared. It was horrible sitting here alone. No one to talk to or distract me from whatever would happen next. I wished now I'd found the courage to tell Maya, begged her to come with me.

A minute later someone called a name. The younger woman dropped the magazine on the coffee table, disappearing into a room at the end of the corridor.

I gazed at the clock on the wall. Watched the minutes tick by. Eventually a girl around my age appeared, walking up to the older woman, widening her eyes in an embarrassed *let's leave now* sort of way. She didn't even glance in my direction, just made for the door like she couldn't get out of there fast enough.

The woman got up and trailed after her. Her mother, I guessed, noticing the resemblance, and couldn't help wondering why they were here.

None of your business, I told myself. They were probably asking themselves the same about me.

"Laurie?"

A lady with short dark hair was smiling at me across the waiting area. I followed her, stomach heavy with nerves, into a room much like Mum's at the surgery: a desk and two chairs, an examination bed behind a screen. The doctor or whoever she was sat down, and I perched on the other seat. She smiled at me again, clearly trying to put me at ease, then scanned the form I'd filled in earlier.

"My name's Debbie. I'm one of the counsellors here. Are you happy for me to call you Laurie?"

I nodded.

"So you've come to us for pregnancy advice?"

I cleared my throat. "Yes."

"Do you think you may be pregnant?"

I opened my bag and handed her the test stick. She studied it for a moment then gave it back. "If you don't mind, we'd like to do another, just to make sure."

My heart flip-flopped with a sudden rush of hope. "Could it be wrong then?"

Debbie inhaled, pressing her lips together. "Unlikely, Laurie, to be honest. Those things are usually pretty accurate."

"Okay."

"But all the same, we like to repeat them. So we can be certain."

She handed me a little pot for the urine sample, pointing to the adjacent toilet. "I'll be in here." She gave me another of the warm smiles the clinic seemed to excel in. Do they train them to do that? I wondered, as I locked myself in the loo. Or maybe you just had to be a really nice person to work here.

It took me ages to pee, even though I'd drunk a glass of water before I left home. Nerves, I guessed. But eventually I had a small sample to hand back to Debbie, who disappeared for a few minutes.

Please god, I prayed, crossing my fingers and tucking them under my legs so no one could see. Please let me be wrong.

"All right," said Debbie as she reappeared, sitting back down. A sheet of paper in her hand. She fixed her gaze on mine, her expression friendly but impossible to read. "Our test confirms that you're pregnant."

I closed my eyes, trying not to cry. For a moment, for a tiny, tiny moment, I'd still been hoping that maybe the one I did last week was wrong, that just possibly everything might be okay.

"I take it this isn't good news?" I heard Debbie say.

I shook my head, squeezing my eyelids tighter. But the tears leaked out anyway. An instant later I was sobbing. Debbie picked up a box of tissues and offered it to me; I pulled out a couple, pressing them hard against my eyes.

It was hopeless. Tears gushed out, soaking the tissues. Then my nose began to run and I had to wipe that too.

"Take your time," Debbie said gently. "No hurry."

For some reason the kindness in her voice made me cry even more. It took several minutes to pull myself together, to open my eyes and face the woman opposite. She was gazing back at me, her expression full of concern.

"I'm guessing this has come as something of a shock."

"Yes." My voice sounded wet and gurgly.

"Have you talked to anyone else about it?"

I shook my head again.

"All right, we can discuss your options, Laurie. But do you mind if we go through a few details first?"

I nodded, and she glanced at my form again. "You're fifteen, am I right? Sixteen next August?"

I nodded again.

The counsellor made a note of something on my form, then looked back up. "Can you tell me the first day of your last period?"

"July twenty-fourth." I had it by heart now.

She wrote it down, then picked up a calendar, her pen hovering over the dates. "So that would make you…nine weeks pregnant."

"No, I…I know when…" I swallowed. "The date it happened. It was August seventh."

Debbie smiled. "We always date a pregnancy from the first day of your last menstrual period."

"Oh. Okay."

"But you're sure of the date of conception?"

I cleared my throat again. "Yes. It only happened that one night," I added, my cheeks burning. "I mean, ever. For me."

Debbie put down her pen. Gazed at me. "Right. And does he know…the father?"

The father. The words sliced into me. *The father.* Another sharp pang as I remembered Charlie.

"Laurie?" Debbie spoke again. "Are you in contact with the father?"

"Yes," I said. "I mean I see him around." We were still avoiding each other – keeping our distance seemed easier if we took it literally. And I was still missing him desperately, a constant hollow ache in my heart. "But I haven't told him," I added.

"Can I ask you why not?"

I shrugged. I didn't know how to answer. Didn't know how to admit that I was scared telling Charlie would frighten him off completely. Destroy any chances of us getting back together.

"And you haven't told anyone else? Your parents?"

"No."

"Are you planning to?"

I shook my head vigorously. "I'd rather deal with it myself."

The counsellor's face softened. "So you're really on your own with this, aren't you, Laurie? No friends around you can talk to either?"

I shook my head again. God knows, I'd thought about telling Maya. Every day I'd considered taking her aside, letting it burst out. Imagined the relief of it. Not having to handle it all on my own.

But how could I do that to my friend? Make her keep a secret like that? It wouldn't be fair. And to be truthful, I couldn't face her knowing. Maya was…cool. Really nice. But her parents were pretty traditional, uptight about things. I couldn't honestly be sure how she'd react – not when it came down to something like this.

And then there was Charlie. I felt certain Maya would guess immediately it was him. It would be all over my face. How would she deal with that?

Her knowing…while he didn't.

It just felt wrong.

"So let's run through your options, Laurie." Debbie's voice was soothing, yet efficient, bringing me back to the reality of my predicament. "You can, of course, choose to continue this pregnancy and keep the baby. Or you have the option of giving the child up for adoption. Or, there's a third possibility, which is to go for a termination."

"A termination," I echoed, forcing myself to say the word. Face what it meant.

She nodded. "I know it's not an easy decision to make, but for many people it's a better option than continuing the pregnancy. The best option for them. But ultimately, it's something only you can decide."

"How would it be done?" I asked, almost stammering. "The termination, I mean."

Debbie glanced down at her notes. "I'm afraid you're too late for a medical abortion – the abortion pill – so you would be looking at a surgical procedure."

I must have winced because she smiled at me reassuringly. "You can have it done under sedation, Laurie, or a general anaesthetic if you prefer."

She let her words sink in before speaking again. "Have you had any thoughts about what you might like to do?"

Had I had any thoughts? I know it was just the way Debbie phrased it, that she didn't mean anything by it, but the question was so ludicrous I nearly laughed.

Had I had any thoughts?

Every single moment of every single day – seven days since I stared down at that blue tick on the pregnancy stick

– this had been the only thing I *could* think about. I'd drifted through a week of school on autopilot. There in body, but my mind elsewhere.

Could I have Charlie's baby?

Impossible. It was insane even considering it. I couldn't begin to picture a future where I had a child, not even years and years from now. It wasn't that I never wanted kids, but it was something so distant, so far ahead, that I couldn't remotely imagine what it would be like.

But the alternative…could I possibly bear to get rid of it?

Just asking myself the question brought ice to my guts. Turned up the volume on the nausea that had crept into my daily life. Round and round it went. Thought after thought after thought. But never an answer. Just cold hard numb shock at finding myself in a position where I even had to decide.

"Laurie? You're taking GCSEs next summer, right?" Debbie's voice pulled me back again. "Have you decided what to do next?"

I *had* decided, I wanted to say, though I supposed now that was up in the air. "I was going to stay on to do A levels."

"Right. And what then? University perhaps?"

I nodded. "Though I'm not sure what subject."

"Of course, it's not impossible to get qualifications and study for a degree while being a mother, Laurie, but it can be tough. Especially as a single parent. Babies and small children take up a lot of time and energy, so you'd need to factor that into any decision you make."

I blinked. "I know."

I remembered when Walt was born. I was just eight, but even so, I was shocked by the amount of noise and mess and work a baby entailed. He seemed to be forever crying, or needing a fresh nappy. I can still recall the exhaustion on Mum's face, hearing her get up in the night. The way, as Walt got older and more mobile, we had to be so careful to keep things out of his way. Things he might choke on. Things he could break.

Oh hell, Mum would kill me, I thought with a surge of panic. She'd be so upset. And Dad…I know Dad would tell me he'd support me whatever I decided to do, but Mum wouldn't be able to disguise her disappointment, her distress at me wrecking my future so completely.

"I can't work out how it happened," I blurted. "I keep going over it. I mean, we only did it twice."

"On different occasions?"

"That one night," I coughed. My throat felt prickly with embarrassment. "We used a condom both times."

Debbie smiled in sympathy. "They can be tricky. If you're new to them."

I felt my cheeks smart again.

"It's possible it came off and neither of you noticed. Or maybe one had developed a small tear – if it was beyond its use-by date, for instance.

"I don't think…" I stopped myself.

Shit. Why hadn't I checked? It hadn't occurred to me that anything could go wrong. If I'd known, I could have come here, got the morning-after pill I'd read about on their site.

If I'd had any idea…this would never have happened. And Charlie couldn't have noticed a problem either, or he'd have said something.

"The good news," Debbie continued, "is you're not that far on. You've come to us in plenty of time."

I had? It felt to me like I'd been clueless…careless. Hadn't even realized my period was overdue, not till weeks after.

The counsellor must have noted the surprise on my face, because she reached out and put a hand on mine. "You'd be amazed, Laurie. It can take months for some girls to discover they're pregnant. Sometimes they don't even realize until the baby arrives."

I'd heard stories of that, women going into labour with no clue they were even pregnant. It seemed so difficult to believe. How could you not even notice?

"I feel really tired," I said. "And sick too."

"That's normal. Typical symptoms for early pregnancy. Don't worry, it's not a sign that there's anything wrong."

Oh, but it *was*, I thought, tears springing to my eyes again. It was a sign that there was something wrong. This whole situation was very, *very* wrong.

And I had absolutely no idea how I could ever put it right.

Chapter 25

When I got home, I found Mum in the kitchen, rooting through the freezer after something for supper. She glanced up as I came in.

"Laurie." Her face broke into a smile. "I was wondering where you'd got to."

"You're back," I said, trying to hide my agitation. I'd been counting on Mum being at the surgery till late; Tuesday afternoons she had an asthma clinic, and it always ran over.

"Clinic was cancelled." Mum pulled out a packet of chicken pieces and straightened up. "These will do. Your dad's making a stir-fry tonight."

I stared at them, pale pink and flabby in their clear plastic packaging. My stomach lurched.

Oh god.

I darted upstairs before I could even think of an excuse. Shut myself in the bathroom just in time. As I kneeled on the floor, my stomach gave one violent heave, and I was sick into the loo. There wasn't much; I'd barely eaten today. Even the thought of food made the nausea worse.

A minute later a knock on the door. "Laurie?"

Damn. Mum must have heard me. Or wondered why I'd charged off like that.

"Laurie? Are you all right?"

I pulled myself to my feet, turned on the tap, gulped down some water. Wiping my mouth, I opened the door.

"I think I've got a stomach bug." I forced myself to make eye contact for a few seconds before letting my gaze shy away.

Mum reached out and put her hand on my forehead. Frowned. "You don't feel hot. When did this come on?"

"This afternoon," I lied.

"You're awfully pale." She examined my face. "You have been for a while, I've noticed. You should drop into the surgery so I can run a blood test. Check your iron levels are okay. How are your periods?"

Heat rose to my cheeks. "Why?" I snapped.

Mum blinked at me in surprise, but didn't comment on my tone. "Well, Laurie, if they're particularly heavy, you could be anaemic, that's all. Pop into the surgery tomorrow after school, I'll take some blood."

"I can't," I said quickly. "I've got netball practice."

This was actually true, though I didn't feel remotely up to it. Last week I made myself go along, even though I nearly passed out, I was so tired.

Mum frowned again, her forehead creasing. "Can't you come in afterwards? I'll be there till six."

"Look, I'm fine," I said, in a breezy tone that I hoped

would make her back off. No way could I risk Mum taking any blood. You could tell someone was pregnant from a blood test, couldn't you? "It's just a twenty-four-hour thing. Loads of people have had it at school."

Mum looked dubious. For a moment I thought she was going to insist. "Well, we'll see. But if you're not feeling better by the weekend, you're definitely having that test, all right?"

I nodded. "Sure."

Mum extended her hand again and rested it on my cheek. "I worry, okay, sweetheart? It's what mothers do."

Her expression was so loving it brought tears looming again, though I couldn't believe I had any left. I'd cried so much this last week I'd had to nick a concealer from Katy's stash of make-up, use it to disguise the redness around my eyes.

I leaned forward and gave Mum a hug, hiding my face in her shoulder as I searched for the words to fob her off. "Honestly, I'm fine. You can stop worrying."

It was such a blatant lie that I was amazed when she released me with a smile. Astonished she couldn't see through it instantly.

"Let me know if you feel up to eating anything," Mum said, turning to go back downstairs. "Perhaps you should have a lie-down in the meantime."

I retreated to my room, feeling a mix of guilt and relief. Guilt about lying to Mum. Relief that I'd got away with it, and had some time alone to mull over my visit to the clinic.

"Can I make a suggestion?" Debbie had asked, as she handed me a clutch of leaflets.

"Okay."

"I'm not here to tell you what I think you should and shouldn't do, but what I will say is it might be easier if you told your parents – and sooner rather than later. I know it feels very hard to break news like this, and yes, you may face some strong reactions, but in my experience most girls in your position find it's better in the longer run."

She had eyed me for a moment before guiding me back to reception. "This isn't the sort of thing you should face alone, Laurie."

I got those leaflets out now, and picked out the one titled *I'm Pregnant – What Are My Options?* I read it through carefully.

You are the only person who can decide what is best for you, it said, *and this may not be the same decision that your partner, friends or family would make.*

What decision would they think was right? I wondered. Mum had never had a termination, as far as I knew. And Maya, what would she do in my shoes?

She'd never end up in your shoes, said a voice in my head. She was way too sensible. I shook it away, thought about Charlie. What would he want, if it was up to him?

I had no idea.

Focus on yourself, I reminded myself. Could I really bring a child up on my own? Or with Charlie? Or was the right thing to end it now, before it could ruin everything?

It seemed an impossible question. How could I know? Either way, I might regret it for the rest of my life.

I gave up. Stashed the leaflets at the bottom of my underwear drawer, where there was no chance they'd be discovered. Dad usually did the laundry, leaving my clean stuff in a basket for me to put away.

I lay on my bed. Not feeling quite so sick now, but I was dizzy and my tummy ached with lack of food. I should try to eat something, I knew that, but I couldn't face joining everyone downstairs.

Why was I so reluctant to tell Mum about this? I asked myself again. I'd thought about what Debbie had said all the way home. I knew it made sense – Mum was a doctor, for god's sake. She'd know what to do, how to arrange things.

But somehow I couldn't bring myself to do it. It wasn't just that I was embarrassed, admitting to Mum that I'd lost my virginity. No, it was more that of all the girls in my year to end up pregnant, it made no sense that it was me. Mum had always been so upfront with me and Katy about contraception and stuff, making it clear we could go to her any time we felt the need.

I was the last person who could claim ignorance. Who could say she didn't know how to protect herself.

Maybe that was part of it. Maybe the way Mum had always stressed the importance of taking precautions was the reason I felt so ashamed now. I'd let her down. Even after all her efforts, I'd royally screwed up.

I felt stupid. Careless, despite knowing Charlie and I had been careful. But it wasn't only that. Behind all Mum's openness and advice was a clear message – getting pregnant when you didn't want to be was something you should do everything to avoid. After all, why else would she be so concerned?

Because it had happened to *her*, I thought. I was pretty sure I'd been an accident. Not that Mum or Dad had ever said so, god no. But people had often commented on the fact my sister and I were so close in age. No one chooses to get pregnant again just weeks after they've given birth, do they?

Downstairs I heard the back door open and shut. Walt running into the lounge and turning on the TV. I pictured him, snuggled into the corner of the sofa, sucking his thumb.

Mum and Dad were always on at him about it, but whenever Walt watched television, his hand strayed to his mouth. You'd tell him to stop and he'd take it out, and a few seconds later, it was back again. Mum was always fretting that it would ruin his teeth.

And there it was, I realized. The biggest reason I didn't want to confide in Mum or Dad. The reason I had to handle this on my own. Not just their disappointment. But the heartache it would cause both of them. The worry. They'd had enough of that, in the last few years, with Dad. I'd seen the anxiety etched on Mum's features as she'd dealt with his low moods, the atmosphere they left in the house.

And the extra work she'd had to take on, to compensate. All the admin as well as seeing patients. I had no idea if Mum minded being the only breadwinner, but I was sure of one thing. My parents didn't need any more stress in their lives.

I was afraid. Afraid that if I told them it would prove too much for Dad. Send him spiralling back down again. Afraid that the extra worry would take its toll on Mum too, on top of all that added work.

What Debbie had said was right – owning up to my parents might well make things easier for me. I could let Mum and Dad take some of the strain, help me come to a decision.

But one thing was clear – telling them would only make their lives harder.

Chapter 26

"You coming to the team meeting?"

I shook my head and Maya frowned. "What gives with you at the moment? You used to love netball."

"I still do."

"Yeah?" Maya gave me her no bullshit stare. "You missed practice on Wednesday, and now you don't want to come to the meeting."

"I'm not feeling up to it," I said weakly.

Maya chewed the inside of her lip. "So what do you want me to say to Mrs Arnold?"

"Tell her I'm sorry?" I shrugged. "That I'll be there next week." I had no idea if that was true. Probably not.

Maya eyed me for a few seconds longer then left me to it. Tagging on the end of the lunch queue, I bought a plain roll and a bottle of orange juice, and headed out to the patch of bare grass at the back of the sports hall.

I was in luck. No one about. It was a warm day for early October, but it was always windy round here; most people preferred to sit over by the science lab, where it was more sheltered.

I chose a spot by the large holly bush. It kept the worst of the breeze away. Sitting on the grass, I picked at my roll, tearing off little pieces and chewing them slowly. I'd found that if I ate plain food, a bit at a time, the nausea subsided for a while. I washed down each mouthful with a sip of juice, feeling the sweetness on my tongue, the surge of energy it gave me a few minutes later.

I'd reread the leaflets Debbie gave me three days ago. Pored over every word. It was normal to experience all this, they said, but it was still hard to believe that you could feel so ill and yet be okay. How did women stand nine whole months of it? And for more than one child?

"Mind if I join you?"

I glanced up to see Tom peering down at me. I forced a smile, and he took it as an invitation, flopping onto the ground beside me.

"What brings you round here?" I asked, wondering for a moment if he'd sought me out.

"Avoiding my dad," Tom said. "He's been on at me to spend lunchtimes at the study club. He's determined I'll get top grades next summer."

I gave him a sympathetic look. At least for most of us school was another world, somewhere we could escape whatever might be going on at home.

Tom examined the remnants of my bread roll. "Is that your lunch?"

I shrugged. "Wasn't very hungry."

His expression remained blank, and I tried to think of

an excuse to get away. I could go and sit in the drama studio; it was usually empty at lunchtime.

"Shouldn't you be at netball practice?" Tom asked. "You're in the first team, aren't you?"

I almost laughed, impressed Tom had even noticed there were two teams – most boys never paid any attention to "girls" sports. But then Mr Rochester sometimes helped out in the PE department; maybe he talked about that sort of stuff at home.

"I...I'm not feeling too good," I said. "Still getting over a bug."

"Right." Tom squinted into the distance, then sat down next to me. He really did look like his dad, I thought, taking in his thick brown hair, his broad shoulders.

"Laurie..." Tom started, then hesitated. "Listen, it's none of my business, I know. Tell me to sod off if you like. But...that test I saw you buying..." He cleared his throat, steered his gaze to mine. "Was it by any chance positive?"

I tried to inhale, but the breath wouldn't come. I stared out over the patch of grass leading to the wooden fence surrounding the school. There was nothing to see, but I wasn't looking anyway. My eyes were hot with the effort of not crying. Despite my struggle to stay in control, a tear broke free and rolled down my cheek.

"It was, wasn't it?" I felt Tom's hand on my shoulder, giving it a squeeze. I dropped my head and a sob escaped from me, a small, sudden burst of noise. I swallowed, trying to pull myself together.

"Yes," I said finally. What was the point of lying?

Tom knew. One glance at my face would have told him the truth.

"Shit, Laurie. I'm sorry. I'm assuming that wasn't something you'd planned at all."

I laughed, briefly. "You could say that."

Tom removed his hand, and I looked at him pleadingly. "You won't tell anyone, will you?"

For a second he seemed almost annoyed, his features stiffening slightly. "No, Laurie, I won't tell anyone you're pregnant. Why would I?"

He sighed and studied the ground, pulling at a blade of grass. "Listen, you're not the only one with secrets, all right?"

I turned to face him. "What do you mean?"

Tom's eyes flicked to mine then away again. I had the sense he was struggling with something, coming to some kind of decision.

"The thing is…" he began, trying to maintain eye contact, but clearly finding it difficult. He inhaled, and for a second I thought he was going to change his mind. Keep his secret to himself.

"The thing is…I prefer boys."

A pause where I let this sink in. "You mean you're gay?"

"Yeah…I guess."

I tried not to look shocked, though truthfully I was. I'd had no idea. Not that it mattered, but you kind of assumed people were straight. As a default.

"Okay," I replied. "I didn't know."

"No one does." Tom brought his knees up to his chest. Rested his elbows on them. "You're the first person I've ever told."

My eyes widened. Unsure what to say. Why me? And why now?

"So now you know my big secret," Tom continued. "And why I won't go round blabbing yours."

"Okay," I said again, feeling a strange mix of emotions. Surprised, yes, and sorry for this boy who'd held in his secret for so long. God knows, I'd only carried mine for a couple of weeks, and that was bad enough.

I was grateful too, knowing Tom had confided this to reassure me. Or maybe, like me, he just needed to tell someone. To not have it bottled up, festering inside.

"Was it Charlie?" Tom asked, out of the blue.

I sniffed. Nodded. "That obvious, huh?"

He shifted his weight, straightened his legs then bent them again. "Not really. Only if you were paying attention."

Only if you were paying attention? Why would Tom be paying any attention to me, or who I liked? Especially considering he'd just told me he was gay.

Then the penny dropped.

I remembered that night, down on the beach. Tom watching me and Charlie. It wasn't me he'd been interested in – it was *Charlie*. I almost laughed at the irony. Charlie being jealous, thinking Tom was competition.

"He was always eyeballing you," Tom said. "Charlie,

when he thought no one was looking. He'd tease you too, winding you up. Show off when you were around. You know, classic boy stuff."

I tried to think back. Already it was hard to remember how things had been between me and Charlie, before that night together – even though it was only a couple of months ago.

Had anyone else noticed? I wondered. Had Maya?

"I take it you haven't told him?" Tom asked.

I shook my head. I'd barely glimpsed Charlie these last few days, though Maya was still trying to intervene. Yesterday she'd suggested the three of us go to see that new Bond film together, but Charlie had ducked out, apparently, making some excuse about helping out his mother.

"As if," Maya had told me afterwards, clearly furious. "Who does he think he's kidding?"

I'd felt sorry for Maya, and a little for myself – a few months ago I'd have loved a trip out like that – but I was relieved he'd said no. It saved me from having to hide this from him as well as Maya. Buying me time while I decided what the hell I was going to do.

"So, are you planning to tell Charlie?"

I sighed. Debbie had asked the same question – and I didn't know the answer then either. "Do you think I should?"

Tom considered this for a minute or two. I liked that about him. The way he didn't jump to any snap conclusions. Didn't reach for the first thing that came into his head.

"I guess that would depend," he said eventually.

"On what?"

He gazed at me. "On what you want to do, Laurie."

He didn't ask what that might be. And I was so grateful it made me feel tearful again. But he was right. If I decided to keep the baby, Charlie would have to know; after all, there'd be no way to hide it. But if I didn't…

"Have you told your parents?" Tom asked.

I shook my head again. "Have you told yours? That you're gay?"

He shook his.

"Are you going to?"

Tom hugged his knees. Over on the netball courts, faintly, I heard Mrs Arnold give a short sharp blast on her whistle. "I suppose so. Eventually."

"They'll be okay about it, won't they?"

Tom shrugged. "I dunno." He turned his face into the wind. "What about my dad? How would it be for him being, you know, the teacher with the gay son?"

"Tom…I don't think it's like that any more. I mean, this is Brighton after all. Being gay isn't such a big deal, surely?"

He snorted. "You reckon? Well, I guess you haven't been paying much attention, especially to the boys in this school and the crap they say. You'd think being gay was some kind of terminal disease. Contagious too."

"You must hate being here," I said.

Tom laughed. "No shit, Sherlock. Counting off the days till I can leave."

"How many?"

"Two hundred and sixty-two to my last exam. But Dad wants me to stay on to do A levels."

"And you? Is that what you want?"

Tom turned down the corner of his mouth. "Not really. Dad's fixated on me becoming a lawyer or something big in the city – you know, a job that earns lots of money."

"And you don't want that?"

He shook his head. "Doesn't make you happy, I reckon. Being loaded. And you have to work insanely long hours, what I've heard."

I shifted my weight on the grass, ignoring another spike of nausea inside. "So what would you do, if you had a choice?"

Tom scratched the top of his ear. "Not sure. I'd like to work with animals, maybe…something outdoors. I'm sick of being cooped up all day."

"How about music? You're into that, right?" I remembered the project he did in English once, making a poem from different lyrics from his favourite eighties bands: Bowie and The Cure, Prince and Elvis Costello, REM and The Smiths. Miss Jackson had been so impressed she got him to read it to the whole class.

Tom laughed. "Yeah, right. I love it, but I'm not stupid. I know I've got about as much musical talent as this blade of grass."

He plucked one then tossed it into the air, where the wind picked it up and blew it round the corner of the sports hall. We sat in silence for a couple of minutes, listening to the other girls yelling to each other on the netball court. A final blast from Mrs Arnold's whistle.

"Anyway, how about you, Laurie?" Tom asked. "I guess you're on a deadline, right? When do you have to decide?"

"In a week," I said. "Maybe two."

Debbie the counsellor had told me not to leave it too long; made me an appointment for next week. I didn't want to think about why. It didn't seem fair you had to make a decision this hard in such a hurry.

Tom examined my face. "I'm not saying what you should do, Laurie. But do you think Charlie could handle it…if you decided to go ahead?"

"How do you mean?"

Tom shrugged again. "I just can't see him, you know, doing all that dad stuff…"

He didn't spell it out. He didn't need to. Charlie wasn't exactly the sort of person you'd picture pushing a buggy. Or changing a nappy. Or doing any of the things most fathers do.

Maybe one day – but not yet.

"I can't even imagine how shitty this must be for you," Tom stretched his legs, then stood up. "I wish I could help."

"What would you do –" I blurted, suddenly needing to know – "if you were me, I mean?"

Tom gazed down at me. "I don't know, Laurie. I can't answer that."

He sniffed, looked at his shoes then back at my face. "But I'm sure you'll make the right decision. The right one for you. That's all that counts – everything else is just bullshit, okay? Do whatever's best for you."

"Thank you," I said, taking the hand he offered and letting him haul me to my feet.

"Any time." Tom smiled. "Seriously, any time you want to talk, Laurie, just ask."

He picked up his rucksack. Swung it onto his back.

"You know what…" He paused, thinking. "Scratch what I said earlier. Actually I reckon you should tell Charlie."

"Really?"

"Yeah. I think he should know, Laurie. And I think telling him will help you make up your mind. Get things clearer in your head."

I nodded, though I wasn't convinced it would make things any easier. But he was right about Charlie needing to know.

After all, this was his child too.

Chapter 27

I went home first, got changed. It took me a while. Even my loosest jeans were becoming uncomfortable, digging into my stomach. Eventually I found a large safety pin in the bathroom cabinet, used it to join each end of the waistband, creating a little more room.

I cycled round to Charlie's. It was quicker than waiting for the bus, and I hoped the exercise would perk me up. But halfway there I felt so sick I had to get off and walk. It was another warm autumn day, and I arrived at Alice Road hot and breathless.

Not to mention terrified. The whole way I'd been dreading telling Charlie, rehearsing the words I'd need. Never getting beyond that first simple sentence.

I'm pregnant.

How would Charlie react? I wondered, over and over again. How would he respond? I thought about what he'd said a month ago, about waiting, about holding off from anything serious till Nicole lost interest. Would this change his mind? Bring us back together?

Or would it scare him off completely?

What if he flipped out? Told Maya perhaps? Or even Mum or Dad? Could I take that risk?

Don't be stupid, I repeated to myself. You *have* to talk to him, Laurie. He has a right to know.

It was only as I wheeled my bike along Alice Street that I realized Tom was right. This was what I'd been waiting for, to make my decision. When I said the words, when I saw Charlie's face, I'd know what to do.

That would tell me everything.

I'd forgotten to bring a padlock, so I parked my bike behind the building, away from the view of the road. Going round to the front, I rang the bell for the bottom flat. Heard it chime inside, a cheerful sing-song at odds with my mood.

I closed my eyes. Pulse racing so fast I felt light-headed and jittery.

It seemed an age before I heard any movement inside. Before the front door finally swung open.

My heart sank.

Not Charlie. His mum.

I felt crushed with disappointment. Charlie always answered the door if he was in.

"Laurie," Nicole said, looking less than pleased herself.

Shit. Why was she here? Friday afternoons she was usually working at that cafe on the seafront. I blinked at her for a moment or two, trying to come up with an excuse for my sudden visit – though not long ago I didn't need one.

"Is Charlie in?" I asked simply. Maybe he was having a nap. Or listening to music with his headphones on, didn't hear the doorbell.

"'Fraid not. He's gone to the shops."

I hovered on the doorstep, trying to think what to do or say. Nicole just stared at me. There was something intense in her gaze, and I remembered what Charlie had told me, about her threat to tell my parents.

I turned to go. This would have to wait.

"Why don't you come in?" she asked suddenly. "He won't be that long."

I spun back. My surprise must have shown on my face because Nicole's lips twitched, but she held the door open. I went into the living room, feeling mortified. What could I say to Charlie's mother? She had to be wondering why I was here, out of the blue, when I hadn't been round in months.

"Where's Charlie gone?" I asked.

"Up to Churchill Square. He needed some new trainers." Nicole stood there, studying me. She was dressed in her trademark short flared skirt and Dr Martens. In some ways she looked barely older than me, though you could see the years in her face, the fine lines around her eyes, around her mouth.

I sat on the sofa, mentally kicking myself for not texting Charlie first, checking he was home. But I hadn't wanted to alert him, didn't want him making some excuse, or ringing back to ask what it was about. I had to do this face-to-face.

What to do now though? My head spun as I tried to work it through. Even if Charlie came home soon, there was no way I could talk to him with his mother in the flat. And if I left, she was bound to tell him I'd been here. I was afraid – stupidly irrationally afraid – that he would give me the slip. And if I didn't do this today, I might change my mind. Might never find the courage to try again.

In the kitchen the song finished on the radio and cheerful voices discussed the band. I glanced at Nicole, feeling increasingly awkward.

There was something odd in the way she was examining me. She was fidgety. Agitated. She'd always been a bit hyper, rushing around, getting frustrated at little things like missing keys, or the mess we made – Charlie, Maya and me – on the occasions we'd hung out here.

But this was different. Nicole seemed…nervous. Eyeing me like I was here to break bad news.

Which I suppose in a way I was.

"Do you want something to drink?" she asked eventually.

I nodded. "Yes, please."

"Tea? Coffee? Or there's peppermint, if you'd prefer."

"Peppermint would be nice." Though really I had no idea, having never drunk it, but I couldn't stomach tea or coffee since I'd got pregnant.

In truth, I didn't want anything. I was feeling weird, dizzy almost, as if I was losing my grip on the world around me. But at least it would release me from Nicole's unnerving scrutiny for a few minutes.

What should I do? I wondered again as she retreated to the kitchen. When Charlie came home, I'd need an excuse to get him out the flat again. But what? My mind was blank. I couldn't come up with a single thing.

Oh god, this was ridiculous. I stood up, about to tell Nicole I was leaving, when suddenly the world folded in around me and everything went dark.

"Laurie?"

A voice in the distance, a pressure on my arm.

"Laurie? You okay?"

Music in the background, something light and floaty. A girl singing, her voice full of sunshine. Like nothing had ever gone wrong in her life, and nothing ever would.

I forced my eyes open. Charlie's mum was peering down at me, looking frantic. "Jesus, you gave me a scare," she said, and I realized I was lying in a heap on the floor. "You just sort of crumpled."

I opened my mouth to speak but no words came out. The world was still reeling, a sensation of falling, even though I wasn't moving.

"Shall I get a doctor?" Nicole sounded genuinely worried.

I heaved myself into a sitting position. "No," I croaked, then cleared my throat. "No need. I think I just fainted."

I'd read in one of those leaflets Debbie gave me that fainting was quite common in early pregnancy. Low blood sugar, I guessed. I should have made an effort to eat more.

I tried to get to my feet, but my legs felt impossibly shaky and I sank back against the sofa.

"I'll call your mum." Nicole reached for her phone.

"No!" I snapped, my voice too sharp.

Nicole frowned. "Why not, Laurie?" Her stare more intense.

I swallowed. I couldn't think of a reason, but no way did I want Mum seeing me in this state. She'd insist on taking me straight to the surgery and giving me a full check-up.

"It's…" I groped for an excuse. "I'm fine, really."

Nicole kept her eyes fixed on me. "You don't look fine, Laurie. You don't look well at all."

"It's nothing." I tried to make myself appear brighter, but there was an insistent buzzing noise in my head that wouldn't go away.

Please god, don't let me faint again. *Please.*

"Do you have a biscuit or anything?" I stammered. "I think I just need something to eat."

Nicole blinked, then vanished into the kitchen, returning with half a packet of Rich Tea. "Probably a bit stale" – she sounded more offhand than apologetic – "but they should do the trick."

I pulled one out and ate it, while Nicole perched on the armchair opposite. Watching.

"Why exactly are you here, Laurie?"

Her question was so sudden, and her tone so…serious, it caught me off guard.

"I came to see Charlie," I mumbled, but somehow even the truth sounded lame.

His mother's scrutiny didn't waver. "It's a bit random, isn't it?"

I opened my mouth. Closed it again. Unable to find the energy to speak at all.

Nicole smoothed down her short skirt. She was wearing tights with a bright floral pattern that clashed with the rest of her outfit.

Then again, everything about Charlie's mother clashed somehow. The way she looked sort of young – her clothes and make-up more like the girls at school would wear – yet was obviously older. That sense of someone fragile, easily upset – yet scary too.

Even Charlie's relationship with her seemed full of contradictions. Despite her frequent absences, he insisted they were close. He always defended her if you said anything about how she behaved, and put up with her rages, rather than getting angry himself.

I remember once, when Maya and I were here, she accused him of stealing a ten-pound note from her purse; instead of arguing, Charlie hunted round the flat until he found it, tucked into a pocket in her handbag.

Nicole had thanked him, I'd noticed, but never apologized for the accusation. And Charlie didn't point out how unfair she'd been. Just seemed grateful everything had calmed down.

"Laurie…" Nicole hesitated. Clearly battling with herself.

I gazed back at her, waiting.

She inhaled. Cleared her throat. "You're not pregnant, are you?"

I was so blindsided by the question that my expression gave me away immediately. "No," I stuttered, getting to my feet, hoping to fob her off with outright denial. "Why would you think that?"

I sounded a great deal less than convincing.

"Sit down, Laurie." Nicole's tone so forceful I instantly obeyed. "Tell me the truth. That's why you're here, isn't it?"

How???

How on earth could she know?

Could Tom have told her? But when? I'd only confessed to him a few hours ago. Anyway, why would he? He'd promised he wouldn't say anything to anyone. And he didn't even know Nicole.

The world tilted and swayed again. I closed my eyes, trying to steady myself.

"You are, aren't you?"

Her voice closer. I looked up to see Nicole standing right in front of me. I didn't reply. I couldn't. I was shaking now. Tears leaking from the corners of my eyes.

How had she guessed? It wasn't that obvious, was it?

"Shit." Nicole sank onto the other end of the sofa, then leaned forward, cradling her head in her hands. "Shit, shit, *shit.*"

I flinched. She sounded desperate. Close to furious.

"How did you know?" I asked, my voice quavering.

Nicole laughed. A short sharp bark of a laugh. But she didn't answer. Just lifted her gaze to the ceiling, blinking. Trying not to cry herself, I realized.

Oh hell, this was awful. *Awful.* I should never have come. I should have dealt with this on my own. I willed myself to get up and leave, but my body felt leaden. Defeated.

"How far gone are you?" Nicole turned to me.

"Nearly ten weeks."

She gritted her teeth, her lips narrowing to thin lines. "And you've taken this long to tell anyone?"

"I didn't know. I just didn't think it was possible… I mean, we were careful."

Nicole's face twitched again with something unreadable, then she leaped to her feet, pacing the length of the small living room.

"Jesus Christ," she muttered, more to herself than me. "What were the bloody chances?"

I swallowed. I thought about explaining, telling her that we used a condom, then remembered she already knew.

"I don't know how it happened," I said instead.

Nicole's head whipped round. Her expression was… bewildering. Fierce. Accusatory.

"I'm sorry." My voice broke into a sob. This was dreadful. Worse than I could possibly have imagined. "It was only once… I mean just that evening… you know that… I didn't realize…"

I started to cry in earnest. "I should have… we should have been more careful. I thought we *had* been careful."

Nicole's gaze softened a little. She picked up the mug of peppermint tea and handed it to me. "Here, have some of this. It'll make you feel better."

I took it from her, hands trembling so much it was an effort not to spill any. Made myself drink half of it in one go.

It tasted horrible. Like watery mint sauce. But the sensation of warmth pouring down my throat steadied me a bit. Nicole got up and went back into the kitchen. Returned with a glass of red wine and sat in the armchair opposite.

Where was Charlie? I wondered desperately, glancing at the time display on the TV. I'd been here half an hour. Nicole had said he'd be home soon.

"Does Charlie know?" she asked, as if reading my thoughts.

I shook my head.

"Are you planning to tell him?"

I took another sip of the revolting tea. "That's why I'm here."

Nicole pressed her lips together. Didn't speak for a minute while she digested this, just took several large gulps of wine.

"Have you told your parents?"

I shook my head again.

"Anyone?"

"No." It wasn't quite true – I'd told Tom after all, and Debbie at the clinic – but I couldn't see any reason to mention that.

"So Charlie has no idea then?" Nicole repeated.

"No."

"And you're certain it's his?"

"*Yes,*" I said, my face flushing. Not bothering to hide the indignation in my voice. "I have to go."

I put the mug on the coffee table and stood up, but Nicole's hand shot out to stop me.

"Wait. Please."

I yanked my arm away, but stayed put.

"Laurie, I'm sorry." Nicole cleared her throat. Composed herself. "I shouldn't have asked you that. I know you're telling the truth." She closed her eyes briefly before fixing them on me again. "So have you decided? What you're going to do?"

"I've been to the clinic," I said, sidestepping the question I couldn't yet answer. "I'm going back on Monday."

"Okay." Her expression was thoughtful. She stared at the floor for a moment. "You know, don't you, that the same thing happened to me?"

I didn't respond, unsure what to say.

"I wasn't much older than you when I got pregnant with Charlie, and I've never told him – Charlie, I mean. I've never told him how it happened…who with…though of course he knows I was very young at the time."

"What did happen?" I asked, wondering if I even wanted to know. Charlie had always clammed up whenever we'd questioned him about his father. And now I wasn't sure I wanted to hear it from Nicole; it felt disloyal somehow – me knowing, and not him.

"Same as you," Nicole shrugged. "One-night stand."

A flash of pain in my chest. A one-night stand. Was that how Charlie's mother saw this?

Was that how Charlie saw it?

"I never told his dad I was pregnant," Nicole continued, oblivious to my distress. "Never wanted to. Which was just as well, because I'd have had no idea how to contact him. He was half Jamaican – lived over there most of the time."

Impossible not to catch the bitterness in her tone. Nearly sixteen years on and this was clearly still very raw.

I gazed down at my knees. Asking myself where all this was going, and how I might escape. I'd given up on the idea of telling Charlie, at least for today.

"You're not going through with it, Laurie, are you?" Nicole kept her green eyes focused on mine. She was wearing so much eyeliner they looked almost black.

Through with what? What was she asking me?

"You're not going to keep the baby, I mean," she said, seeing my confusion.

"I don't know." I turned away so my face wasn't so easy to read. Or hers.

We both remained silent for a while. On the radio in the kitchen The Beatles came on. "All You Need is Love".

I wondered what Charlie would make of this, if he came back now. How on earth we could explain it, the two of us, sitting here, my tear-stained face. Nicole's air of desperation.

"Laurie," she said finally. "Don't do this."

"Do what?" I forced myself to ask.

"Have a child now…at your age. It will ruin your life."

Something ignited inside me. "Did it ruin yours?" I asked, defiant. "Are you saying Charlie wrecked everything for you?"

She sighed. "Laurie…"

"Is that what you think? That Charlie screwed everything up?" I couldn't believe I was saying this. Or how angry I sounded.

I *was* angry, I realized. Suddenly furious. At Nicole. At Charlie. At this whole messed-up situation. The fact that I was sitting here now, discussing this with someone I disliked more and more by the minute.

"No, Laurie, that's not what I'm saying." Nicole's tone more appeasing now. "I know it sounds like it…it's hard to explain. I love Charlie. He's everything to me…you know that, don't you?"

I nodded. At the same time not sure I believed her. Sometimes it didn't feel like that at all.

"But that's the point, Laurie. A child takes over everything…your time, your energy, your heart, leaving little room for anything else. If there's something you want to do with your life, do it first, before you have kids. That's all I'm saying."

"And what if there isn't?" After all, I hadn't yet decided what A levels to take next year, let alone what I'd do afterwards.

Nicole sighed again, more heavily. "It's not just about

207

you, though, is it?" She narrowed her eyes at me. "What about Charlie? What about what he might want to do with *his* life?"

"He still could," I protested. "He doesn't have to give anything up. If he doesn't want to be with me, I could manage on my own."

Could I? I wondered. Did I actually mean that?

"Be a single mum, you mean?" Nicole snorted. "Laurie, I've been there, done that. Got the bloody T-shirt. It's hard. *Really, really* hard. Not having someone else to help out, to depend on, to give you a break. And not only that…"

She paused. Collected her thoughts. "It makes the chances of there ever being someone a lot lower…don't you see?"

"You're saying, what…no one else will want me if I've got a child?"

"I mean it'll be much harder to establish another relationship, Laurie. A great deal harder than you can possibly imagine."

I stared at her. For the first time in my life, I found myself feeling almost sorry for Nicole. She looked sort of sad. Though I'd never liked her, suddenly I could see how difficult her life had been, how much she'd given up for her son.

And I could understand better why Charlie had gone off to Norfolk like that. Why he hadn't wanted to upset her.

Perhaps he felt he was a burden, was aware how much his life had cramped hers.

"You know, don't you, that Charlie wants to be a pilot?" Nicole declared. "It's all he's ever wanted. Even as a little kid, he was obsessed with planes."

I nodded. Anyone even slightly acquainted with Charlie knew that about him. He was always talking about it, where he was going to go, all the things he'd see.

"I'm his mother," Nicole continued. "I know my son. The truth is he'd never leave you to bring up a child on your own. He'd insist on…on being involved."

Hope welled up inside me. A flood of relief that perhaps I wouldn't have to deal with this alone.

"And that would ruin everything for him, Laurie." Nicole's words froze something inside me. Even her hand felt cold as she leaned over and put it on my arm. "You see that, don't you?"

I stared at her, my mind whirring. Was that true? Would being with me…having our child…would it stop Charlie following his dream?

My heart ached. I couldn't make him give that up. I couldn't do that to him.

"I'm not trying to persuade you, Laurie. You have to believe me, that's not what I'm doing here," his mother added, her voice dropping to a whisper. Her grip on my arm grew tighter. "But I think you should…be aware. Know what you would be getting yourself into…if you… if you decided to go ahead. Especially…"

She stopped.

"Especially what?"

Nicole bit her lip. Hesitating.

"What is it?" I repeated.

"The thing is, Laurie…I wasn't going to tell you this. I know how you feel about Charlie and I didn't want you getting hurt…"

She paused again.

"What?" I hissed, frantic now to hear it.

"I think Charlie might have someone else. Another girlfriend, I mean."

A pain under my ribs like I'd been stabbed. All the air in the room seemed instantly to disappear. I fought for breath as my world started reeling again.

A girlfriend?

But Charlie said we were waiting.

Just until things blew over.

"He's not ready for anything serious, don't you see, Laurie? Yeah, sure, he'd do it. He'd stick around if you had the baby, but really I know he doesn't want to be tied down. He's not ready for that kind of commitment yet. Can't you see that?"

What about the commitment I made? I wanted to shout at her. Having sex with Charlie…losing my virginity to him…it hadn't been something cheap, something I'd simply tossed away. It had been a gift, a promise for the future. Something I thought he'd value as much as me.

"Laurie?"

I tuned her out. Her voice an echo in my head as I scrambled to my feet and made for the door, afraid Nicole might try and stop me again.

But she didn't. She didn't come after me as I grabbed my bike and wheeled it to the road, leaning on the handlebars for support.

Trying to breathe.

Trying to stay upright.

Trying not to collapse again as my whole world shattered around me.

Chapter 28

No sign of Mum or Dad's cars on the drive when I got home, the house quiet as I let myself in. Relief swept over me. No way I wanted anyone seeing me in this state.

I poured myself a glass of water from the kitchen tap, gulping it so fast I was left panting for air. I felt winded. Woozy. Like that time Charlie, Maya and I were playing with a rugby ball down on The Level, and he accidentally ran into me, his head landing right in my stomach.

I put my hand there instinctively, though there was nothing to feel except the soft swell of flesh. Hard to believe something was living in me. Growing. I felt hollow. Like someone had scooped out my insides and yet somehow, miraculously, I was still alive, still breathing.

I ran another glass of water and drank this one slowly, staring out over the back garden. Dad had obviously cut the grass today; the lawn looked short and neat. I tried to focus on noticing things, the details of the world around me, rather than the thought revolving around my head. Like that strip of text that slides across the bottom of the TV screen when some disaster happens.

Charlie has a girlfriend.

He has met someone else.

I waited for the words to penetrate, for the pain that would follow when the shock wore off. I'd believed him. All the stuff he'd said about just taking a break – I'd really believed he meant it. Even though we'd barely spoken these last few weeks, I'd clung to the hope that he'd been genuine about wanting a future for us.

Despite everything, despite whatever decision I might make, part of me had been praying this would work out okay. That it wouldn't be the end, the end of us. That we would survive.

Charlie has someone else.

He didn't wait. He doesn't care.

I closed my eyes and tried to take it in. But surely it couldn't be true? He wouldn't have done that, would he... so soon after?

No, I decided, I didn't believe it. Didn't accept what Nicole had said, or her motives for saying it. I needed to speak to Charlie, now, face-to-face. Hear from his own lips that it wasn't true, that his mother was just trying to come between us. Trying to convince me to do what she wanted.

Hope rose again, bright as sunlight. I had to find Charlie, talk to him. I needn't tell him...about the baby. Not yet.

Charlie has someone else.

I took my mobile out of my pocket. Rang his number.

Somewhere, faintly, a phone began to trill. A familiar

ringtone, the chorus of that dance song that was so popular last year. I frowned, but then the call cut off.

Call ended appeared on my screen.

Upstairs the music stopped just a heartbeat later.

My breathing shallowed. My pulse began to thump in my head. Loud, getting faster. I walked out of the kitchen and stood at the bottom of the stairs, gazing up.

I rang his number again. This time it went straight to voicemail. "Hey, this is Charl…"

I ended the call.

He'd turned off his phone.

I slid off my trainers. Clutching my mobile in one hand, the other gripping the bannister for support, I walked slowly, quietly upstairs.

No hope now. No confusion.

Somehow I just knew. Somehow I was certain as I reached my room and looked inside, Charlie wouldn't be there. He wouldn't be lounging on my bed, waiting for me to come home. Eager to tell me we'd held out long enough. To tell me that everything would be all right, that we'd find a way through this.

I barely needed to glance around my room to confirm what I already knew.

No Charlie.

I turned towards the closed door at the end of the landing. Nothing in my head as I approached it. Nothing now, except a whole universe of emptiness. A black hole at the centre of my heart.

When I reached it, I paused, then twisted the handle and pushed it forward.

Without a sound, the door to Katy's bedroom swung open.

But I already knew what I was going to see.

PART FIVE: NOW

Chapter 29

I'm sitting on Katy's bed, in the aftermath of her barbecue, staring at that picture on Charlie's phone. My mind blanking out, unable to take in what I'm seeing.

There, in that photograph taken at Fishbourne palace, back before the Easter holidays. A month before Mr Rochester died.

Charlie laughing.

His tooth.

Broken.

My hands are trembling from the shock. From what this means.

So Mr Rochester didn't do it. He didn't break Charlie's tooth. Charlie lied. He lied, and now a teacher is dead. Tom's *father* is dead.

I lean back and close my eyes, trying to shut out what I've seen, but Charlie's smile is there, hovering, another after-image burned in my brain. *Charlie*, I ask in my head, *Charlie, why would you do that? Why would you lie?*

Suddenly a noise from the phone. A blast of music. I jump. Open my eyes to see Katy's name on the screen.

I hold my breath, gripped by indecision. Then swipe to accept the call.

"Hello?" Katy's voice.

Does she know? I wonder. Does my sister know Charlie lied about the fight with Mr Rochester? Is it possible she didn't notice his tooth was broken before that?

"Hello?" Katy repeats. "Anyone there?"

Her picture on the screen, under her name. Her blonde hair in a ponytail. Wearing red lipstick and a confident smile.

"*Hello?*"

"It's me," I say finally.

A noise on the other end of the phone, half a sigh, half a groan. "You've got Charlie's mobile then."

Katy sounds pissed off, like I've stolen it or something. Maybe she's worked out that I'm in her room, snooping.

"Yep."

A few seconds of silence, then I hear Katy turn and speak to Charlie. "S'okay. Laurie's found it."

Charlie's voice, saying something I don't catch.

He lied, I think, trying to get my head around it. Charlie lied about Mr Rochester breaking his tooth. Perhaps he lied about all of it.

I still can't believe it.

How could he do that?

How can he live with himself?

"Laurie?" Katy again.

"Yeah?"

"Just leave it there. We'll be over soon."

I don't reply. I'm thinking. Deciding.

"Katy," I say quickly, before I can change my mind. Before she rings off. "We need to talk."

"Jeez," she mutters under her breath. "Sure, Laurie, the place is a bit of a mess. Don't worry, we'll deal with it before Mum and Dad get back." She says this in a weary, sing-song tone that suggests I'm the biggest loser on the planet, and it's beyond her how she puts up with me.

"I know," I say simply, and wait for her response.

"Good. So we'll be there in half an—"

"No, Katy," I add slowly and deliberately. "I mean I *know* about Charlie's tooth."

If she's innocent, she'll have no idea what I'm referring to. For once in my life I'm praying for her impatience to up a notch, for some kind of arsey comeback.

But when my sister speaks, eventually, her voice is small and quiet. "Know what exactly?"

"That he lied."

I wait for Katy to ask what on earth I'm talking about. She doesn't.

A long silence while both of us digest what this means.

"Look, Laurie, I'm not sure what you imagine…" Katy is trying to sound exasperated but I know my sister. She's scared. I can hear it in her voice as she tries to think of some way to bullshit me.

"It's in the photo, Katy. On Charlie's phone. Taken on that trip to the Roman palace. You can clearly see his tooth was broken back then. *Before* he accused Mr Rochester."

This time she shuts up. She doesn't even have a go at me for nosing through Charlie's pictures.

"Laurie, please—" Katy stops. She whispers something to Charlie, her tone low and urgent.

I press the button to end the call.

Chapter 30

I don't leave Charlie's phone in Katy's room. Instead, I shove it in my bag and go straight out, guessing Charlie and my sister will be on their way over. I turn left at the bottom of our road, avoiding the route they'll take, walking fast in the opposite direction.

I've no idea where I'm going till I see a bus coming towards me. Number 77. The one that runs every weekend to Devil's Dyke, a local beauty spot up on the South Downs.

I run to catch it at the bus stop. Pay my fare and take a seat at the back, where I sit with my eyes closed, head resting against the glass, my mind buzzing.

Charlie lied. And my sister knew.

Charlie lied, and Tom's dad is *dead*.

And Katy said nothing.

Ten minutes later, the bus stops and everyone gets off. Most make a beeline for the pub and cafe, a few veering towards the ice-cream van in the car park. I head over the fields to the point where the Downs drop steeply into the vale, and sit on the grass, near where a group of hang-gliders are taking off and landing.

It's a glorious summer day, small clouds drifting across the bright blue sky, perfect cotton-wool puffs. The breeze in my hair. The sound of sheep bleating on the hillside, a dog barking in the distance.

In the village below, a cricket match is in full swing; nearby, several tractors plough a field, a crowd of seagulls trailing in their wake. Beyond, the vast expanse of the Sussex Weald stretches to the horizon. On a good day, you can see all the way to Surrey and Oxfordshire, Dad told us, the time he brought me and Katy up here to fly our kites.

Despite everything, I can't help smiling at the memory, remembering how my sister claimed my kite flew better than hers, stomping off in a temper when Dad refused to make me swap. Even then, I think. Even when we were young, Katy always wanted what was mine. Resented my presence in her life, as if my being here at all somehow detracted from hers.

I sigh. Lie back in the grass. Above me, half a dozen hang-gliders hover and swoop on the air currents bouncing off the Downs, their chutes in primary colours – red, blue, yellow and green. I watch them, envious. It looks so peaceful up there, drifting around, so weightless and free.

Is that what Charlie craves? I ask myself. Is flying his way of escaping the world, everything here on the ground?

A plummeting feeling as my mind returns to what I've discovered on his phone.

Why?

The question revolves round my head, spiralling and

looping like the hang-gliders above. Why did Charlie pretend Mr Rochester broke his tooth?

Was any part of his story true?

Did Mr Rochester do anything at all?

But *something* happened, I think, remembering that gash on Charlie's forehead. Fresh, seeping blood.

Above me, one of the hang-gliders dips and falters, making my heart thud with alarm until his chute catches another updraught, lifting him to safety.

My thoughts snap back to Charlie. There's only one explanation I can come up with. Only one reason why Charlie would lie: because he wanted to get Mr Rochester into trouble.

Serious trouble.

He pretended the teacher broke his tooth, knowing he'd be suspended. Knowing it would spell the end of his career. Though Charlie hadn't bargained on what happened next, I think, recalling the head's announcement in assembly. The moment Charlie charged out of the hall, his face pale with shock and dismay.

No, he never meant it to go that far – I'm sure of that much.

I close my eyes, inhaling the scent of damp earth and crushed grass. Why? I ask myself again. What could Charlie have against Mr Rochester? Why would he want to get him into trouble?

Charlie never had a problem with him, as far as I knew. Mr Rochester was the kind of teacher who got on with everyone. Not like Mr Tames or Ms Ryan, who clearly loathe teaching, oozing dislike and mistrust of any pupil unfortunate enough to land up in their class.

I sit up, retrieve Charlie's phone, and study the picture again. Then find my own number in his contacts and send the photo on to myself. In my bag my mobile beeps, letting me know it's arrived.

This way, even if Charlie deletes it, I have a copy.

Proof.

I gaze down at the screen, at the orange smiley sticker, so happy and cheerful. I can't resist. I bring up Charlie's messages and scroll through.

Some from Nicole. A number from friends at school. Several from Maya. Most, however, are from my sister. I force myself to open the first few and glance through. Each one a punch to the guts.

Can't wait to see you in your prom gear. You're gonna look fab! Katy texted a couple of days ago.

You too, from Charlie. Most of his replies are short. Charlie was never much into texting.

I carry on scrolling, going back in time, trying to skip anything too romantic. Even now, even with what I know about Charlie, I can't handle it.

Then I find what I'm looking for. Sent from Katy, later that day, the Monday we heard Mr Rochester had died. *You okay?*

Oh god…what have I done? Charlie had texted back. *This is all my fault.*

No reply from my sister. Presumably the rest of that conversation took place face-to-face.

Shit. It explains so much about how Charlie has been since. Silent and withdrawn. Not to mention drunk, I think, remembering how many times I've seen him pissed.

And it explains why Charlie felt compelled to go to Mr Rochester's funeral, despite all the very good reasons for staying away.

Guilt.

Charlie is consumed by guilt.

I'd thought at the time it was a bit misplaced. That he shouldn't blame himself for what happened. But now? Charlie has every reason to feel responsible.

I took in another breath, pushing down a swell of emotion. Charlie and me. Both of us feeling like murderers. Though neither of us ever meant it to be that way.

I should go to the police, I realize. Or tell Dad when he gets home, let him deal with it. But even as I know this would be the right thing to do, I also know I won't do it.

Not yet. I need more time to think. To decide.

Why? I ask myself. Do I still love Charlie? I can't…won't answer that. But we've grown up together, shared so much. I can't just dob him in without…

The phone in my hand vibrates, followed by a burst of ringtone. I put it straight through to voice message. A minute later my own mobile sounds from the depths of my bag. I ignore that too.

They can wait.

I get to my feet, make my way across Devil's Dyke, past the family picnicking on the grass, past the hikers and the sightseers taking in the views. Right round to the other side of the hill, where Brighton spreads like a ribbon below, buildings glinting in the sunlight; beyond them the pristine blue of the sea, clouds casting slate-grey shadows on the water.

From here everything looks impossibly tiny. Even the tower block of the Royal Sussex hospital to the east of the city; in the other direction, the tall chimney at Shoreham Power Station. Both look no bigger than Lego bricks.

Suddenly I'm desperate to talk to someone. And I realize who.

Tom.

I want to tell him what I know – and ask what I should do. Though of course I can't. How could I tell him his father's death may have been triggered by a lie?

It would destroy him. And he'd probably destroy Charlie in return. No, there's only one person I can talk to. The one person I least want to confront.

Charlie himself.

At that moment there's another vibration from my bag, the sound of the text alert on my phone. I relent and have a look. Katy.

Laurie, where are you? Please come back. I'm at home on my own. There's something important I have to tell you.

Chapter 31

Katy's standing at the sink when I get home, elbow deep in soapy water, cleaning the oven trays. I don't think I've ever seen her do that before. Helping out with the housework is never exactly high on my sister's list of priorities.

I glance round the kitchen. It looks immaculate, all the rubbish tidied away and the work surface gleaming. A black plastic sack by the back door, ready to go in the wheelie bin.

My sister doesn't say anything when I arrive, just gives me a hesitant smile as she dries her hands on a tea towel and slips off Mum's apron. Underneath she's wearing skinny jeans and a tight T-shirt. She's also lost weight, I notice, and wonder if all this business with Charlie has taken its toll on her too.

"You want a cup of hot chocolate?" she asks. "I've got some proper stuff Sophie left here last night. You know, made with real chocolate."

Coming from my sister, this offer is so bizarre I simply blink. In a flash I can see how this is going to be. Katy playing super nice, and there can only be one reason for that – she wants something from me.

"I'm fine," I say curtly. "So what did you need to tell me?" I sound harsh, but I don't want to be here. I want to get hold of Charlie. I want to hear the truth from him.

Katy glances at the clock on the kitchen wall. Gone midday. I know she's worrying about Mum and Dad arriving home.

"Let's go to my room," she suggests.

I follow her up, sit on the chair at her desk while Katy perches on the corner of her bed. She looks nervous, fiddling with a strand of her hair, the way she does when she's on edge.

"Do you have Charlie's phone?"

I nod, but make no move to take it from my bag.

My sister sighs, obviously fighting a surge of irritation. "I'll give it to him. Save you the bother."

I stare her out. "It's not going to make any difference, Katy. I've already got a copy of that picture."

She chews her lip, remaining silent. If her plan was to get Charlie's phone back and delete the evidence, it's backfired. But surely she wouldn't drag me here just for that? Katy isn't stupid. It must have occurred to her that I'd take precautions.

To what end? I ask myself. What exactly *am* I going to do with that photo?

I've no clue, I realize. But I'll have a better idea when I've spoken to Charlie.

"Listen, Laurie, I can see this looks bad, but you don't

230

know the half of it," Katy speaks up. "This really isn't Charlie's fault."

"So tell me," I say. "Tell me what really happened."

Katy sighs again, dropping her hands to her lap. "It was his mum, Nicole. He did it because of her. It's not his fault, Laurie. You can't go and say anything."

This all spills out fast and urgent, in a pleading tone I haven't heard in ages. Not since the last time she wanted something from me: to borrow some money perhaps, or persuade me to do her chores.

"You don't know him like I do," she adds, forgetting I've known him all my life. A lot longer than she has.

And yet, says a little voice in my head, maybe she's right. Maybe I don't know Charlie, not really. Maybe my sister has seen sides of him I can only guess at.

"He lied," I say. "Charlie lied about Mr Rochester and now he's dead."

Katy swallows. "It's not like you think."

"So tell me what it *is* like," I snap back, and even as I say it there's a pain in my heart. How did it ever come to this? Katy knowing secrets of Charlie's that I have no inkling about.

"The thing is he…" She stops. Regroups. "It wasn't as if *nothing* happened with Mr Rochester. It's more that Charlie…he exaggerated it a bit. Played it up."

"How do you mean, *exaggerated*? And why would he even do that?" And what did Katy mean about Nicole? How was she involved in all this?

"He found out that his mum—"

A blast on the doorbell. We both freeze for a second, then I go downstairs to open the door, assuming it's a delivery or something. But find Maya standing on my doorstep.

I get a weird mix of emotions. Part of me pleased to see my friend; part of me wishing she'd disappear so I can hear what Katy was about to tell me.

Maya doesn't notice my agitation. "Hey, you're in!" She grins. "I called you loads of times. How come you're not answering your phone?"

Hell, that must have been her ringing when I was up on the Downs. I'd assumed it was Katy. Never thought to check.

"You not going to let me in?" Maya frowns. "This isn't a bad time or anything, is it?"

I shake my head and hold the door open, unable to think of a decent excuse. As I follow her into the hallway, I see Katy coming down the stairs, looking pale and anxious. She scowls at Maya, then disappears into the kitchen.

"Wow." Maya leans in to whisper. "What's with her? Lost her broomstick or something?"

Normally I'd laugh. Right now I actually have some sympathy with my sister.

I head up to my room, Maya on my heels, hoping I can turn this into a short visit. I'm anxious to finish talking to Katy before Mum and Dad get home.

Maya nabs the window seat, turning to me with an

excited expression. "You'll never guess!" She's beaming with delight, brimming with whatever's brought her rushing round.

"What?" I try to sound interested rather than impatient.

She makes a little squee sound and claps her hands. "Douglas Lloyd has asked me to the prom!"

I swallow, feeling wounded. What about me? I thought Maya was desperate for us to go together, especially now Charlie's out the picture. Our pact in pieces.

But why shouldn't she go with Douglas? I remind myself. Why shouldn't she like someone? That whole pact we made, it was stupid. Not taking into account the future. How it would change everything. How *we'd* all change.

"That's brilliant, Maya," I say, hoping I sound like I mean it.

"But you'll still come, right? It's not like I'll be glued to his side or anything. We'll just have a few dances."

I nod, lacking the energy to argue. Or even to think about the prom, now only four days away.

Maya glances round my room. Gets up and checks in my wardrobe. "You still haven't got your dress, have you?"

"Mum's taking me shopping tomorrow afternoon," I lie. "After my last exam."

Maya presses her lips together. Her doubtful look. Then blinks it away. "So Douglas says his dad is going to hire a limo, and there's plenty of room for all of us…" I tune out for a minute, wondering what Katy is doing. Praying Mum and Dad are taking the scenic route home. "…and I know

233

we can't have actual champagne, right, but you can get this fizzy pear stuff and it tastes really similar…"

"Sounds great," I say, trying my best to seem enthusiastic. Hoping Maya will leave it at that.

Her face falls. "You're angry with me, aren't you? For saying yes to Douglas."

I inhale, try to focus on my friend. "Of course not. Really. Douglas is nice. I'm sorry, it's just I've got a lot on my mind."

Maya fixes her brown eyes on mine. "Is it Charlie?"

My heart skips a beat. Why is she asking me that?

"I mean, all those rumours about him. How Mr Rochester did it because of Charlie reporting him. Has your sister said anything?" Maya asks this in a hushed tone, obviously worried she might be overheard. Her eyes drift to my bedroom door, as if imagining Katy standing outside, listening to every word.

Perhaps she is. I wouldn't put anything past my sister.

"No," I lie again. "It's just exams…results, I mean."

"But you've got nothing to worry about," Maya says breezily. "You'll get straight A stars, right across the board."

I wouldn't bet on it, I think, remembering the English paper last Tuesday. My struggle to focus on the questions, formulate an intelligent answer.

I look up to see my friend studying me with a disheartened expression. Like she's given up on me. "I'm not an idiot, you know, Lee. Just because you won't talk to me, it doesn't mean I can't work things out for myself."

I stare at her. Open my mouth to speak.

Maya holds up her hand. "Don't bother. Don't make something up, or make any more excuses. If you don't want to…can't confide in me, it's okay. I can live with that. Just stop pretending that you're all right when you're clearly not."

I gaze back at her, eyes glazing again. More than anything I want to confess everything I've just learned about Charlie. About my sister's part in all this. Ask her what on earth I should do.

But how can I? How can I dump this dilemma on Maya? Tell her that Charlie – our oldest friend – is someone we hardly know any more.

Besides, I suspect she'd push me to report him and Katy, would argue it was the right thing to do. And I'm not sure I can bring myself to do it.

It's my problem, I realize. Another thing I have to face on my own. Like the pregnancy. My dilemma. My decision.

"Anyway, I've found somewhere that has fantastic jewellery," Maya says, changing the subject. "In the Lanes. It's open Sundays, and guess what? They do clip-on earrings."

"Cool," I say, making myself look pleased. Though Maya had her ears pierced when she was small, I've never fancied the idea.

"We could go there this afternoon," she suggests. "Check out something for the prom."

"I can't." I seize on an excuse. "Mum and Dad will be

home in a minute, and I promised Walt I'd take him to the park." As fibs go, it's hardly convincing, but no way can I go into town with Maya. I have to talk to Katy. And then I need to find Charlie.

Most of all, I have to work out what the hell I'm going to do.

"I could go tomorrow," I add, trying to sound keen.

Maya frowns again. "But you just said you're going dress shopping with your mum."

"We can meet up afterwards," I improvise, hating all the lies I seem to be telling these days. "That way I'll have my dress and you can help me pick something to go with it."

Maya's shoulders slump. "Okay," she says. "It's a date." She gets up, grabbing her bag. "I'll leave you to it then. Text me about tomorrow."

I follow her downstairs. By the door, she stops. Then turns and pulls me into a hug. "The prom is going to be fun," she says. "We're going to have the best time, I promise. And next year, it'll be a fresh start. We can put everything behind us."

My friend gives me a meaningful look, and for a moment I wonder. How much does Maya know? Could she possibly have guessed the truth?

But which truth? What happened between me and Charlie?

How I feel about him?

The pregnancy?

I'll talk to her, I resolve, as I go off to find Katy. Once

the prom is over, I'll talk to Maya and try to smooth things over between us. But right now, I have to pin down my sister, get her to tell me what's really going on.

There's no sign of her in the kitchen, however, or in her room. The bathroom is empty, and even the garden is vacant. And tidy, I notice. Everything back in its usual place.

But my sister has vanished.

Chapter 32

This time Charlie answers the door. He gazes at me for a moment, then steps back to let me in. Like he's been expecting me all along.

Which I suppose he has.

"Katy here?" I ask, praying she isn't.

"You just missed her." Charlie walks into the living room, leaving me to follow. "She went into town with Jo and Sammy. To see about getting her hair done for next week."

I'm open-mouthed with surprise. How can my sister even think about the prom at a time like this? Then it occurs to me this might be an excuse – perhaps she's gone to offload, or ask their advice.

But would Katy risk telling anyone else? I wouldn't rate the chances her friends could keep their mouths shut.

"What about your mum?" I ask Charlie.

"She'll be back soon. Do you want to go out?"

"Okay."

He picks up a bottle of beer from the coffee table and drains it. I glance at the clock on the wall – nearly two.

Is that his first today, or have there been more? How does he get hold of all this booze anyway?

Grabbing his hoody, Charlie trails after me. Automatically we head to the seafront, walking in silence, both lost in our thoughts. When we reach the paddling pool on the main parade, Charlie nods at the nearby kiosk.

"Want anything?"

I shake my head.

"Me neither." He sinks onto an empty bench and stares at the ground between his feet. I'm not sure I've ever seen him so forlorn. Or so wrecked. He has dark circles round his eyes, and looks like he's lost even more weight.

Like he's falling apart, I think, as I sit at the other end of the bench, observing the crowds. Most of Brighton and Hove seem to have piled down to the seafront for a Sunday afternoon in the sun. A mob of kids are playing in the paddling pool, laughing and squealing and kicking water at each other. Impossible not to remember the fun we used to have here, the three of us. Back before everything turned bad.

I glance at Charlie, but he has his eyes fixed on the horizon now, seemingly unaware of all the activity around us. Or that I'm sitting here next to him. It doesn't bother me much. It's easier like this. Not looking at each other.

"Katy said you found my phone," he mumbles eventually.

I take it out of my bag and hand it over. Charlie examines it briefly, then stuffs it in the pocket of his jeans. "Thanks."

"I saw that photo," I say, wondering whether to mention

I have a copy. Decide not to bother – Katy's probably already told him.

Charlie doesn't move. Doesn't respond.

"It was taken on that trip to Fishbourne, wasn't it? A month before you said Mr Rochester assaulted you."

Still no reply.

"Your tooth was chipped back then, Charlie."

His hands grip the edge of the bench, the skin tightening over his knuckles. "I never meant it to turn out like that, Lee," he says, under his breath. "You have to believe me."

I wait for him to continue, but Charlie lapses back into silence. A group of adults, some in their fifties at least, glide past on rollerblades, chatting as they go. In the sandpit next to the paddling pool, two boys are having an argument – one hits the other with a plastic spade before the parents rush in to intervene.

"Are you going to tell me what happened?" I ask after several minutes.

Charlie closes his eyes. Leans forward, head hanging. Lets out an audible groan. I can tell he's been waiting for this. Rehearsing what he's about to say, trying to figure out the best way to explain. Even after everything that's happened, how much has changed, in some ways I can still read him like a book.

"Nicole." He clears his throat. "My mum," he adds, as if I might somehow need reminding. "I got back from school one night…the night before it kicked off with Mr Rochester. Found her crying in the kitchen."

He pauses, gazes out to the horizon, then back at me. "She was really upset, Lee. And I mean *really* upset. She was off her head too, had drunk most of a bottle of wine."

"What was she upset about?"

"She wouldn't tell me at first, but in the end I got it out of her." Charlie sniffs. Wipes his nose with the back of his hand. "I mean, it was horrible, seeing her in that state – I couldn't just let it go."

I picture Nicole Forrest drunk and crying. It isn't hard to imagine. It was always there, that sense of someone on the edge. "So what did she say?"

Charlie inhales. "She told me she'd been having an affair."

"An affair?" I frown. "What do you mean?" Nicole Forrest is single, as far as I know – at least, Charlie has never mentioned there being anyone.

"With a married man. It had been going on for over a year, and he…this man had just broken up with her."

"Why?" My frown deepens, as I ask myself where this is leading.

Charlie's face seems to spasm. I can't tell what emotion is behind it, but it's clearly strong. "His wife found out, about the affair, I mean. She gave him an ultimatum – her or Nicole."

"And he chose her? His wife?"

"Yeah," Charlie nods. "Dumped my mum by phone."

I digest this for a moment or two. "Do you know who he was?"

Charlie doesn't answer. Just looks at me. Waiting for me to catch up, I realize. To catch on.

"Mr Rochester." I say it more for confirmation than as a question.

"Yep." Charlie drops his head again, rubs his forehead with the heel of his hand. "Everyone's favourite biology teacher was screwing my mother."

He closes his eyes, then laughs as he opens them again. A hard, bitter sound. "They met at the parents' evening in Year Ten. Nicole said he was flirting with her, though I didn't notice. You know how you never see stuff like that when it's your own parent?"

I nod.

"I guess she was right, though," Charlie continued, "cos when they bumped into each other a few weeks later Mr Rochester invited her out for a drink. It went on from there."

"And your mum told you all this?" I try to picture Mr Rochester with Nicole. It seems impossible – but then it's always impossible to imagine teachers outside school. Having an actual life.

"Like I said, I got it out of her eventually." Charlie turns to face me again. "She's not as bad as you think, Lee. I know you don't like her much, but she tries…to be a decent parent, I mean. It's been hard for her, not having anyone else around. Her being so young when she had me."

I remember Nicole saying that to me last year, and the truth of this stings. Has it always been so obvious, how much I dislike his mother? Again I wonder if Charlie knows what happened between me and her. Could she have told him?

She promised she never would.

Swore she would keep my secret.

I push the thought away. "So you did what? Decided to have it out with him?"

Charlie kicks at the ground, speckled white with the traces of old chewing gum. "Basically yeah," he says quietly. "I didn't intend to…I didn't plan it or anything, Lee. I didn't mean for it all to go so badly wrong."

"Okay," I say, though of course it wasn't.

"But when I went into school the next day…I dunno…I remembered the state my mum was in, and I just wanted to tell him." He glanced at me again. "I needed…I don't know. Looking back, I'm not sure what was in my head. I was angry, Lee…upset that he'd screwed with my mother like that. It didn't feel right he should get off the hook so easily. Walk away as if nothing had ever happened."

His gaze flicks over my face, but he doesn't see what's building inside me. Doesn't notice the anger in my eyes.

"I mean, he left me with the mess, didn't he? My mum in pieces. He told her he loved her, she said, promised to leave his wife. And then suddenly…" Charlie flattens his hand, makes a cutting gesture, then balls it back into a fist, tight with emotion. "You can't just dump someone, you know. You can't lead them on like that, then toss them away when you've had enough."

"*Oh yeah?*" The words erupt from my mouth before I can stop them. I almost laugh, though it's not remotely funny. I'm just so astounded. How could Charlie, *of all people*, actually say that to my face?

He sees my expression and finally catches my meaning. His cheeks flush and he turns away. I blink back tears of indignation. *Not now*, I tell myself. You didn't come here to deal with this now.

"So you what...?" I ask after a long pause where I pull myself together. "You confronted him?"

Charlie clears his throat again but still won't look at me. "I waited till after school. He...Mr Rochester always went to the lab after last bell – you know, clearing up, getting things sorted for the next day. I walked in and shut the door behind me and came straight out with it. Told him I knew."

"And he, what...hit you?"

"Yes...no...not exactly." Charlie groans again, closing his eyes as he remembers. "He didn't mean to. He was trying to explain, to calm me down and...I dunno, I just flipped... There was a scuffle. Mr Rochester tried to push me away and I lost my balance, caught my head on the side of the bench."

"So that was an accident?" I point to the mark on his forehead, fading now to a thin red line.

Charlie nods, his hand going up automatically to feel the scar. "He was devastated when he saw what had happened. Offered to drive me to A&E. But I walked out.

Came straight over to yours."

"To speak to Katy?"

Charlie nods again, still avoiding my gaze. "I had to talk to someone, Lee. I didn't know what to do. But your mum made me call Nicole and she went ballistic. Insisted we report it. And I let myself believe it would be right to…you know…" He pauses, reluctant to say it.

"To accuse an innocent teacher of assault."

Charlie swings round. "He wasn't innocent, though, was he, Lee? He got involved with my mum and then dumped her. He led her on."

Anger rises up in me again. "But that's not illegal, is it? That's not a crime, like falsely accusing someone. Getting them sacked."

The words tumble from my mouth, out of my control. "And it's not as if *you'd* ever do anything like that, is it, Charlie?" The sarcasm in my tone unmistakable.

"That was different," he mumbles. "That wasn't the same thing at all."

I nearly get up and walk away, have to grasp the edge of the bench to stop myself doing it. Or worse. I feel like smashing my fists into Charlie's face. Nearly overwhelmed by the urge to hurt him.

And suddenly I understand. Why Charlie did what he did. I understand how easy it would be to give in to that impulse. To hit out, if not with your fists, with words. With accusations.

Charlie swings round, grabs my hand. Tears glinting in

his eyes. "Lee, you have to believe me. Please. I had no idea what would happen next. No clue. I thought Mr Rochester would just get a warning or something. Maybe suspended for a bit."

"*How could you think that?*" I pull my hand away and jump up, my voice louder, not caring that all around us a dozen gazes swing in our direction. "Assaulting a pupil is major shit, Charlie. He'd have lost his job at the very least. He could have been prosecuted."

"Lee, *please…*" Charlie hisses, noticing all the curious onlookers. "Please just sit down and hear me out."

I sit back on the bench.

"It was Nicole…" he continues, voice lowered. "I wanted to let it go. I told her it was an accident, but she insisted he was the responsible adult, that he should have to account for himself, and face the consequences. Said she'd report it herself, if she had to."

"But the thing about the tooth, Charlie…it was an out-and-out lie."

He shuts his eyes briefly. Groans. "I don't even know why I went along with it. I've gone over and over it in my mind. I just got sucked into it all." He rubs his face with his hand. Blinks.

"It's hard to explain…how it got so serious, so quickly. The school asked if I had any other injuries and Nicole jumped in and made me show them my tooth. And I went along with it…couldn't face having it out with her in front of the head and everyone. And then they insisted on getting

the police involved and they questioned Mr Rochester…
it all just escalated, Lee."

I close my eyes. Around me all the noises of the seafront
– the cries of gulls, the rumble of traffic on the road
behind, the sound of children squealing and laughing. In
the distance, a drift of music from a bar. I push it all away.
Try to imagine what it must have been like. Try to give
Charlie the benefit of the doubt.

"So she did it to punish him," I say, eventually. "Your
mum got you to make up—"

"Not make up," Charlie protests. "I wasn't lying, not
really. I just didn't tell the whole truth."

Maybe that was why I hadn't picked up the signs that
night at the Indian, I think. It was Katy, wasn't it, who
brought it up, said that stuff about his tooth? I remember
Charlie looking uncomfortable, but I'd assumed that was
because he didn't want her talking about it.

"I never meant it to go so far, Lee," Charlie repeats, in a
pleading tone. "But once Nicole started it, I couldn't do
anything, could I? Not without getting her into trouble."

He blinks a few times. Close to tears. "You don't
understand." His voice subdued. "She's all I've got. All the
family I have."

"That's not true. What about your grandfather?"

Charlie snorts. "I hardly know him. Anyway, he's not
very nice. He turned his back on my mum when she got
pregnant. Wouldn't speak to her for years."

I frown. That seems a bit old-fashioned. Do people even

care about that stuff any more? Then I remember how scared I'd been to tell my parents. How I'd dreaded their reaction, the impact it might have on them.

Charlie reads my expression and his face clouds. "Apparently he didn't like the fact my father was half Jamaican."

Blimey, I think, taken aback. I get a pang of sympathy for Charlie, thinking how that must make him feel.

"So how did you really break your tooth?" I ask after another few minutes have passed, Charlie having lapsed into silence again, his expression miserable, his posture defeated. As if confessing all this had cost him everything.

His mouth twists. "I fell over at a party. Smashed into a wall. Like I said, it was a weak tooth."

I bite my lip, trying to sort things out in my head. "So Katy knew all along the tooth thing was a lie?"

"Yeah." Charlie's cheeks flush, like even admitting this is some kind of betrayal. "She was there when I broke it."

"She said the fight with Mr Rochester was over your work. So she knew that wasn't true? She knew then what it was really about?"

Charlie sighs. "It's the story we agreed, to cover up all the stuff about Nicole and the affair. But then…after he… you know…" He looks up at the sky. Blinks. "We never thought that was going to happen, Lee. And afterwards, we were both too scared to tell the truth…"

I think of my sister, asking myself why she played along with it all. Why Katy didn't try and persuade Charlie to come clean before more damage was done. She'd just kept quiet. Hoping, I guess, that it would all blow over.

They suit each other, I realize. I've spent so long wondering why Charlie went off with Katy – apart from the obvious physical stuff – and here it is. They suit each other. Katy doesn't challenge him, or give him a hard time. Katy lets Charlie live the life he wants – an easy one.

Because I can see more clearly now. Charlie is weak – it was easier to go along with his mother than stand up to her. Easier to let people believe a terrible lie than tell the truth.

We sit there, each locked in our own little world, oblivious to everything around us. In the end it's Charlie who speaks first.

"What are you going to do, Lee?"

The exact same question I'm asking myself.

What am I going to do?

"I think you should put things right," I say after a pause.

Charlie swings round, dismay on his face. "How, Lee? How can I go back now and say I lied? You can't imagine how often I've thought about it. I've nearly done it, several times, but it wouldn't just be me in the shit, would it? It would be Nicole too. I can't do that to her – she's cut up enough about all this as it is."

I raise my eyebrows.

"I'm not kidding, Lee. She was in pieces when Mr Rochester killed himself. Even worse than when he dumped her. It was all I could do to stop her going to the funeral.

That's half the reason I went, in case she turned up, caused trouble."

I nearly laugh. The irony seems lost on Charlie. That he was the one who made the scene. Who caused the trouble.

"But he died, Charlie," I remind him. "Someone died."

Charlie looks stricken. Almost as if he's hearing the news for the first time. I imagine what it would be like, waking every day to the knowledge of what you've done. Having to keep it secret, locking it inside while trying on the outside to look like someone who's not being eaten hollow by guilt.

But of course I already know how that feels.

For a second or two I wonder if I should tell him what Tom mentioned after the funeral, about things having been rough at home for some time. About Mr Rochester being on antidepressants. But I'm not sure Charlie deserves to hear it. Not sure he should be let off the hook that easily.

I glance over. He's shaking his head, to and fro. Then I see he's crying.

"I killed him, Lee. I killed him. You think I don't know that?" He swipes at the tears running down his face, smearing them across his cheek. "Every single day, that's all I think about. How I told a stupid lie and now he's dead."

It's then I remember that night on the beach, when Charlie swam out to the pier and I thought he'd drowned. And everything that followed. I can see now. That's all it takes.

One mistake.
One moment where you make the wrong decision.
And lives are lost, or wrecked for ever.

Chapter 33

I don't go home after leaving Charlie on the seafront. I walk to the allotments in Weald Avenue, looking for Dad. Guessing he'd head straight up there as soon as they got back from Hampshire. With any luck, I might catch him alone.

Weald Avenue is a big site: three hundred plots, bare in winter, all brown soil and withered stalks, but now a riot of green. Most just the usual veg patch; others more like cottage gardens, criss-crossed with little paths, full of flowers, wind chimes and statues.

What they all have in common, however, is some sort of hut. And not just your bog-standard wooden shed. You'll find every colour and shape here. Some new. Some so rickety they look as if they'd blow down in the next breeze.

I make my way towards Dad's patch, over in the far corner. It's nothing special, a series of raised beds laid out with different fruit and vegetables. Straight paved paths. A small shed, stained dark blue, where he keeps a little gas stove to boil water for his tea.

But I like it here. The ordered rows of crops. The neat

square of lawn where Dad puts his deckchair in summer. Walt's flower garden and, at the end, a small pond teeming in spring with newts and tadpoles.

Just being here makes you feel calmer somehow. Whatever mood you're in when you arrive, you always leave in a better one.

And mine lifts when I see Dad standing by a row of leeks, staring at the ground as if willing them to grow. I study him for a minute as he peers closer, reaching out to pluck something from one of the leaves.

It makes my heart feel weirdly full, watching him. Remembering that period where he did nothing much. Just sat around the house. Absent, somehow, though he was always physically there.

The allotment almost went to ruins back then. Weeds invaded all the beds. The shed roof leaked after a storm, rusting the tools.

So the day Dad put on his jacket and headed back here, we knew he'd turned a corner. He always said the allotment was his version of the local pub – only cheaper and healthier. He loved the sense of community, chatting to the other gardeners. It's the reason he hung on to the plot, after Walt was born and we moved to a bigger house and garden, with plenty of room for vegetables.

Maybe it was this place that saved him, I think, remembering Tom, feeling a mix of sadness and relief. My dad made it through.

"Hey!" Dad spots me, enveloping me in a hug when

I go over. No sign of Walt. Thankfully.

"Good weekend?" he asks, after a brief rundown of their trip home. The Sunday traffic. Walt sulking when his Nintendo ran out of battery.

"It was okay," I say, trying to look like I've been doing nothing much. At the same time figuring out how to steer the conversation towards what I need to know.

Dad looks me over. "Nice of you to drop in. We were wondering where you'd got to."

"Down the beach. Taking a break from revision." I keep my voice bright and offhand, examining the leeks. Notice some of the leaves have neat little arcs cut into them.

"Beetles," says Dad, following my gaze. "I've been trying to spot the buggers, but I swear they hide when they hear you coming."

This makes me laugh, but Dad has already picked up on my mood. "What's up, love? You all right?"

"Fine," I say, though it's very far from true. I feel badly shaken by my confrontation with Charlie. And no more certain what to do. "Is it a crime to lie about something that's happened? You know, if you say someone did something, and they didn't."

Dad's eyes linger on mine. "Well, I suppose it would depend."

"On what?"

"On what the consequences were, Laurie. For instance, if you lied in court and caused another person to go to jail for something they didn't do, that would be perjury.

Equally if you lied in court to try and get someone off the hook."

"What if it never got as far as court?"

"Well, then they could be prosecuted for perverting the course of justice. Again, it depends what happened, love." Dad gives me a serious look. "Can you tell me?"

"It's nothing," I say quickly. Maybe too quickly. "It came up when we were doing citizenship at school, a topic on justice. I thought it was interesting."

"It is. I often wonder if I should have become a lawyer, rather than go into the police."

I gaze at Dad, a little surprised. It never occurred to me that he has regrets. That he might feel he'd taken a wrong turn in life.

"I thought I might do law next year, for one of my A levels," I pretend. "So can you still be prosecuted if you're under eighteen?" I keep my tone light, casual.

"Yes, you can."

"And what would happen if…you know, if you were found guilty?"

Dad presses his lips together, thinking. "Well, in theory you might be sentenced to spend time in a juvenile detention centre. But again, it would depend on what you'd done. If it wasn't too serious, and it was a first and only offence, then you'd probably end up with community service."

"Could a good lawyer not get you off?"

Dad's eyebrows narrow. "Do you need to know this

stuff? For school, I mean? I thought physics was your last exam."

"Not really. I'm only interested because we were studying a newspaper article," I invent, praying Dad will believe me. "About a sixteen-year-old girl who lied about a...sexual assault at school." I hope this is enough to put Dad off the scent.

"And what happened?"

"The teacher lost his job...and got very depressed and ended up in hospital." It's as close to the truth as I dare go.

Dad runs his tongue over his teeth, leaning on his spade. "Impossible to say for sure, Laurie, but that girl would be in a lot of trouble if it was proven her allegation was untrue."

"Would it stay on her record? I mean, after she'd been prosecuted. Would it affect her chances of getting a job? Pursuing a career?"

"It could. Generally you don't have to tell employers about previous criminal convictions, but in some cases they can check."

Would that include airline pilots? I wonder. I'm guessing it would, but I daren't ask. It would give Charlie away for sure.

"Okay. Thanks," I say. "You've been a great help."

Dad seems less than convinced. He gives me a long look. "You certain there's nothing you want to tell me, Laurie?"

My breath stalls. Oh god, has he guessed?

"Of course not." I force myself to laugh. "Stop being so paranoid."

Dad grins. "Sorry. Old habits die hard." But there's something in his eyes, something watchful. Almost suspicious. Still, what can he do? Suspicions are nothing without evidence.

And only I have that.

The question is, what on earth am I going to do with it?

Chapter 34

It takes ages to get to sleep that night. It's all going round and round my head, like a mantra.

What am I going to do?

I doze into the morning, woken now and then by the sounds of the house. Mum getting up, clattering around the kitchen. Dad taking Walt to school – still another three weeks till he finishes for the summer.

Katy's voice, saying something in the hallway. "…back this afternoon…" is all I catch.

I feel a rush of relief. I know I'll have to confront my sister sooner or later, but right now, later will do just fine.

I fall back asleep, waking again to the sound of the front door closing, the rev of an engine reversing over the drive. I get up and look out of my window. See Mum's car pulling away.

Monday isn't one of her morning surgeries, is it? I frown, trying to think through the fog of tiredness. Maybe she's popped in to catch up with some paperwork. Or gone to the shops – though we usually have our groceries delivered.

Pulling on my dressing gown, I go downstairs. See from the kitchen clock that it's gone eleven.

I really have overslept.

I make myself a cup of milky coffee and take it back up to my room, propping myself up in bed with my physics file. The exam isn't till two, and thankfully I'm not expected in school first – the revision classes finished last week.

What am I going to do?

The question forces its way to the front of my mind, displacing all thought of kinetics.

A rock and a hard place, I realize. And me stuck in between.

If I tell the school, the police, that Charlie lied, that Mr Rochester had been innocent, Charlie might be prosecuted. Possibly even go to prison. And every chance his career as a pilot will be ruined.

But if I stay silent? Delete that photograph from my phone? Another secret, festering inside me. Everyone believing Mr Rochester killed himself out of guilt for assaulting a pupil. Tom and his family having to deal with the stigma for the rest of their lives.

And Charlie, what would it cost him, to keep it quiet? Can he live with what he did so easily?

No, I think, remembering all the times I've seen him drunk recently. That haunted, hunted look he has now. He may not have the guts to own up, but his secret is leaking out in other ways.

Outside I hear a car pull up in our drive. The slam of the

door as someone gets out. Mum, I guess; Dad's at college today. I wait for the sound of her key in the door, but suddenly there's a ring on the bell.

I hold my breath. Maybe it's Charlie, I think wildly, though I know that's stupid. He'd call me first. Must be the postman, needing a signature. Or one of those religious people who come round, trying to convert you.

Pulling on jeans and a T-shirt, I go downstairs and open the front door. Sure enough, it's not Charlie.

It's his mother.

Nicole is standing in our porch, fiddling with her car keys. She looks like she dressed in a hurry, a green cotton cardigan shoved over a dark red dress. Flip-flops on her feet. No make-up either, her eyes disconcertingly bare without their usual smudge of eyeliner.

She gazes at me for a moment, then pushes past with barely a nod. I stare after her, astonished by her rudeness.

"Laurie…" She pauses in the hallway. Clearly making an effort to keep her voice measured. "Are you on your own?"

Then it hits me. Charlie has told her.

He's told her that I know.

"Mum's just gone out," I stammer. "I don't know when she'll be back."

"Well then, I won't beat around the bush," Nicole says, reading my expression. "You know why I'm here."

"Give me a minute." I shoot upstairs before she can object. Shut myself in the bathroom and run the tap. I take a few deep gulps of water, trying to pull myself together.

I'm shaking, I realize, as memories come flooding back. Just the sight of Nicole. I haven't seen her since…

"Laurie?" Her voice calling up. "You okay?"

Oh god, what am I going to do? Stay here till Nicole gets fed up and leaves? Or Mum comes home? But I know Charlie's mother. She won't give up. If she doesn't have this out with me now, she'll wait till later.

I splash some water on my face. Glance in the mirror.

I look pale. Frightened. Like I did back then. Back when my life veered right off course.

"Laurie? Are you coming down?"

Turning from my reflection, I grab a towel and wipe my face.

Nothing for it but to face the music.

Nicole's sitting on the sofa in the living room. If you could call it sitting. More like hovering, as if ready to fly at me any moment. I stand by the fireplace. Give myself the advantage of height.

"Charlie said…" Nicole pauses. Rethinks whatever she was about to say. "I think he might have…might have given you the wrong impression."

My jaw tightens. "You mean about what happened with Mr Rochester?"

Nicole nods, glancing out the window, as if checking we won't be interrupted.

"Listen." She turns back to me. "I know he shouldn't have

lied about Paul breaking his tooth, but..." She stops again.

"But what?"

Nicole bites her bottom lip. I see her pressing her thumb against the jagged edge of her car key.

"It was my fault, all right? *My fault*. If I hadn't told Charlie about Paul...he wouldn't...wouldn't have confronted him like that. And I was the one who insisted on reporting it to the school and the police."

"Why?" I ask, keeping my voice steady. "Why would you do that when you knew Mr Rochester hadn't done anything wrong?"

"But he *had*," she snaps, her small features hardening. "Believe me, Laurie, he'd done plenty. He rang me and just—"

"I don't mean that," I cut in. "That was wrong, I agree, but it was between you and him. But he didn't do anything to Charlie, did he?"

Nicole stays silent.

"*Did he?*" I repeat, more insistently.

"Not exactly...Charlie said it was an accident, that he fell. But it should never have happened, should it? Paul should have—" She stops. Rubs her forehead. "Laurie, please, *listen* to me. I know what we did wasn't strictly—"

"Wasn't strictly what?" My voice rising as a wave of emotion rocks me on my feet. "Wasn't strictly true? Wasn't strictly right? *Wasn't strictly legal?*"

Nicole swallows. "It looks bad, yes, but you weren't there, Laurie. You don't know the full story."

"I know why you did it." I put a hand on the mantelpiece to steady myself. "You did it to punish Mr Rochester. You dragged Charlie into your mess."

I take a step forward, my fist clenched. I'm suddenly furious. Anger coursing through me, erupting. Molten.

Nicole's eyes widen. This clearly wasn't the reaction she'd been expecting. Not like before. Me broken, terrified.

I think of Tom, of his devastation after the funeral. He's lost his father. His *father*. And because of what? Because this woman couldn't handle being rejected.

How does she think *I feel*? I want to scream at her. What if I'd punished Charlie the way she did Paul Rochester?

"Laurie, please, calm down," Nicole says, her voice almost a whine. "All I'm asking is that you don't say anything, okay? That you just keep it to yourself." She gives me a pleading look. "*For Charlie's sake.*"

I stare back at her, struggling to take in her words. My head full of memories. All the horror of last year.

Everything I went through.

Everything I did.

Exactly what Nicole wanted, though I thought I wanted it too. Thought it was the best thing.

The lesser evil.

"Charlie's suffered enough, Laurie," I hear her saying. "Consider how bad it's been for him, all of this. What Paul…" Her hands fidget with her car keys. "…I never imagined he'd kill himself. Never. If I'd known for an instant what state of mind he—"

"So you lied," I yell. "And it backfired. Backfired big time. And now Charlie's life is screwed and you want me to keep my mouth shut—"

Nicole jumps to her feet. Takes a step towards me, her keys still in her hand.

"And meanwhile Tom and his mother are going through hell," I continue, unable to stop. The words bursting out of me.

Nicole narrows her eyes, unintimidated by my fury. "I know what this is about," she hisses, finger jabbing towards my face. "This isn't about Charlie, or Paul or Tom or anyone. This is about *you*, isn't it? About what I said to you last year. *This is about what YOU did.*"

I stare at her, open-mouthed.

Inside my head that video starts playing again, the one I forced myself to watch on YouTube. A chasm opens, so wide I'm teetering on the edge. About to fall.

Blood splatters, red on white.

Glistening.

"This is your stuff, Laurie, that much is clear. You're angry with both of us. Me and my son."

I open my mouth. Nothing comes out. My head is reeling. I clutch the mantelpiece for support.

Nicole's eyes are slits, her brow creasing into a deep frown. "You're punishing us – me and Charlie – for what *you* did."

The world spins. I feel like I might black out. "You said it was for the best," I whisper. "You said it would ruin my life, and Charlie's."

Nicole snorts. An ugly sound. "Don't try and pass the buck onto me, Laurie. I never told you to get rid of it. You made that decision all by yourself."

I try to swallow, but it's as if my throat has closed up. My breathing feels like something I have to focus on. Make happen.

"And you're jealous," she continues. "Jealous that Charlie chose Katy instead of you. You can't stand that, can you? That he prefers your sister."

I'm so winded I can't speak. My mouth opens and closes but still nothing comes out. How can she think that? How could she possibly think I'd report Charlie *out of jealousy*?

"I'll tell him." Nicole takes another step towards me, bringing her face right up to mine, her voice clear and steady. "You breathe one single word to anyone about this, Laurie, and I'll tell him and everyone else what you did."

"Tell us what?" says a voice behind us.

We both spin round, mouths gaping in surprise. Mum is standing in the doorway, clutching a Co-op carrier bag, staring at the pair of us.

"Tell us what?" Mum looks at Nicole and then back at me.

I close my eyes briefly.

This cannot be happening.

This cannot be happening.

Nicole sticks out her chin. "I suggest you ask Laurie." Her expression tight and defiant.

"And I suggest you *leave*," Mum replies, in a tone no one

265

usually argues with. She stands back to let Nicole through. But Charlie's mother doesn't move. Clearly deciding what to do.

"*Right now*," Mum repeats, louder.

There's a look on my mother's face I've never seen before. Determined. No, more than that. It's the look of someone ready to pounce, ready to take on anyone – anything – in defence of the child she loves.

"Clare," Nicole says, "you've no idea wha—"

"I'm not interested in a word you have to say." My mother's voice has a hard, final edge. "I come into my house and hear you threatening my daughter. If you don't leave immediately, I shall call the police."

Nicole glances at me. Hesitates for a few more seconds, then strides out of the front door, slamming it behind her.

We both absorb the impact for a moment before Mum turns to me, checking the time on her watch.

"Right, Laurie. Go and get into your uniform, while I make some lunch, then I'll drive you to your exam. And when you get home, I think you should tell me exactly what's been going on."

PART SIX: THE PROM

Chapter 35

Half of Year Eleven appear to be waiting outside The Grand as our limousine draws in. Most clumped together on the steps leading to the ballroom, watching the new arrivals.

Our driver pulls up right outside, giving everyone a grandstand view as we clamber out of the limo. Douglas first, holding out his hand to Maya. I manage on my own, lifting the hem of my dress as I step onto the pavement, my other hand clutching the little evening bag Mum lent me.

A flash of light in my eyes. I glance up to see a photographer aiming his camera in my direction.

"Smile," he calls, lining up another shot.

My face freezes. I'm too nervous, and uncomfortable. The sleeveless powder-blue dress Mum and I found in a tiny shop in Sydney Street is beautiful, but tight around the bust. It's hard to breathe deeply and my shoes are too high, already pinching my toes and making my feet ache. Not to mention the clip-on earrings I got in that shop Maya suggested, digging painfully into my earlobes. It's all I can do not to reach up and pull them off.

How on earth am I going to make it through the whole evening? I ask myself, as I follow Maya and Douglas up the steps to the Empress Suite. I nearly bottled out as it is, but Mum persuaded me to change my mind. "You only get one prom," she said. "You'll regret it if you don't go."

I doubt it, but here I am anyway. Less for my sake than for everyone who worries about me.

Especially Mum.

Especially now she knows.

"Come on, we can't miss the show," Maya says, as she and Douglas squeeze onto the top step to watch the other arrivals. She looks gorgeous and elegant in her slim blue dress with its beaded neckline. Douglas, wearing a white tuxedo with a red bow tie, keeps glancing at her appreciatively.

I feel a pang of envy. I get the sense that this is going to be a big night for my best friend in more ways than one. Tomorrow, I reckon, Maya and Douglas will be well and truly an item.

"Look!" She points at a classic red Mustang cruising along the promenade. It draws into the little layby outside the hotel and Rory Jenkins and Alicia Rice get out to a riot of applause and whistles from everyone waiting. A few minutes later, Janey Robbins and her crowd arrive in an actual horse-drawn carriage, the two white ponies unfazed by all the cheering and honking from the Brighton traffic.

I check around me, wondering if Charlie and Katy are here already. I heard my sister tell Mum she and Jo were going to Sammy's to get ready, planning to hook up with Charlie, and Sammy's boyfriend Frank, before coming to the hotel.

"Here's Tom!" Maya waves as he pulls up below us. Nothing flashy, just an ordinary car. I glimpse the woman behind the wheel. His mum, her face pale and drawn as she leans to kiss Tom on the cheek.

"Good luck," she mouths as he gets out, before filtering back into the flow of traffic.

I'm about to go over and say hello when a pink stretch limo glides into view. Sammy and Jo waving out the window, grinning at everyone.

Here we go.

The chauffeur opens the passenger door and Sammy appears, stumbling as she tries to stand on a pair of insanely high heels. Frank climbs out after her, followed by Jo and Dan.

No one else emerges for a second or two. I'm just wondering if Katy and Charlie have changed their minds – decided to skip the whole thing – when my sister clambers out of the car. It's practically the first time I've set eyes on her since our conversation in the kitchen three days ago. Katy's hardly been home, and when she has, she stayed holed up in her room. Avoiding everyone.

So this is the first time I've seen her in her prom dress. Strapless, drawn tight round the waist, with a bodice covered in sequins and gems of different shapes and sizes. The skirt is long and flared, but it's the colour that's so captivating: pale green satin, overlaid by a light blue chiffon that gives it a beautiful, shimmering two-tone effect.

The stylist they hired to come to Sammy's has made a fabulous job of Katy's hair, sweeping it to the left and twisting it into ringlets, leaving one blonde tendril to frame the other side of her face. She's topped it off with a lovely diamanté hairband, and her make-up is amazing, her eyebrows groomed into perfect arches, while her skin has a dewy, almost other-worldly, sheen. Her lips, highlighted with pale pink gloss, look impossibly full.

My sister is stunning.

Radiant.

No wonder Charlie picked her, I think, wishing now I'd made more effort. Feeling dowdy in my plain dress and minimal make-up, though both Mum and Dad made a big point of telling me how nice I looked before I left.

Katy stands there, gazing about for a moment or two before leaning back into the car. Speaking to someone.

Charlie.

A few moments later he emerges onto the pavement and my heart stops. Charlie looks amazing, despite the weight he's lost. I've never seen him all dressed up before – apart from the suit he wore to the funeral. But this is different. The tuxedo looks as if it was made for him, close-fitting, a big black cummerbund round his waist. A bow tie in the exact shade of shimmery sea-green as Katy's dress.

We're a couple, it seems to declare. We belong together. Made for each other.

272

I wonder whose idea that was – Charlie's or my sister's?

A second later he turns his head, eyes widening as he clocks me. A moment's hesitation, then he looks away. Katy slips an arm through his, her gaze sliding over me like I'm not even here.

Maya touches my shoulder. "You okay?" she asks, as Charlie, Katy and their entourage sweep up the steps and into the ballroom.

"Fine." I muster a smile as we follow them inside.

Just get through tonight, I tell myself. Everything else can wait till tomorrow.

Chapter 36

The Empress Suite looks incredible. All the tables covered in floor-length white cloths, topped with starchy linen napkins, glasses sparkling in the light reflected from the chandeliers. Each crowned too with a floral bouquet; roses and honeysuckle and sweet peas that smell like they've just come from Dad's allotment. Above, tethered to the centre of the table, pastel balloons, complementing the colours of the flowers.

Once everyone has arrived, we sit down for the meal. I'm with Maya, Douglas and some friends from his tutor group. Charlie and Katy, thankfully, are seated at the opposite end of the ballroom, sparing me my sister's blank gaze.

I manage the first course – a simple salad – despite my nerves, my misgivings about being here at all. But halfway through the main meal – salmon quiche with baby new potatoes and assorted vegetables – it all gets too much. I make an excuse to Maya and head to the loos on the ground floor, relieved to find them empty.

Locking myself in one of the stalls, I lower the lid and

sit down. Five minutes, I tell myself, making the most of this oasis of quiet and calm, a break from the exhilaration of a hundred-plus kids determined to have the night of their lives.

I hardly feel like celebrating, not after all the drama since Mr Rochester's death. I'm tempted to make an excuse and leave, but as Mum pointed out, this is the last time we'll all be together. Next year everyone will scatter, some staying, going into the sixth form, others off to different colleges. A few starting apprenticeships with local firms. The idea of it makes me feel sad. Things coming to an end.

I'm so lost in my thoughts I don't hear the door to the Ladies' swing open. It's only when I emerge a few minutes later that I see Katy leaning over the basin, checking her make-up in the mirror.

She turns to face me. No surprise on her features. Knowing I was here.

She must have followed me in.

"Well, have you told her?" Katy asks, with no preamble.

"Told who? What?" I wash my hands, wondering if I should leave before this kicks off into something both of us might regret.

"I saw you talking to Mum the other day," my sister declares, jutting out her chin. "In the summer house."

Damn. I thought no one had spotted us. Dad was out with Walt, and I assumed Katy was at Charlie's – or off doing prom stuff with Sammy and Jo.

"So, what did you say to her?" Katy demands, in a tone

I know only too well. The one she uses when she's determined to have her own way.

I dry my hands, stalling for time. My mind flashing back to that hour in the garden, me still in school uniform, fresh from my last exam. Desperate to get it over with before I lost my nerve.

"I got pregnant," I told Mum as soon as we were inside the summer house. "I was pregnant and I had an abortion."

I watched Mum's face as I said it. Saw the dismay, the shock. A few seconds of pure reaction before she regained control.

"Oh Laurie." Her eyes filled with tears. "Why on earth didn't you tell me?"

"I was so scared," I mumbled. "I didn't want to upset you…and Dad, especially after everything you'd been through."

"No." Mum shook her head, grabbing my hands and squeezing my fingers as if this were all a mistake she could argue away. As if by contradicting me, she could wind back time and make me see sense. "You should have told me, Laurie. I should have been there for you. I should have been the one you could turn to."

No anger in her voice. Just a world of regret.

"Charlie?" she asked, seeing I was too choked up to speak.

I nodded. And Mum's expression said everything. That she'd always known what I felt for him, what he meant to me – even, possibly, before I knew myself.

"Laurie, are you going to tell me what you said to Mum

or not?" Katy's question drags me back. I look up to see her eyes glistening with tears.

And it hits me. She's scared, I realize. Not just angry, which is pretty much her default emotion.

But why confront me now, three days later? Why not before? Maybe she's been drinking, I think, working up her courage. Or perhaps she's simply set on ruining my evening.

I clear my throat, levelling my gaze at hers. "It was nothing about you. Or what happened between Charlie and Mr Rochester."

"Yeah, well I'd pretty much guessed that. You reckon I'd be here otherwise?"

She has a point. If Mum knew anything about Katy's part in all this, my sister would be grounded for the rest of her life.

"So are you going to tell her?" she asks. "Or Dad?"

"I don't know," I admit, and Katy takes a step towards me, her expression full of resentment.

"Okay, Laurie. So how exactly are we supposed to enjoy tonight with you holding both of us to ransom?"

I stare at her. I'm right. I can smell alcohol on her breath, something heady and sweet. They must have drunk it before they arrived – either that or they've sneaked some into the hotel.

"Katy," I say, pushing down the urge to retaliate. "Now isn't the time, is it? We can talk about this tomorrow."

I promised myself I wouldn't spoil tonight for anyone.

Me included. Whatever is going on in our lives, whatever may be about to happen, I want this prom to be a good memory – or at least not a bad one.

My sister, however, isn't having any of it, rolling her eyes in a gesture of barely suppressed frustration. "God. I thought you actually *cared* about Charlie."

I don't respond. What the hell does she expect me to say to that?

"How could you even consider dumping him in it, Laurie? Why go out of your way to wreck his life like that?"

"Think about it," I reply, my voice rising despite myself. "Charlie *lied*, for god's sake. Mr Rochester is *dead* – probably because of what he did."

"No." Katy shakes her head. "No, we can't be sure it was because of that…there was loads of other stuff going on. Charlie said Mr Rochester's life was a mess."

How does he know that? I ask myself, then remember Nicole. I guess Mr Rochester confided in her. And he was having an affair, after all – proof enough that things weren't exactly great at home.

"But, Katy, even if that wasn't why Mr Rochester killed himself," I argue, "think what Charlie's accusation has done to Tom, to his family. It's destroyed his father's reputation. They have to live with it, even if he doesn't."

I picture Tom, crouching at the back of the crematorium. His head in his hands. Desolate. Desperate.

My sister leans over the porcelain sink, blinking. Trying not to cry. Despite everything, I feel a pang of sympathy.

She really cares about Charlie – that much is clear. Sometimes I imagined she went off with him simply out of spite, to get one over me in the never-ending game of one-up she seems to play in her head.

Maybe I was wrong.

"Why are you protecting him, Katy?" I ask. "You understand, don't you, this is serious shit you're helping to cover up here. The least you could do is persuade him to own up. Deal with it."

Her eyes dart around the toilets. She looks cornered, in the grip of some sort of panic. "What choice do I have?" she wails. "I love Charlie. I don't want to lose him. I know what he did was wrong, but I understand why he did it and I don't think he deserves to be punished."

She stops. Chews the corner of her lip, her expression morphing to something darker as she turns back to me. "That's not why you're doing this though, is it? It has nothing to do with Tom or his family. Oh sure, you'd like to think that. Good old Laurie, always doing the right thing."

Katy tips her head up, struggling to contain her emotions. "The simple truth is you want to punish Charlie. You just want to get back at him for what he did."

Punish him.

Her words almost an echo of Nicole's.

Has Nicole carried out her threat of three days ago? Gone ahead and told Charlie about the baby?

Told my sister?

I shut my eyes, feeling dizzy. I'm not sure I can deal with this. I want to go home, get out of this dress and these stupid shoes. I want to crawl into bed and pull the duvet right over me and never, ever have to think about any of it again.

"I'm right, aren't I?" My sister's voice in my head, full of bitterness – and a kind of triumph. "You're jealous. You can't stand the fact that Charlie chose me, can you? That he didn't want you."

"What did he tell you?" I stammer, holding the basin for support.

Please god, I pray. Please don't let anyone walk into the middle of this.

"He told me *everything*, Laurie. Not that it was exactly news to me. It was so bloody *obvious*." There's such venom in her tone I almost flinch.

"Everything? What do you mean?"

Katy sighs. One of her *how can you be so stupid* sighs. "Charlie came round to talk to you, last year, after the pair of you had some kind of bust-up."

He did? Charlie never mentioned it. When? I wonder, but know better than to ask my sister.

"You were out," she continues, "so he said he'd wait. We took a couple of Dad's beers and sat in my room. And that's how I got it out of him."

Got what out of him? I want to scream, fizzing with frustration. But I try not to show it. Try to hide how much Katy is getting under my skin.

"Here's the thing, Laurie." Her eyes level with mine. "I'd already worked it out – what happened at Ria's party. It wasn't hard. You were so miserable, and after that night everything changed, didn't it? You and Charlie barely spoke any more."

I gaze at her, amazed Katy had even noticed. I haven't given my sister enough credit, I see now. I'd assumed she had zero interest in my life.

"And it didn't take much to get Charlie to admit he'd slept with you – especially after a few bottles." She laughs. "You know what a lousy liar he is."

"Not that lousy," I snap back. "He had everyone convinced Mr Rochester attacked him."

Katy shrugs. "That was different. He just had to fudge things a bit." She says this like it was a small thing. Something insignificant.

I let it go. I get the sense nothing I say will make an impression on my sister. I close my eyes, try to steady my breathing. Forcing myself to see this through.

"Anyway, I persuaded Charlie he was best off leaving you alone," Katy says casually, as if relating the plot of some film rather than the way she ruined my life. "That it was in your interests as well as his."

"Why?" I ask, making myself look at her. "Why would you even do that?"

My sister shrugs again. As if the answer was obvious.

I take a step towards her. Get my face close to hers. "Seriously, why do you hate me so much, Katy? Why do you always have to be so fucking *mean*?"

Her eyes widen a little. I don't think she's ever heard me swear before. "I don't hate you, Laurie. Don't try and make this my fault."

"I'm not." My voice quavering with emotion. "I'm wondering why you're so keen to make everything *my fault*. What's *that* all about, Katy? You want to have this out now, so let's do it."

I'm tired of running away. Biting my tongue. If my sister is hell-bent on a fight, she can have one. But Katy takes a step back, turning to examine herself again in the mirror. Her flawless, beautiful face.

The eyes in the reflection lock on mine. "I dunno, Laurie. Maybe it's because you're always so bloody perfect. Getting the best marks at school, all the attention. The best friends."

"What do you mean?" I frown. "You've got friends. What about Jo and Sammy?"

Katy snorts. "Yeah, right. Every time my back's turned they're bitching about me."

She was jealous, I realize. Jealous of my friendship with Charlie and Maya.

"You always get what you want, don't you?" she says, her voice fuelled by resentment. "Always have. Mum and Dad, they dote on you, give you all the attention. Darling Laurie. The clever one. The nice sister. The *good* sister. Did you ever stop to ask yourself how that makes me feel?"

I gaze back at her reflection. She's right. I'm not sure

I ever have – I've been too focused on how Katy makes *me* feel.

"Of course Mum and Dad don't prefer me over you." I try to keep my voice steady. "I suppose they just…" I pause, searching for the right words.

"Just what?"

"Find me *easier*, okay? Easier to handle. Easier to live with."

Not any more, I think, remembering Mum's face when I told her about the abortion. Her anguish plain to see, despite her efforts to hide it.

"This is my fault," she'd whispered. "I let you down. You should have felt able to come to me, ask me for help."

That was worse somehow. If Mum had been angry, if she'd been disgusted, I could have handled it. Maybe. All along I'd been afraid she'd never forgive me, but that wasn't even the issue, I saw – the person Mum couldn't forgive was herself.

As she leaned forward, clasping me into a hug that lasted a full minute, I knew that this would break her heart a little. For the rest of her life, Mum would blame herself.

And nothing I could say would ever change that.

"I'm sorry," Katy says out of nowhere.

I turn to look at her properly. She's studying me with an expression I can't read. Faint trails in her make-up where tears have tracked her face.

"I'm sorry," she says again. Genuine regret in her voice – or a good imitation. What game is my sister playing now?

I wonder, as she grabs a tissue and presses it to her cheek. Carefully, not wanting to smudge her makeover.

"I knew you liked him, Laurie. I could see what Charlie meant to you. So I took him from you. And yeah, I did it deliberately, just to piss you off."

Her eyes slide from mine then back again. "And then I realized I really liked him."

I stand there, stunned by her honesty. "You didn't take him away," I stammer. "Charlie didn't have to go along with it. He had a choice."

"Really, Laurie, it's not so hard to get them to make the wrong one." Her mouth forms an apologetic smile. "You've got a lot to learn about boys."

"All boys?" I ask, thinking of Tom. Of Douglas. Are they all so easy? So easily led? Or is my sister judging people by her own standards?

Katy watches my reaction, gauging the effect of her words. "So, I'm sorry," she repeats. "You have my apology, and now I'm asking you not to ruin everything."

Her mouth quivers, and for an instant I look past the make-up, past the hairstyle and the lovely dress and see my sister for the young girl she is. Confused and vulnerable.

Just like me.

Just like all of us.

"I can't..." I stumble on my words. "I can't promise you that. It isn't that simple."

Katy hovers, motionless, for a couple of seconds, then gathers herself up, pulling her shoulders back and smoothing her hair with a hand. She heads for the door, leaving me standing there, dazed, my world tipping and reeling, gazing after her.

Right at the last moment, before she disappears off into the crowd in the ballroom, my sister turns back to me.

"Well, I guess I can't blame you, Laurie, for wanting to get your own back – on Charlie and me." Her expression resigned. "But if you want to know the truth, I always thought you were better than that."

Chapter 37

By the time I get back to the ballroom, the tables have been cleared and music is blaring from the mobile disco. Most people are on the floor dancing, wearing happy, excited expressions: their exams behind them, a summer of freedom ahead.

I'm relieved to see Maya jumping around to "Call Me Maybe", along with Sophie, Douglas and a couple of his mates.

At least I'm not spoiling my best friend's big night.

Over in the corner, I spot Katy leaning into Charlie, deep in discussion. I watch as Jo and Frank go up and grab them by the hand, pulling them both onto the dance floor. Katy and Charlie start shuffling around, but you can tell their hearts aren't in it, their bodies too tense, the smiles on their faces too fake.

"Laurie!" Maya waves me over. I go to join her, then notice Tom heading towards the lobby. Suddenly, I feel a strong urge to talk to him, to check how he's doing. Hoping that will somehow help me to make up my mind.

"Back in five," I mouth to Maya, and try and catch him

up. But Tom's not in the lobby, or by the cloakrooms.

Where did he go?

I exit the hotel, crossing the road towards the beach. It's still light, but the sun is low on the horizon, and the seafront quiet; too late for day trippers, too early for the crowds that descend at night on the pubs and clubs.

Leaning over the railings, I survey the lower promenade. No sign of Tom anywhere. I pick my way down the steps, gripping the handrail to stop myself tripping in my heels. I glance around when I reach the bottom, but Tom is nowhere to be seen. Perhaps he's gone down to the water – impossible to see over the hump of the shingle.

I steady myself against a wall and slip off my shoes. No way to cross the pebbles in these things. As I straighten, I feel a hand on my arm. I spin round. Find myself face-to-face not with Tom, but Charlie.

"Shit," I say, breathless. "You scared me."

"Sorry." He gazes at me with an expression I can't read. As if he'd rather be anywhere but here; at the same time like he has nowhere else to go. "I thought for a minute you'd gone home," he adds.

I shake my head. "Just needed some fresh air." I glance behind him to see if Katy's on his heels, but Charlie's alone. Followed me, I suppose, to pick up where my sister left off.

"Can we talk?" He nods at a nearby bench.

I scan the beach once more for any sign of Tom, then give in. Cross to the seat, carrying my shoes. I feel faintly ridiculous being outside in a prom dress, but what the hell.

This is Brighton; pretty much anything goes.

Charlie sits next to me, hitching up the trousers of his tux to allow room for his knees. I still can't take in how different he looks, remembering the old T-shirt and faded jeans he wore down here last Sunday.

Only four days ago, I realize. It feels more like for ever.

"I just wanted…" Charlie pauses. Looking uncomfortable.

I sigh. "Yeah, I know. You're wondering if I've decided yet, what I'm going to do."

Charlie nods, his cheeks flushing. Clearly embarrassed his motives are so transparent.

"I don't know," I say honestly, watching a mob of gulls squabbling over an abandoned bag of chips.

"So you haven't told anyone? Katy said you were talking to your—"

"Mum, yeah." I let it hang for a few seconds. "Like I told my sister, I didn't say anything about you."

"And you're not going to?" Charlie's eyes lock on mine. I can't bear the hope I see there. Can't bear that all he cares about is getting off the hook.

Has he really no idea what he's done?

I know he said it tormented him, that he thought about it all the time. But right now I wonder if all he really worries about is himself. About what will happen if he's caught.

I should have stayed at home, I think. This evening has become a looming disaster, everything converging in on me. I can feel my mood plummeting, tipping into something darker.

"Sorry, Lee," Charlie says, when I don't answer. "I didn't want to spoil your night. I'll leave you to it."

He gets to his feet, starts to walk away.

Something cracks inside me. A heat building. The anger I'd barely kept a lid on last time surges up again.

Urgent. Overwhelming.

"My sister." The words burst out before I can stop them.

Charlie pauses. His features tight as he turns back to me.

"My *sister*," I hiss, as the rage erupts. Refusing to stay down any longer.

"Lee—"

"Of all the crappy, shitty, terrible things you could have done, Charlie, why did you go off with my sister?"

He swallows. Looks away.

"You said we were going to wait, Charlie, and I *believed* you. I actually believed you. Then barely a month later I find you in bed with *Katy*."

Charlie won't meet my eyes. "It…" He stops. Swallows again. "It just sort of happened. I'm sorry."

"*Just sort of happened?*" I mimic. "You just sort of happened to sleep with my sister?"

"I…" He stands there, glancing around as if someone might come to his rescue. "She…"

"She what…?" I say, my tone sarcastic. "She *forced* you?"

Charlie shakes his head, his expression miserable. "Not exactly."

I think back to what Katy said earlier. *You've got a lot to learn about boys, Laurie.* The contempt behind her words.

For Charlie's weakness. For being so easily led. For being so...*easy.*

"You have no idea what that did to me, have you?" I'm shouting now. No longer caring who might hear. "No idea what I was going through. What I had to deal with on my own."

"No, really, Lee, I get it. I totally get it. I know I behaved badly, I—" He holds up his hands to calm me down, but it only makes me more furious.

"No, Charlie." I leap to my feet. "No, you really *don't* totally get it. You don't get it at all. While you were busy being all loved up with my sister, I had to deal with the mess you left me in. And I don't just mean the fact that you broke my fucking heart."

Charlie closes his eyes. Shutting me out. "Look, Lee, this isn't the time—"

"There's something you should know." I say it quickly, before there's any possibility I can change my mind. "*I was pregnant.*"

The second time this week I've said those words.

On this occasion I keep my gaze averted, but I hear his sharp intake of breath. I stare down at my bare feet, at the smudges of red polish on my toenails, done in a hurry. Blood pounding in my head as I wait for Charlie to say something.

But he doesn't speak.

Finally I force myself to look up. Charlie's frowning at me, face clouded with confusion. Like he simply can't process what I've just said.

"*You were pregnant?*"

"From that night," I add, in case he could be in any doubt. "When we were together."

His mouth drops open, the shock on his face unmistakable now.

So Nicole hasn't told him.

"But that's not possible." He shakes his head as if I might have imagined the whole thing. "No way. We were careful. *I was really careful.*"

I stare at him in disbelief. "You're saying, what…*that I'm lying*?" I ball my hands into fists, overcome again with the urge to punch him. "So you need *proof*, Charlie? Cos I have it. Notes from the clinic, the hospital."

"No, I don't mean—"

"So you're what? Accusing me of sleeping around? Getting knocked up by someone else?"

"But we…" Charlie stammers. "I used condoms. I made sure—"

"Yeah, well, it didn't work, did it? They have a failure rate, Charlie. They're not infallible."

He blinks. I see his breathing shallow. "Oh god…" he groans and I watch his expression change to one that pulls the plug on all my anger.

Charlie looks devastated. Like I've just told him the world is about to end. "So you…" His eyes flit to my stomach then back to my face. "So you…?"

I nod, watching his expression alter again. Still shocked, yes, but something else as well.

He looks appalled. Not like Mum, who was clearly sorry and upset. Charlie looks more…distraught.

Like I've done something terrible.

Unforgivable.

Darkness engulfs me as the world drops away and I'm back there, at that hospital. Crying from the moment I get out of the car, Nicole hurrying me past the throng of protesters grouped outside the building.

"C'mon," she urges, ushering me inside.

I try not to look at their placards. Try not to hear what they're chanting, but I'm crying harder as we reach the reception. Crying when the nurse and then the doctor ask me again if this is really what I want to do. Crying as Nicole watches me, face tense, clearly wanting this over as soon as possible.

I'm crying as I sign the forms. Still crying when the nurse leads me away and the doctor administers the injection.

And then, it stops.

In that white, sterile operating room, the drugs close round me like a spacesuit, insulating me from everything.

From myself.

Nothing but a blank space in my head, the warm fuzz of sedation. I'm gone, like an echo, drifting into an endless blankness, away from the Earth and everything that matters.

No light.

No sound.

Just a pinprick figure disappearing out of view.

"*Lee?*" Charlie's voice. A million light years away.

I ignore him, lost in afterwards…the pain as the sedative wore off in the recovery room. Only some of it physical. A deep, sharp ache. The aftershock of the ordeal. But even that wasn't the worst.

"*Lee?*"

I keep my eyes tight shut, blocking Charlie out. Still back there, as we exit the clinic, Nicole holding me up, hurrying me to the car.

Not fast enough.

That woman's face in my head, her features distorted with disgust. "*MURDERER!*" she screams, shoving her placard in front of me. "*How could you kill your own child?*"

"Lee?" Charlie's hands on my shoulders, shaking me. "Lee, *why*? Just tell me why?"

I open my eyes. His face full of anguish and disbelief. "Why, Lee? Why didn't you tell me?"

No breath in my lungs. I blink hard, trying to stay in control. Trying not to start crying again. "I'm sorry," I whisper. "I'm so sorry, Charlie. I came round to talk to you, but you were out. And then your mum…"

"What about her?" He grips me harder.

"I told her…or rather she guessed. She guessed why I was there, and she…"

"She…what? What did Nicole do?"

"She persuaded me not to tell you."

Charlie slumps back onto the bench. Makes balls of his fists and presses them into his eyes, hands trembling.

"She said it would ruin your life, Charlie...both our lives. And then there was...Katy."

A sob. Almost a choking sound. I watch as tears run down Charlie's cheeks again, like the other day. This time he lets them fall, doesn't raise a hand to wipe them away.

"You did it because of...Katy?" he whispers. "You're saying this –" he looks down at my stomach again – "is my fault?"

I shake my head, though of course, that's not quite true. When I caught them together, in my sister's room, I made up my mind. There was no future for us – for me and Charlie. That much was obvious.

If I had his child, I'd be on my own. Alone.

But it wasn't really about them, I see now. It was everything. It was my future – and Charlie's.

Because what Nicole had said was true. How could he become a pilot, flying high and carefree, with the weight of fatherhood hanging round his neck before he'd even begun?

Finding him with my sister just confirmed it was the right thing to do. Or so I'd thought.

But here, now, I'm wondering all over again if I made the right decision.

What if I got it all wrong?

What if I made a terrible mistake?

Tears blur my vision as I look at Charlie, his expression mirroring the face of that protestor. Her anger, her disgust, haunting my dreams, my waking hours. My heart full of despair as I wait for the same verdict to emerge from Charlie's mouth.

Murderer.

Despite what everyone said – the counsellor at the clinic, the doctors, those nurses, Mum – it feels like I'll never get that word out of my head.

Something snaps.

I leap up. I don't pause. I don't even look back. I just run, feet bare, along the seafront. Dragging air into my lungs. Ignoring the pain building in my chest, in my legs, in my head. In my feet.

I run all the way to the pier. Heads turn as I dash through the entrance and along the wooden boards. I keep running, the thump of my heart so loud I can barely hear the music coming from the funfair. I run, dodging everyone around me.

People are leaving, I realize. The pier is closing for the evening.

But I don't care.

I keep going until I reach the end.

"Miss?" A man's voice in the background as I approach the railings, peering at the sea churning below. "Miss, I'm afraid you need to leave."

I ignore him, watching the waves crash around the struts of the pier.

Murderer, shrieks the woman in my head. *Child killer.*

And Charlie's face, the moment I told him. His shock, his anguish.

His grief.

I lean over the railings. Beneath me, the sea swells and churns. But it's low tide, not that deep. Not enough water to cushion the impact.

"Miss," the man calls again. "We're closing up."

I don't look at him, keeping my eyes fixed on the waves below as I think of Mr Rochester. Was this why he did it? Just to make it all go away, all the voices in your head. All the impossible decisions. Hurting people whichever way you turn.

To make everything stop. Once and for all

"Miss!"

I lean further over the railings, feeling the breeze in my hair. My heart beating. All the life inside me still.

And all the reasons not to do it come crashing back.

Mum, Dad.

Walt.

Maya.

They'd be devastated, I think, remembering Tom's face outside the crematorium. Ending my pain would only be the start of theirs.

"*Lee.*"

I take a deep breath. Step away from the barrier, turning to see Charlie racing towards me.

Chapter 38

"Shit, you scared me," Charlie pants, pulling me into a hug so tight I can hardly breathe. Like Mum, he doesn't let go for a full minute. Maybe two.

Finally, he releases me. "Lee? You okay?" Charlie gazes down at me, his expression full of concern. I'm shaking, I realize. All the shock, all the adrenalin of the last few days – of the last couple of minutes – catching me up.

"I think so," I say, though I'm far from sure.

"I'm so sorry." Charlie's voice cracks with emotion. "About everything. All of it. Disappearing on you the way I did. Getting you pregnant, then going off with Katy. How I reacted just now – it was such a shock, Lee. I didn't mean anything by it."

"Pier's closing now," says the security man behind us. "I have to ask you both to leave."

"No worries, we're going." Charlie takes my arm and escorts me off the pier and along the lower promenade.

"Please, Lee," he says, pausing. "Give me a chance to get my head around all this. To explain."

"I need to sit down," I say. All at once I'm so tired my legs feel like they might crumple beneath me.

Charlie nods towards the beach, then glances at my bare feet. Without a word he picks me up and carries me over to where the pebbles shelve into the water. It's only as he puts me back down that I remember. Last time we were here – on this beach together – it was that evening.

Ria's birthday.

Back before it all started.

"Here." Charlie takes off his jacket and lays it across the stones. "Don't want you wrecking that lovely dress."

I shoot him a wobbly smile and lower myself onto it, still feeling trembly. Charlie sits beside me, leaning over to wipe a scuff off his shiny black shoes.

I gaze at my feet. The toes on my left foot are smeared with blood. Must have cut myself on something when I was running.

"Lee, please will you hear me out? Let me explain?"

I nod, too exhausted, too shaken to argue.

"Listen, I know I've screwed everything up." Charlie pulls me round by the shoulder, forcing me to meet his eyes. "I got scared, Lee. Terrified. About us, I mean. It wasn't that I didn't like you, though I know that's how it must look. It was because I liked you too much…"

He stops, seeing my sceptical expression.

"Seriously, Lee. After we…you know…it hit me. That you and me, we could never be anything casual, that there was too much between us. It kind of freaked me out, to tell the truth, and once we'd…after that night there was no going back, was there?"

I turn towards the sea, saying nothing. Feeling a little queasy, like everything inside has come crashing down.

"Lee, I needed space, that's all. Time to think."

I close my eyes. Find my voice. "Is that what you were doing when I walked in on you and Katy? *Thinking?*"

I stare him out till Charlie looks away, sheepish. "That's the bit I can't explain. But please believe me, I never meant it to happen."

He grabs my hand. "I missed you, Lee. I know I said we should wait and everything, and I knew that would be easier if we weren't hanging out together. But I missed being around you – and Maya. I wanted to try and make it all okay again, so I came round to talk but you were out and she…Katy was—"

"When?" I cut in.

Charlie frowns. "When what?"

"When did you come round? What day?"

He gazes into the air as he thinks. "I dunno. A couple of weeks after we talked at the beginning of term, a few days before…before you found us together. I came round after school."

He stops. "Hang on, it was a Tuesday, cos usually I have football practice but that week it was cancelled."

I work it out in my head. It must have been the day I went to the clinic, first talked to that counsellor. When else? I'd been home most of the time.

Jesus. We probably missed each other by minutes. Seconds even.

What might have been different if I'd delayed for half an hour? Put off going to the clinic for a little bit longer?

"God, I feel so bad about Katy," Charlie blurts. "I haven't been fair to her either, Laurie. I just let it happen. And it was easier to let it happen again, and then you walked in on us and it was too late."

I fix my eyes on him. "And now? Why are you still with her then? Why all this time, Charlie? Right under my nose. In my face?"

Charlie flushes. "I dunno. I'd blown it, hadn't I? You and Maya didn't want anything to do with me after that – not that I blame you. But I was..." He pauses, looking embarrassed. "I guess I was lonely. And Katy's sort of easy to be around. She...you know, doesn't take stuff too seriously. And she can be pretty funny."

Doesn't take stuff too seriously? I turn away again, pushing down my hurt. Is that how Charlie sees me? Too serious? Too intense?

Maybe he's right, I think. Maybe I'm not as fun, as frivolous as my sister, though god knows it's a side of her I rarely see.

"The thing was, Lee, I wasn't even sure you liked me that way."

My head whips back. "How do you mean?"

"Katy said you saw me as a friend. Nothing more."

My eyes widen. "She said that?"

I knew you liked him...I could see what he meant to you...
So I took him from you.

Katy's words echo in my head. So she lied to Charlie. Told him I didn't care. I feel a wave of loathing for my sister. And something else. A kind of pity. That she had to stoop so low. That she has to live with herself and what she's done.

"But you knew I liked you," I protest. "We *slept together*, Charlie. And you knew I didn't want to stop seeing you – after all, that wasn't my idea."

Charlie shrugs, pulling a face. "I thought maybe you'd changed your mind. That day we spoke at school, you know, after it happened, you made me swear not to tell anyone – I thought perhaps you were embarrassed about the whole thing."

He inhales, squeezes his eyes shut for a moment. "Christ, I've made such a fucking mess of everything, haven't I?" His voice full of misery. "I listened to Nicole, to Katy, when all along I should have been listening to you."

I gaze at him. Head hanging, hand rubbing his jaw like someone just hit him.

"I'm sorry," he says. "I'm sorry about Katy, I'm sorry I broke your heart, and I'm sorry about the baby, for what you had to go through. I'm sorry I wasn't there for you, and I'm sorry about the way I behaved just now. It was so much to take in."

I don't reply. Don't tell him it's okay. Don't pretend to forgive him. We remain silent for a minute or two, absorbing the noise of the traffic on the road running along the seafront, the music drifting from one of the pubs under the arches behind us. A man shouting in the distance, too far away to make out what he's saying.

We should go back to the prom, I think. People will be missing us, wondering where we've gone. I'm about to get to my feet when Charlie's phone rings. That stupid tune again. He pulls it from his jacket and glances at the screen.

I see his features stiffen.

"Don't go," he says to me, then gets up and makes his way further up the beach. Out of earshot.

I glance back at the Palace Pier. At the water swirling around the huge iron pillars that keep it suspended over the sea.

How close did I come? I ask myself, then think of Mr Rochester. Was that an impulse, or something he planned? Just a moment of madness, like mine, an urge to make it all stop?

If he'd had someone there, someone he could talk to, would he still be alive? Was it all down to chance?

I push the thought away, shivering in the breeze picking up off the sea. Too much. Too morbid.

Up on the promenade, I hear Charlie say something into his phone. His voice tight with anger, though I don't catch the words. I twist round. See him pacing up and down, his features rigid with tension.

Katy, probably, demanding to know where he's got to. Giving him a hard time for deserting her on her big night.

An hour ago I might have found it in myself to feel bad for her. Just a little bit. But I'm still smarting from Charlie's revelation.

My sister's lie.

A crunch of stones. Charlie picking his way back towards me, feet sliding on the shingle. Agitation on his face, his eyes restless, jaw stiff with emotion.

"What is it?" I ask.

Charlie swipes a hand over his mouth.

"What is it?" I ask again, more insistent. Dread pools in my stomach. What else has gone wrong? What else *could* possibly go wrong?

Charlie slumps onto the stones, looking like the sky just fell in. He avoids my gaze, staring out to sea, at the sun sinking towards the horizon.

"Charlie? What the hell is going on?"

He turns back to me, his skin pale with shock. When he speaks his voice is shaking.

"Lee, you wouldn't even believe me if I told you."

Chapter 39

"Charlie, for god's sake *just tell me*."

What now? is all I can think, with a shiver of fear. Hasn't the worst already happened?

I stare at him, trying to fathom what could have made him so upset. Has something happened with Katy? Has she dumped him?

Finally Charlie takes a deep breath, blowing it out between his teeth. Sits back down beside me. "Promise you won't freak out?"

"I promise," I say, at the same time wondering if it'll be one I can keep.

He sucks in another lungful of air. "Earlier, when you told me you got pregnant, I meant it when I said I'd been careful. I couldn't understand how it could possibly have happened."

"Okay."

"So you remember I nicked the condoms off Nicole?" Charlie asks. "From the box in her bedside table."

I nod, cheeks flushing. Asking myself why he's bringing this up. What's the point?

Charlie runs his hand over his head, fingers skimming the buzz of curls erupting again. Behind him, the sun sinks into the sea, a perfect circle of orange sliding over the horizon.

"Laurie, listen. I think I know what happened...*how* it happened."

"What do you mean?"

This time it's Charlie's face that reddens. He closes his eyes briefly before he speaks. Gathering strength. Searching for the right words.

"Nicole told me a story once. About someone she knew, a friend of hers, who was seeing some bloke who didn't want to get married. So she...this friend...got a needle and pierced all the condoms. Through the wrapper so you couldn't tell, not unless you were really looking."

I frown. "Why on earth would she do that?"

Charlie sighs. Sounding a bit like Katy when she thinks I'm being dim. "So she'd get pregnant, Lee. And then he'd have to stick with her."

I study him, perplexed. I can't work out what's more bizarre: that Nicole would tell her own son a story like that – or that anybody would ever contemplate doing something so awful.

"Nicole got really drunk after Mr Rochester died," Charlie continued. "The day of...his funeral. Really pissed, like when he dumped her. And she said something...about how it had all backfired. How she'd done a terrible thing and it had gone horribly wrong."

"What?" I ask, but my stomach tightens. I've an awful feeling I already know.

"I asked her, several times, but she wouldn't say. Just kept shaking her head, saying she was sorry."

Oh god. *Oh god...* "You don't think...?" I stare at Charlie, horrified. "But no one would actually *do* that, would they? Not really. It's so..." I can't even put it into words. Can't get my head around what Charlie is implying.

He swallows. Lowers his voice, even though there's no one around to overhear. "Those condoms we used, Laurie. I didn't mess up. I even checked the date on the packet, to make sure they were okay. I wanted to get it right because it was my first time too, you know that."

I did know. Remember him telling me, whispering to each other in the dark. It was what made it so special.

The first time, for both of us.

For an instant I'm back there, bathing in the glow of that perfect night. The feel of Charlie's skin against mine. The warmth that radiated off him. The rightness of it all.

"I didn't screw up, Lee. I read the instructions while you were in the loo, did everything just like they said. Like they showed us at school."

I shut my eyes. Open them again. "Are you saying you think your mum did that?" My stomach hollows with disbelief. "You're telling me that Nicole...tampered with them? The ones we used?"

Charlie nods, his face crumpling with emotion. Tears in his eyes now. Tears of anger. Of anguish.

"But that's crazy!" I gasp, almost breathless with shock. "No way, Charlie. That's insane."

"Yeah," he mutters. "Isn't it? Fucking insane." He turns away and I see his hands are trembling.

"How do you know, Charlie? How can you be sure?"

"I rang her, just before I got to the pier. She didn't pick up, so I left a message. Asked her outright."

"*And?*"

"That was her just now."

My heart freezes. "So what did she say?" My voice rising with panic and frustration. "Did she admit it?"

"Not exactly. But she didn't deny it either. Just kept repeating she was sorry. Sorry for everything."

"Jesus." I place both hands onto the shingle to steady myself. To counteract the feeling that the ground is dropping from beneath me again. Trying to get all this straight in my head.

Surely it can't be true?

"Why?" I stammer. "Why would she even do something like that?"

Charlie rubs his forehead, the way you do when you've got a headache. "Why do you think? She was crazy about Paul Rochester, claimed he'd talked about leaving his wife. In Nicole's own screwed-up, twisted way I expect she thought she was just clinching the deal."

He pauses, clears his throat. "She's always wanted another child, you see. The chance to do it properly…you know, in an actual family. She has this thing about being a single mother. Feels people look down on her, judge her."

"That's ridiculous," I say thinking of all the kids at school with only one parent. None of them behave like Nicole – or use it as an excuse. I close my eyes. Trying to take all this in. Do I believe any of it? It seems so…far-fetched. Impossible.

And yet…and yet it makes an awful kind of sense.

I groan, as pieces of the last year start to rearrange themselves, falling into place. Why Nicole had been so desperate for Charlie to distance himself from me. How she'd guessed so quickly why I'd gone round to see him.

She knew.

She knew those condoms were useless. She knew I could have got pregnant.

I flashback to her expression as she answered the door that afternoon. The look that passed across her face when she saw it was me.

Dismay, I realize now. Nicole had been waiting for that visit. Had been dreading me turning up on the doorstep, looking for Charlie.

I feel a rush of anger…of bitterness. Nicole could have stopped it happening. She could have warned Charlie – or me. I could have taken the morning-after pill, made sure I never got pregnant in the first place. Nicole could have spared me everything that followed.

But she didn't. Too scared, I suppose, too embarrassed to expose herself. To reveal how low she could sink in her attempt to trap Mr Rochester.

God. I feel another surge of hatred for Nicole, a pierce of cold that makes me shiver. But with it the beginning of something else – sympathy? forgiveness? – as I realize how terrible this must be for Charlie.

On top of everything else.

After all, he didn't ask for this mess either. Like me, he never did anything to deserve it, had got caught up in something outside his control. And, like me, he'll have to live with the consequences for ever.

I glance over. Charlie's looking out across The Channel, his head silhouetted against the sunset. The sun has all but disappeared, but the sky is still a blaze of orange, the colour deepening by the minute.

Just like that night last year, when all this began.

"You okay?" I ask.

Charlie sniffs. Swipes a hand across his face. "Not really. Another piece of my life that's totally fucked up, isn't it? My relationship with my so-called mother. The number of times I've stuck by her, because I felt sorry for her, felt guilty for screwing up her life. I know you don't get it, Lee. Why I stick up for her, but there's always been this…" He trails off.

"Always been what?"

"I dunno." He picks up a stone and hurls it at the water, but it falls short, hitting the shingle with a sharp flinty crack. "It's always been the two of us, when it came down to it. Like I said, Nicole's all I've got – and I'm all she's got. How do you turn your back on that?"

He falls silent, and we listen to the lap of the waves against the shore. The drone of traffic behind us. I study the orange glow on Charlie's skin, a tinge of fire reflected from the sky. It reminds me of the warmth there was between us that night. Like a gorgeous sunset – beautiful, but fleeting. Short-lived.

But still something I wouldn't have missed for all the world.

"I've messed everything up," Charlie says, his voice flat and mournful. "Especially us."

I don't answer at first. What can I say?

It doesn't matter? I forgive you?

Then it comes to me.

"We all have," I murmur. "We've all done things we're not proud of."

All of us – me, Charlie, Katy and Nicole. And Mr Rochester, I think, with a wrench of sadness.

So many mistakes. So many consequences.

"I guess," Charlie says, with a resigned tone that makes my heart ache even more. "But there's no way back, is there?"

I watch the last blaze of sunset fade from the sky, ushering in the twilight. More of a chill in the air now, making me shiver in my sleeveless dress. I look towards the ruined pier further up the beach, remembering Charlie's plunge into the water. And later, what we did that made the whole world feel new. Like something fresh, something exciting to be explored. Everything full of hope and possibility.

Then I think of the trail of events it set off. What it led to – me lying, dazed, in that hospital bed. Feeling like my life had ended in that operating room.

I sense something shift inside me, finally. I can see now, what happened in that hospital was a link in a chain that stretched way back, to before Charlie and I even got together. Back when Nicole met Mr Rochester. And my heart feels lighter suddenly. Less burdened.

It wasn't all my fault – or Charlie's.

It just was.

"No, we can't go back," I agree, "but we can go forwards." I'm remembering that nurse. The one who sat by me in the recovery room while I came round. What was her name?

Barbara.

I recall her face, plump and worn. The way she held my hand, giving me a tissue as the sedative wore off and it all came rushing back to me. Why I was there. What I had done. And I remember now what she said, just before I left the hospital. Words crushed from my mind by that protester outside.

"I know you feel terrible, honey, but for what it's worth, I think you've done the right thing. Only it might take a while for you to be able to see that."

I'd gazed at her, too choked up to speak.

"You're young," she added. "This will fade. There's plenty of time, you know, for it all to come good in the end."

She was right, I think, turning to Charlie, but find him pointing upwards. "What's that?"

I follow the line of his finger. See, just above the horizon, what looks like a star. Only brighter. And moving. Slowly gliding towards us.

"ISS," I say, smiling despite everything.

Charlie frowns. "ISS?"

"The international space station. You know, the one that orbits the earth."

"You sure?"

I nod. "You can always tell. Too large and bright to be a satellite, and no red lights, so definitely not a plane."

We sit transfixed, watching it grow closer.

"There's really people up there?" Charlie asks.

"Yep. A crew of six."

I can't help myself. I do what I always do when I'm with Dad and Walt, tracking its journey across the night sky. Raise my hand and wave.

"Go on." I nudge Charlie.

"Don't be daft. They can't possibly see you."

"That's not the point." I lie back on the stones and watch it pass overhead. Reluctantly, Charlie lifts his hand and waves too. A few seconds later the space station fades into the neon glow above Brighton.

"You'll be up there one day," Charlie says.

I shake my head. "I'm going to be a doctor."

"Really?" Charlie frowns again. "But I always liked the idea of you being an astronaut. Both of us up in the sky."

"Yeah, well. It's not exactly likely, is it? Hardly the same as training to be a pilot."

He shrugs. "So? Someone's got to do it, Lee. Why not you? I reckon it'll be normal one day, going up into space."

"You think?" I manage a smile too. "I doubt it somehow. Not in our lifetime."

"Well, if I'm right and you're wrong, it doesn't matter. You could still go into space if you're a doctor. They'll need medical people up there too, on Mars, or wherever. You could do both."

I laugh, then think about it. Maybe Charlie's right. Maybe anything could happen. And I realize how much my life – my hopes – have shrunk in the last year. Pretty much down to sheer survival.

I feel Charlie's gaze lingering. "I'm sorry," he says again. "I wish I could take it all back. Everything. I'd do anything to be able to rewind and start over…" He stops, his voice beginning to crack. "I'm not going to ask you to forgive me, Lee, but I want you to know I don't blame you, for what you did. It was the right thing. The only thing you could do, under the circumstances."

I look at him, tears pricking my eyes again. Aware now how very much I needed to hear that.

"I mean it," he says. "You mustn't blame yourself. I couldn't bear that."

Charlie gets to his feet, extends his hand. "Tomorrow," he says as he pulls me upright. "Tomorrow I'm going to deal with all of this. Put everything right. As much as I can now, at least."

"Okay."

I go to withdraw my hand but he keeps hold of it. "I'm serious, Lee. First thing I'm going to the school, and then the police, and I'll tell them the truth."

I feel his fingers trembling in mine, but something has changed in his expression. He looks lighter, somehow. Less burdened.

The relief of having finally made up your mind to do what you know you must.

However terrible that will be.

However much it will cost you to do it.

Because it's right. And it's the only thing you can do.

Chapter 40

We go back to the prom. Knowing that tomorrow everything changes, we both want to make the most of what's left of tonight.

Somehow.

I head straight to the hotel cloakroom and get my bag. Dive into the loos to tidy myself up. A bit of concealer under my eyes to hide where I've been crying, a dash of lipgloss, then I'm good to go.

I pause for a moment, studying my reflection. Remembering how I did the same at home, that morning after I got back from Charlie's flat. Looking to see what had changed.

Nothing then, but now…perhaps. Hard to put a finger on it. I seem older somehow, though it's not physical. Something in my expression, the look in my eyes. More direct. Less uncertain.

Definitely more experienced.

"There you are!"

Maya breaks away from dancing to Green Day's "Time

of Your Life" and bounds up to me. She seems happy, I'm glad to see.

"Where'd you go? I've been looking everywhere. I thought maybe you'd gone home with Katy."

"Isn't she still here?"

Maya shakes her head. "She got pissed off when Charlie disappeared."

Despite everything, I feel a twinge of pity for my sister. Her big night in ruins. And I wonder how Charlie's confession tomorrow will affect her. Will she stick by him, or cut her losses and leave?

Not my business, I tell myself, turning to Maya. I clasp her hand, leaning in so she can hear me over the music. "Tomorrow, let's go somewhere, if we're not too knackered. Somewhere we can talk."

Maya steps back, narrowing her eyes. "About what?" Concern in her face.

"About everything that's happened."

My friend blinks. "About you and Charlie, you mean?"

I frown. "You knew?"

Maya shrugs. "I knew you liked him, if that's what you mean. You think I could miss something like that? Especially after he went off with Katy."

I gaze at her. Surprised…yet not. Had I really imagined Maya wouldn't notice anything?

"I'm sorry," I say, squeezing her hand. "I'm sorry I didn't talk to you…it was just…I had to do something…very difficult, and I didn't know how to tell you."

Maya's gaze lingers on mine. I can see she's dying to ask more, but biting it back. "Yeah, well I'm not going to deny it pissed me off. Of course I've been angry with you – and hurt that you wouldn't confide in me."

I smile. "Thanks for hanging in there. And not giving me a hard time."

Maya frowns. "What would have been the point of having a go at you? It was obvious you had enough on your plate."

Her face softens, and she leans in, gives me a hug. "Whatever it is, you don't have to tell me, Lee. We're best friends, but that doesn't mean we have to tell each other everything. I'm not going to abandon you, you know – whatever's happened."

"Thanks," I say again. "But I do want to talk. Not right now, though – let's enjoy what's left of tonight."

Maya nods, then glances down at my feet. "Where the hell are your shoes?"

"I left them by a bench outside. Someone took them." Charlie and I spent ten minutes searching along the promenade before we gave up.

"Are these what you're looking for?"

I turn to see Tom standing behind me, hand extended. Dangling by the straps, looped over one finger, are my shoes.

I pull a face. "Actually, I was rather hoping I'd seen the last of them."

Tom laughs, and right then the DJ announces a slow

dance over the speaker. "Grab your partners and hit the floor, let Jessica Simpson take your breath away." An instant later Douglas comes up and sweeps Maya into the crowd, leaving Tom and me side by side.

I glance around for Charlie. See him over in the corner, talking to Dan and Sammy. His eyes flit in my direction, away again.

"Well?" Tom does a little bow, holding out his hand. "May I have this dance?"

I pull on my shoes, let him lead me onto the dance floor. Tom goes all ballroom on me, placing one arm round my waist, clutching my other hand like we're about to waltz rather than shuffle around awkwardly, trying not to fall over each other's feet.

"This for show?" I ask.

"Course not," Tom grins. "I'm guessing you missed the big event of the evening?"

"What was that?"

"Me, earlier. Asking Ryan Benson for a slow dance."

I laugh. "Good for you."

"Yeah, I decided the prom was as good a time as any to come out. Besides, I won't see most of these people after tonight. I'm off to Plumpton College in September."

"That's the agricultural place, isn't it?"

Tom puts on a fake West Country accent. "Arr. Oi be training to be a farmer, young Laurie."

This makes me laugh even more, though it's tinged with sadness as I gaze around at all my schoolmates. Trying to freeze this moment in my mind – the last time we'll all be together.

Nothing will ever be the same again.

"I'm glad you came. I wasn't sure you would." Tom steers me away from the speakers so we can hear each other.

"Me neither," I say.

His eyes sweep across the ballroom. "Wouldn't miss it for the world. Rite of passage, isn't it?"

The DJ puts on Nelly's "Hot in Herre" and half our year start chanting and gyrating, jostling the pair of us.

"Can we sit down?" I suggest. "My feet really are killing me."

We grab a couple of chairs in the corner with a good view of all the bodies writhing on the dance floor. We're practically the only ones sitting it out. Apart from Dan and Charlie, and Toby Arnold and Liz Jeffries over in the far corner, busy necking under the watchful eye of Miss Tozer.

"Actually I need to talk to you," I say to Tom, watching Maya and Douglas flirting with each other, their faces glowing with the promise of things to come.

"What about?" Tom asks.

"Charlie."

Tom's eyes flit to where he's standing, then back to me. "I'm not going to like it, am I?"

I shake my head.

"Then save it, Laurie. Save it for another day."

"Okay."

After all, he'll know soon enough. Once Charlie's told

the school, and the police, it'll get straight back to his family.

But even so I can tell I've punctured Tom's good mood. He doesn't speak for a while, just watches everyone making the most of their big night. When he does break the silence, his voice is quiet.

"God, this has been such a crap year."

"Yeah. Tell me about it." I shift my feet in my shoes. Wince at the pain, then turn to him. "Are you okay though? I mean…not okay, obviously. But, you know…" I try to find the right words.

Tom swivels in his seat. Looks me head on. "I'm fine, Laurie. I mean, it's shit, but I'm hanging in there. I'm coping…*we're* coping."

And tomorrow? I wonder. Will Charlie's confession make things better or worse? I shut my eyes briefly, wishing there were some way to spare Tom all of it. Knowing there isn't.

"How about you, Laurie? Are you doing all right?"

I nod.

"No, I mean really all right. After, you know…" He doesn't spell it out.

I think about this as "Hot in Herre" segues into Lil Jon's "Get Low". Archie Furrows and Harry Stoke break into a daft rap dance, then Alicia and Sophie trump them with some impressive twerking while everyone claps along.

Am I okay?

I am, I realize. Pretty much.

Not happy, no. Not even particularly optimistic.

But inside, something has subsided. Started to recede.

There's nothing more corrosive than a secret, I can see now. How it eats away the heart of you, devouring you from the inside. Sapping all your energy in the effort to keep it suppressed.

I glance at Tom. Catch him watching Charlie before turning back to me with a sigh. "It's taken me a while but I finally get it." He nods at all the kids writhing in front of us. "Most people seem happy enough, appear to be sailing through their lives, but it's just an illusion, isn't it? Deep down, they've all got their own problems, their own issues."

He fixes his gaze on mine. "It's not just us, Laurie."

"I guess not." I watch Jemima Brooker doubled up with laughter as her friends Sylvie and Poppy sidle up to a clump of boys stranded on the outskirts and drag them into the centre of the dance floor.

"You know what I wish?" Tom pauses, his voice choking a bit. "More than anything I wish I could go back and tell my dad what else I've figured out."

"What's that?"

Tom sniffs. Clears his throat. I notice a little nick in the skin where he's caught himself shaving. "You heard of a band called Madness?"

"You're kidding, aren't you?" I laugh. "My mum loves Madness. She went to see them at the Brighton Centre a couple of years ago. I must have spent half my childhood listening to their stuff."

"Do you know 'The Sun and The Rain'?"

I nod. "I love that song. They did that crazy video, didn't they?"

"All their videos were crazy," Tom says. "But I've listened to it a lot recently, and I realized they're right. It's the sun and the rain."

"How do you mean?"

"When you think about it, life is like the weather. No place stays sunny all the time, though it can seem that way when you're little and every picture book has blue skies and a great big yellow sun. But life's not really like that, is it? Nowhere is always sunny – but it doesn't rain all the time either."

"Right…" I say, not really grasping what he's on about.

"What I'm saying, Laurie, what I'm getting at is…you and me, we've had a patch of really bad weather."

"A depression," I say, remembering the word from my geography revision.

"Exactly." Tom sighs, a slow, heavy sigh. "Anyway, that's what I wish I could have told Dad. That eventually the black clouds would pass. That it would all blow over."

I think of my own father. His own cloudy patch, and feel a rush of gratitude that he's weathered the storm. I'm lucky, I realize. It could have been worse.

Much worse.

"Back in a minute." Tom gets up and disappears into the crowd. I scan the room. Maya is still dancing with Douglas, who's clearly struggling not to tread on the hem of her dress. Charlie is nowhere to be seen.

Must have gone home, I think, asking myself how he'll manage tomorrow. Will he take Nicole? Or Katy? What will happen to him? I can't even guess.

"Last song of the evening, folks," the DJ croons into his microphone. "And this one's for Laurie Riley. Everyone grab your partner for a little bit of Madness, because 'Tomorrow's Just Another Day'."

The familiar mouth organ refrain comes on, and from the corner of my eye I spot Tom, his arm around Ryan. Giving me a thumbs up.

"Lee."

I turn to see Charlie standing in front of me, holding out his hand. Beside him, Maya is hanging on to the other, grinning.

"Come on," he says again.

"Please," adds Maya.

I let them pull me to my feet, kicking off my awful shoes, and they haul me into the mob of kids going crazy on the dance floor, flinging themselves around like this is the last night of their entire lives.

Charlie grabs Maya's other hand, and we dance like that, each holding on to the other, shuffling round. Clumsy but happy.

A triangle, I think. Not eternal after all. Or perfect.

But it was, for a while.

And that's enough.

If you have been affected by the issues raised in this book, the following organizations can help:

For advice about pregnancy, contraception and abortion –
Marie Stopes UK
www.mariestopes.org.uk
0345 300 8090

For advice about depression –
SANE
www.sane.org.uk

YoungMinds
www.youngminds.org.uk

Q&A with Emma Haughton

What was your inspiration for writing *Cruel Heart Broken*?

When I was learning French some years ago, the tutor had us translate an article from a French newspaper, all about an incident that had happened in a school in a town near Paris, where a false accusation from a pupil led to a teacher's suicide. A story so intriguing I never forgot it, and eventually decided to use it as the basis for a novel.

As a former journalist, do you find you look to news articles and statistics for ideas for your stories?

I'm always on the lookout for interesting real-life events and situations, as truth is so often stranger than fiction. With my journalism background, I do feel a need to be accurate – I'm happy to embellish situations to make them work in story terms, but not basic facts. For instance, I read up on male suicide and teenage abortion and consulted people with personal and professional experience, to ensure my story was as accurate as possible.

Were you a Laurie or a Katy growing up?

Hmm… I'm going to say I was a bit of both. I didn't work that hard at school. I mucked about a lot and was always getting sent out of class. But I wasn't a mean girl like Katy either, though I spent quite a lot of time hanging out with my friends in the girls' loos! I was always a keen reader, and quite serious on a lot of levels, so I have a good deal of Laurie in me too.

Right then I'd have loved to be on a spaceship heading out towards the stars. I'd watch the planet recede to a pinprick, all my problems left behind. **Laurie wants to be an astronaut – what about you? Are you a secret space fan?**

I dreamed about being an astronaut when I was young. I loved astronomy and science-fiction, and the idea of exploring space and different planets captured my imagination. Unfortunately I turned out to be seriously rubbish at science, and when I first flew in a plane, realized I was actually terrified of flying. So, not much hope of me getting accepted into any space programme. These days I confine myself to reading sci-fi and watching every *Horizon* programme about space and the nature of the universe.

There's a strong sibling rivalry theme in the book – is that something you think many families experience?

I think a lot do, yes. Certainly I was always at loggerheads with my brother. We never really got on, and looking back, I think that's a real shame. We missed out on a lot by not being close.

Having lived in Brighton, why do you think it's such a popular setting for stories?

Brighton is a great mix of different cultures, being both a historic seaside resort and a mecca for alternative lifestyles, so I guess that offers writers plenty of material. It's also a lovely city, with a great vibe, and surrounded by beautiful coastline and the Sussex countryside.

Despite everything that she goes through, Laurie seems reluctant for things to change. How did you feel about leaving school for the real world?

I stayed on to the sixth form, so it wasn't something I faced at sixteen. But after my A levels I couldn't handle the thought of going straight off to university, and ended up taking four years out to travel and work. I needed that long to grow up a bit, otherwise I'm not sure I could have coped with the undergraduate workload.

Your characters have fantastic ambitions. Was it always your ambition to be a writer or did you ever dream of doing something else?

Deep down I always wanted to write, but it never felt like something I could realistically achieve. There wasn't the creative writing culture when I was young, and I assumed it was a gift you were born with. It took me a long time to understand that writing is essentially a craft, something you can learn to do. So I booked myself on writing courses, I persevered, kept revising my manuscript and sending it out. Got rejections aplenty. And then one day the phone rang – my first YA novel, *Now You See Me*, was going to be published. It was something I once never believed would happen. But if you want something enough, you can do it. You really, really can.

Acknowledgements

Many thanks to my agent, Jo Williamson, and my editor Sarah Stewart, along with all the team at Usborne. Thanks to Marie Adams and Chris Murray, for keeping me afloat. James Ridley, I am grateful for all your thoughtful comments along the way, and for keeping me fed in the meantime. Apologies to all my family and friends for the usual neglect while writing this book, most particularly Maggie Jeffries, who I left stranded in a cafe after getting over-absorbed in the copyedits – I hope you think it was worth it, Mags!

About the author

EMMA HAUGHTON worked as a freelance journalist, writing features for a wide variety of newspapers and glossy magazines, before becoming an author. A mother of four, she now lives and writes fiction in Dorset.

Cruel Heart Broken is her third novel.

@Emma_Haughton
www.emmahaughton.com

Also by Emma Haughton

Inspired by a
true story

NOW
YOU SEE
ME...

...but can you trust me?

Emma Haughton

**NOMINATED FOR THE 2015
CARNEGIE MEDAL**

ISBN 9781409563693

Also available as an ebook

Three years ago, thirteen-year-old Danny Geller
vanished without trace.

His family and friends are still hanging on to every last shred
of hope. Not knowing if he's alive or dead, their world is
shrouded in shadows, secrets and suspicions.

This is the story of what happens when hope comes back to
haunt you. When your desperation is used against you.
When you search for the truth – but are too scared to
accept the reality staring you in the face…

Also by Emma Haughton

"Perfect for fans of Sophie McKenzie"
Lovereading4kids on
NOW YOU SEE ME

Some secrets are...

BETTER
LEFT
BURIED

Emma Haughton

ISBN 9781409566700

Also available as an ebook

Brother dead.
Best friend missing.
House ransacked.
Stalked by a stranger.
Attacked in the street...

...And Sarah has no idea why. She never knew her brother
was hiding a dark secret when he died. But now his deadly
actions have led the wolves to her door.
And the only way out is to run.

"An utterly compelling story about crime and intrigue
in which everything surprises."
The Independent's Teen Books of the Year

"Spellbindingly brilliant."
The Dark Dictator

"Emma Haughton obviously has a super power –
she knows how to reel her readers in and won't let them
go until the last line!" Serendipity Reviews

"*Better Left Buried* confirms Emma Haughton's reputation
for taut, well-plotted psychological thrillers."
Lovereading4kids

For more incredible Usborne YA
reads, news and competitions, head to
usborneyashelfies.tumblr.com

@Usborne

@UsborneYA

www.usborne.com/youngadult

HAV